MW00932405

J. N. Chaney

www.jnchaney.com

2nd Edition

TRANSIENT ECHOES

BOOK 2 IN THE VARIANT SAGA

J.N. CHANEY

For my grandfather,
who shared a lifetime of stories
but couldn't stay for mine.

BOOKS BY J.N. CHANEY

The Variant Saga:

The Amber Project

Transient Echoes

Hope Everlasting

The Vernal Memory

Renegade Star Series:

Renegade Star

Renegade Atlas

Renegade Moon

Renegade Lost

Renegade Fleet

Renegade Earth

Renegade Dawn

Renegade Children

Renegade Union

Renegade Empire

Renegade Descent

Renegade Rising

Renegade Alliance

Renegade Evolution

Renegade War

Renegade Peace *(Coming Sept. 2020)*

Renegade Star Universe:

Nameless

The Constable

The Constable Returns

The Warrior Queen

Orion Colony *(with Jonathan Yanez)*

Orion Uncharted *(with Jonathan Yanez)*

Orion Awakened *(with Jonathan Yanez)*

Orion Protected *(with Jonathan Yanez)*

The Last Reaper *(with Scott Moon)*

Fear the Reaper *(with Scott Moon)*

Blade of the Reaper *(with Scott Moon)*

Wings of the Reaper *(with Scott Moon)*

Flight of the Reaper *(with Scott Moon)*

Wrath of the Reaper *(with Scott Moon)*

Will of the Reaper *(with Scott Moon)*

Descent of the Reaper *(with Scott Moon)*

Hunt of the Reaper *(with Scott Moon)*

Bastion of the Reaper *(with Scott Moon)*

The Fifth Column *(with Molly Lerma)*

The Solaras Initiative *(with Molly Lerma)*

The Forlorn Hope *(with Molly Lerma)*

Resonant Son *(with Christopher Hopper)*

Resonant Abyss *(with Christopher Hopper)*

Galactic Law *(with James S. Aaron)*

Galactic Judge *(with James S. Aaron)*

Galactic Jury *(with James S. Aaron)*

Galactic Executioner *(with James S. Aaron)*

Deadland Drifter *(with Ell Leigh Clarke)*

Deadland Wanderer *(with Ell Leigh Clarke)*

Deadland Sentinel *(with Ell Leigh Clarke)*

Ruins of the Galaxy Series *(with Christopher Hopper):*

Ruins of the Galaxy

Galactic Breach

Gateway to War

Void Horizon

Black Labyrinth

Imminent Failure

Terminal Fallout

Quantum Assault

Rise of the Gladias

The Messenger Series *(with Terry Maggert):*

The Messenger

The Dark Between

Star Forged

The Silent Fleet

Dawn of Empire

Worlds Apart

Rage of Night

Heaven's Door

Radical Dreamer

Cosmic Ride

The Sol Arbiter Series *(with Jia Shen):*

Sol Arbiter

Intrinsic Immortality

Digital Chimera

Memetic Drift

Standalones:

Their Solitary Way

The Other Side of Nowhere

Forever Family

CONNECT WITH J.N. CHANEY

Join the conversation and get updates in the Facebook group called "JN Chaney's Renegade Readers." This is a hotspot where readers come together and share their lives and interests, discuss the series, and speak directly to J.N. Chaney and his co-authors.

https://www.facebook.com/groups/jnchaneyreaders/

He also post updates, official art, and other awesome stuff on his website and you can also follow him on Instagram, Facebook, and Twitter.

For email updates about new releases, as well as exclusive promotions, visit his website and enter your email address.

https://www.jnchaney.com/variant-saga-subscribe

Enjoying the series? Help others discover the *Variant Saga* by leaving a review on Amazon.

CONTENTS

ACKNOWLEDGMENTS

As with any book, this one could only exist through the encouragement of the wonderful people in my life. Here's to my family for their endless support; to Sarah, who opened doors I never knew existed; to Geoff, for all the late nights plotting in the basement; to Rob, whose art is a constant inspiration to me; to Valerie, who always knew how; to James, who was there at the beginning; to Chase Nottingham, my brilliant editor; to Vickie, Steven, Corbin, and Dustin; to my amazing beta readers; and to everyone else whose name I left out. You are the reason these worlds exist.

PART I

Man cannot discover new oceans unless
he has the courage to lose sight of the shore.
– **André Gide**

Across the sea of space,
the stars are other suns.
–**Carl Sagan**

PROLOGUE

UNDER A VIOLET SKY ON A DISTANCE WORLD, deep in the heart of a cerulean jungle, a teenage boy ran for his life.

The predator was close behind him, roaring, snapping branches as it crashed through the dense undergrowth, a growing blur in the distance. The boy kept low, clutching an armful of fruit to his chest. He would drop the food if it came to it, but not a moment before. The boy had searched for over a day for something to eat. He wasn't about to give it up.

He leapt over a fallen log, bursting through the tree line into an open field of tall grass. A large cliff stood in the distance, rising two hundred meters above the ground. His camp was at the top. He'd be safe there…if he could make it.

He darted through stalks of glowing blue grass. Rigid stems whipped against his skin as he ran but didn't slow him. After a hundred meters, he stopped, glancing back to see if the beast was still following. Where had it gone?

Silence filled the air, broken only by the blowing wind as it whirled through the valley, hitting his cheeks. He stared at the jungle, waiting.

A thunderous cry sent a flock of birds scattering from the treetops. The monster burst through the shroud of foliage into the open field, stopping a few meters from the grass. Finally in clear view, the boy could see the animal was massive. On all fours, it stood two meters tall. Thick brown hair covered most of its body, save its snout. A pair of crimson eyes fixated on the boy. Below them, two gray tusks large enough to skewer a grown man protruded. The beast's thick calves were like cords of wood. Ropes of muscle underneath the skin stretched and tightened with every stomp.

It reared on its hind legs, towering over the field.

The boy took a step back.

The beast edged forward.

With newfound motivation, the boy exploded into a mad dash toward the base of the cliff. The cries and thunderous footfalls of the predator followed.

As he neared the rock face, he could hear the creature getting closer. A rope dangled before him, lodged safely between two stones. He'd fashioned it over a year ago. It was the only means of reaching the top of the ridge. He slid to a quick halt, kicking dirt and grass into the air. The beast was closing fast.

He tugged the rope, freeing it from the crevice, and climbed, using his feet and only one arm as he hugged the precious fruit close to his chest.

The animal arrived within seconds, ramming into the cliff face, sending a shower of loose stones to the ground. A few hit the creature's tusks, shattering into dust. It shook its head and roared, standing on its hind legs and scraping the rock wall in a vain attempt to follow its prey.

The boy did not look back. As he found the top of the cliff, he clasped the mat of blue grass and pulled himself over the edge. He swung his legs around and collapsed onto his back, releasing the fruit in his hands along with a sigh. The cries of the predator continued in the distance below him, but the fear of death was gone. He was safe.

The buttercream clouds passed overhead, partially blocking the light of the two suns, shading him. He scratched his chin, rubbing the stubble of a half-grown beard. He decided not to move again until the animal had gone, so he stayed on his back, waiting for reprieve.

The beast continued to whine, clawing at the rocks. Slowly, its cries grew softer, and it was not long before the monster turned and stomped toward the forest.

The boy sat up and stretched his arms, cracking his spine. He collected the fruit and headed toward his hut. The cliff was narrow, but widened into a spade shape. It curved and extended roughly eighty meters before dropping off. His home lay in the center between two stone walls under a large tree with wide branches and thick leaves. Beside the tree, a small brook flowed from a crack in the rock, providing fresh water. The hut itself held little space, but the boy didn't mind. He lived alone and had for quite a while now.

After placing the rest in a basket, he snagged a piece of fruit along with his bone knife and went to the stream nearby. The produce was colorful, primarily magenta with dashes of turquoise and yellow throughout the skin. He split it open with the blade and the pink juice washed over his fingers. The smell was therapeutic, a sweet and relaxing aroma which filled his nose and watered his mouth. He bit hard into the fruit, hardly chewing as he gulped the chunks of moist produce down. His tongue barely had time to register the taste, he swallowed so quickly. He gasped as the last of it disappeared, finally remembering to breathe.

Despite the recent contribution, his stomach growled.

After rinsing the knife in the brook, he set it to the side and washed his face. The juice dripped from his cheeks into the stream, filling it with a pink glow. The boy stared into the water, watching as the natural flow of the brook returned. With it, another man's face. Encased in chestnut hair—unkempt and naturally wild—a thin beard persisted over a strong jaw line. The stranger's nose was thin, tucked between a set of dirt-encrusted cheeks. Who was he? What did he want? The boy stared at him, studying the unfamiliar features. The hair, the nose, the neck, the forehead.

But the eyes—yes, those were familiar. Piercing green and calm, the boy knew them well. They had belonged to him once, years ago, before this horrible place had stolen him away. Before he switched the machine off and disappeared—fell through a crack in space and landed on another world.

Those eyes, they remembered a two story apartment, deep in an underground city—the last human colony on Earth—and the family of three who lived there. They recalled the school—teachers and friends, learning and books, laughing and training. People used to say the children there were special.

In those days, the green eyes belonged to the boy alone. Now he shared them with this stranger and his tangled beard.

Terry, a voice whispered in his mind. It was a young girl. He knew her well. *What's a birthday? What does it mean?*

He smiled into the brook, and the man returned it. "It means you grow up and get to start school," he whispered. "It's a pretty big deal."

I wish I could go with you, she said. The words lingered as a gust blew through the peak. The tree sighed overhead, rustling its leaves.

Terry shuddered, swallowing the lump in his throat. He wondered how long the voice would stay today. He usually enjoyed the visits, but only when he initiated them. He didn't like it when they came uncalled. "Janice, go away."

When will you be back? She asked.

As if to answer, a well of tears formed in his eyes, and he gasped. *I broke my promise,* he thought. *I said I'd come back, and I never did. I lost her. I lost them all.*

The more he remembered, the more he wept until a steady flow of gentle sobs bled out of him and poured into the water. The tears fell, distorting the image of the man, colliding with the familiar emerald eyes the boy knew so well.

1

Ortego Outpost File Logs
Play Audio File 264
Recorded: April 12, 2350

FINN: *How long until you come home?*

CURIE: *Not for another week. We're still establishing the outpost.*

FINN: *But you've been gone a month already.*

CURIE: *These things take time. Besides, you're always disappearing to go on some mission or another. Can't I do the same? Go ask Colonel Ross to give you some busywork if you're bored.*

FINN: *I'm not bored. I just miss my girlfriend.*

CURIE: *I know. I miss you, too. But I can't leave my team in the middle of a project. I have responsibilities. We all do.*

FINN: *Can I visit, at least?*

CURIE: *All the way out here?*

***FINN**: Sure, why not?*

***CURIE**: It's desolate and empty. There's only five of us. You'd be so bored.*

***FINN**: Our birthday is in two days, Mei. We always spend it together. Who cares if there's nothing to do?*

***CURIE**: Hm. I'm not sure…*

***FINN**: Don't make me start with the pet names.*

***CURIE**: Okay! You win. Come and be with me in the desert. Let us sit together and stare at the dirt.*

***FINN**: What a softy you are.*

***CURIE**: Just shut up and get here.*

***FINN**: I'm already packing a bag.*

End Audio File

Ortego Reconstruction Outpost
April 12, 2350

Mei Curie sat on a slab of metal debris, staring into the solar fields of the former Ortego headquarters. The panels glistened with the sunlight, unmoving. They looked exactly as they had on the day of the Second Jolt over three years ago, back when the sky erupted and a crater had formed at the edge of this field. Mei had stood here and watched it happen. It still gave her nightmares.

"Doctor Curie?" shouted Sophia Mitchell, but everyone

called her Sophie. Mei stared at the M2280 on the girl's face and neck, otherwise known as a breather, a machine used to filter Variant from the air. It was hard to believe how far technology had come. Before the Second Jolt a few years ago, the idea of walking around on the surface without a protective suit on was laughable. Variant affected all organic cells, killing biological matter from the inside, so any exposure usually resulted in death.

Mei had been genetically engineered from birth to endure Variant, but most weren't so lucky. Instead, thanks in part to the blood of people like Mei, a vaccine had been created. This didn't allow anyone to breathe the corrupted air, however. It only kept their cells from degenerating. So the breather had been created, and with it, a massive step forward in the battle to take back the surface.

Sophie handed Mei a digital pad. "Sergeant Finn called. He said to tell you he's on his way."

"Thanks," she said, checking the report and handing it back. "Let me know when he arrives, will you?"

Sophie nodded and returned to the tent.

Mei sighed, digging the heel of her boot into the wet earth, dragging clumps of dirt toward her. The world was changing. With it, the human race. Each day, progress was being made to bring mankind to the surface. In the last few years, several outposts had been established, the range of the radio towers extended, and most of the hostile threats eliminated. Just as the first Jolt had brought about a great change, the second had created a new age all its own. For the first time in two hundred years, humanity was no longer stagnant.

A horn honked in the distance. Mei turned and spotted a dirt cab a kilometer and a half down the road.

She got to her feet and jogged to the main research tent. "Sophie," she called.

Sophie poked her head out of the flap. "Yes, ma'am?" Despite only being a year younger than Mei, Sophie always treated her with the same respect she gave the older staff. The girl was remarkably intelligent and exceptionally mature for her age. Her thesis on the Ortego Corporation's lesser-known technologies had prompted Mei to look her up, despite a lack of field experience. Unlike most of the senior staff and many of the newer PhDs, the young Sophia Mitchell possessed what Mei considered one of the more valuable personality traits—a penchant for the unconventional. During her training, Sophie had a knack for coming up with outlandish solutions to complex problems. It was why Mei had taken a shine to her in the first place, despite her instructors' objections. "She doesn't follow procedure," Doctor West had said when Mei inquired. "It's as though she's intent on failing her classes."

Mei didn't care about any of that. Where so many others saw failure and a lack of focus, Mei found an ignored creative spark in need of sustenance. Six months after attaining her own doctorate, and shortly before receiving authorization for her new team, Dr. Mei Curie approached Sophia Mitchell about becoming her apprentice, and the girl readily accepted it. Mei never regretted it for a second. "Sergeant Finn is almost here. Let the others know I'll be meeting with him and to only bother me if there's an emergency."

Sophie looked confused. She stepped out of the tent and glanced at the camp entrance. "I didn't receive any transmission. Where is he? I don't see him."

"Down the road. Five minutes out, maybe."

"Sometimes I forget how good your eyes are. I'm a little jealous."

"I'd take your height over my eyes if I could," said Mei, laughing.

Sophie grinned. "Enjoy your time with the sergeant, Doctor."

"I don't know what you mean," said Mei.

Sophie gave her a look that said, *You're not fooling anyone*, and then receded into the tent.

Mei headed toward the entrance to the camp and waited for John's cab to arrive. She was torn about his visit. On the one hand, he brightened her day, and she loved seeing him. On the other, he wasn't a scientist. There wouldn't be much for him to do but sit and stare at the ground, something he was sure to complain about. John was a soldier, an active explorer in the physical world, always on the go, never slowing. It wouldn't take him long before he grew tired of the boredom and isolation of this place.

John's cab soon arrived. He brought the vehicle to a stop near the edge of the solar field. As he hopped out, she could see he still wore his brown and green military uniform. He also had a canteen strapped to his hip and a rifle on his side. John picked up the duffle bag sitting in the passenger seat and swung it over his shoulder. Standing there, he looked daunting, a little more than two meters tall with shoulders twice as wide as Mei's. He beamed an inviting smile at her. "Sorry to keep you waiting, Doc."

She ran and hugged him, barely wrapping her arms around his waist. He buried his nose in her hair, chuckling. She smacked his side. "Missed you."

"I bet you'd miss anyone living so far in the middle of nowhere like this." He glanced around the field. "Took me eight hours to drive here from Komodo Outpost."

"Imagine the trip without the dirt cab," she said.

"I know, I know. I shouldn't complain," he said. "Where's our tent? I need to unload my crap. You set up near the crater?"

"No, we're about two kilometers from the site."

"Why so far?" he asked.

"There's radiation," she said. "We have to wear suits while we're there."

"So it's safe back here?"

She nodded.

"Oh, I almost forgot." He went to the rear of the cab and grabbed another pack. "Here's some extra supplies. It's mostly food."

She opened it and found a bundle of fruit, two bottles of wine, a bag of seasoned soy meat, and even some candy. "Wow, I don't know what to say," she said. "The team's going to love this. They haven't had anything but rations for three weeks…you didn't have to do this, John."

"Sure I did," he said, winking. "The best way in with the natives is food."

Mei took a seat in the main tent next to John, waiting for everyone to show up for the afternoon brief. The tent was ten meters long and five wide, containing a large conference table, half a dozen chairs, a digital display board, and several crates no one knew what to do with.

Sophie entered after a few minutes, followed shortly by Travis, Zoe, and Bartholomew. Once they were seated, it was down to business. "As you can all see, Sergeant Finn has arrived safely," said Mei, standing at the head of the table.

John waved at each of them. "Glad to be here," he said.

"Thanks for the food," said Zoe Masters, a talented computer engineer with dyed red hair and green eyes. Her voice had some rasp to it.

"The sergeant will be here for a few weeks," said Mei. "He's offered to help out where needed, so I've asked him to assist Bartholomew with setting up a third supply tent."

"Great," said Bart, sighing. "You know I'm an engineer, right?"

Mei ignored him. "If any of you need an extra pair of hands, please do not hesitate to ask him."

John sat up in his chair. "I'll be in and out a few times a week, but I'll schedule around you guys."

"You're leaving?" asked Zoe. "Why?"

"I promised Central I'd do some scouting. We've already mapped most of the area, but I figured I'd spend some time filling in the gaps. Gives me something to do."

"Regardless, Sergeant Finn will be happy to assist," said Mei. "Simply let him know ahead of time." She nodded to Sophie. "Your turn."

Sophie got to her feet and replaced Mei at the head of the table. She turned the display screen on, quickly locating a file labeled *Radiation Levels.* "As you all know, I've been studying the residual radiation from the Second Jolt, which we first noticed approximately six months ago." She glanced at John. "Sorry, Mr. Finn. I hope you don't find this too boring."

He shrugged. "Trust me. It's not the first time I've been subjected to a science lecture I didn't understand." He nudged Mei with his foot.

"Fair enough," said Sophie, continuing. "Today marks the end of my first testing period. Here are the results." She touched the file on the screen and a map appeared. "I've been trying to find the source of the radiation, but so far I haven't had much luck. My best guess is it's coming from the rubble of the old Ortego building, but after several scans, I still don't have a good answer."

"That sucks," said Travis.

John raise his hand. "So you don't even know what's causing it?" he asked.

"I was hoping to have a solution by now, but as you can see, I've come up short. Also, you don't have to hold your hand up, Mr. Finn."

John scratched the back of his head. "What kind of radiation is it?"

"High frequency, electromagnetic," said Sophie. "Gamma rays, technically."

"I take it gamma rays are bad?"

"Deadly," said Mei. "It's the reason we're staying as far away from the crater as we are."

"We have the suits, though," said Bart. "They're solid, and the radiation's not so strong. It's annoying since it slows us down, but hey, it could be worse. We can still do our jobs."

"Keep working on the problem, Sophie," said Mei. "We're here if you need help."

The girl smiled and nodded before taking her seat.

"Bartholomew? Zoe? Travis? Anything else?" asked Mei.

Zoe shook her head. "I'm still working on the Ortego Disks we found in the rubble. They're pretty banged up, so it'll be a while before I have anything to talk about. Sorry."

"Nothing here, either," said Bartholomew. "Check again in a week. I should be done with the coil by then."

"Coil?" asked John.

"Framling Coil," he said. "Part of the reason we're here is to research how they work. Central sees value in it as a new source of power."

John glanced at Mei. "Aren't those the things that turn hot air into electricity?"

"The very same," said Mei. "Most were destroyed in the blast, but a few survived." She clicked the display off. "Anyway, unless there's something else, I think we're done for the day."

"Great." John clasped his hands. "I don't know about the rest of you guys, but I'm starving. Who's up for some dinner?"

Ortego Reconstruction Outpost
April 13, 2350

The lead-lined radiation suit weighed almost as much as Mei, but thanks to her Variant-infused DNA, she barely noticed. Her genes gave her the strength of a man twice her size. Lucky, considering how small she was.

What used to be the Ortego building now lay in rubble. Most of the facility had vanished during the Second Jolt, consumed by the explosion. In its place, there was only a crater filled with chunks of stone, FlexCrete metal, and two-hundred-year-old office supplies.

Months ago, when Mei had first come here with her team, she had no idea what to expect. From a distance, the entire building seemed to be pure rubble, nothing more than rocks and metal shards, but such was not the case as it turned out. To her surprise, the basement levels were largely intact, according to the scans Bartholomew had taken. If luck was on her side, she might yet discover something she could use to further her research—a way to make her understand what really happened the last time she was here.

Her heads-up interface appeared over her suit's visor. A green dot blinked in the corner, indicating she had a call. With her eyes locked on the icon, she blinked, accepting the transmission and opening the line.

"Doctor Dwarf, do you read me?" asked a muffled voice in her ear. "Doctor Dwarf, please come in."

She rolled her eyes but smirked. "John, quit bothering me. I'm working."

"I say again, DD, this is Omega Deathblade. Do you copy?"

"Are you okay, John? Do you need attention?" She stepped over a piece of debris. The scattered remains of Ortego littered the field. "I'm not surprised. I told you it was boring here."

"Don't be modest, Doc. You're not even close to boring."

"You flatter me, sir." She edged her way to the side of the massive hole where the majority of the building's remains were.

"Find anything cool yet?" he asked. "Depends on your definition," she said, setting her bag on the ground. She took out her tripod scanner and unfolded the legs. "I'm about to run a scan. Exciting stuff."

John sighed into the mic.

Mei grinned. "Thought so." Her display lit up again with an incoming call. "Gotta go. Travis is calling."

"Farewell, my darling!"

"See you in a few hours, goof." She switched to the other line. "Yes, Travis?"

"Doctor Curie, sorry to interrupt. I'm about to send in the flippies. You might wanna clear out."

"Already?" she asked. "I was about to start my scan." She glanced at the tripod. "Well, go ahead." She hustled to the observation tent fifty meters from the site. Inside, Travis sat in his radiation suit, fumbling with one of the drones—flippies, as Travis called them. Mei was never a fan of the little robots, but they'd proven quite useful when it came to removing debris and hazardous material from the site. They were expensive, short-ranged, and malfunctioned constantly, which was why the contractors back home rarely had anything to do with them. It wasn't until a young Travis Scott pulled the drones from storage and started tinkering with the little machines that they were finally put to good use. He'd retrofitted each of them with FlexCrete, the same material used to create the Ortego building as well as the Maddison Bridge. FlexCrete was the strongest metal alloy known to exist—atomically thin sheets folded repeatedly to produce the most durable material in the world. It kept the flippy's tiny arms from buckling under the weight of heavy objects, while also allowing for its small size. These drones were only about a meter tall, but they were at least five times as strong as an average human. The design reminded Mei of a squirrel. The flippies sat on their back legs and waddled slowly toward whatever target their operators gave them. Once in place, their arms extended into flexibly thin tendrils which could wrap around and lift whatever objects were in the way. Useful and effective.

Travis tapped the head of the flippy with his index finger. "Time to go to work, Stanley." He typed a command into the keyboard on the table, and the robot came to life.

"Only one?" asked Mei.

"I'm sending Mortimer and Jefferson soon. I figured Stanley could start working now while I book the others."

She nodded.

Travis sent a command to Stanley from the computer, and it waddled out of the tent. Once it arrived at the side of the crater, it unfurled its FlexCrete tentacles and got to work. The flippies would collect the rubble and deliver it to a trailer attached to the dirt cab. Travis would then spend several days sorting and cataloging the trash, looking for anything useful. "This should only take an hour," he said, focusing his attention on Mortimer.

"Sounds good," said Mei. "I'll be right back." She stepped out of the tent and walked toward the dirt cab. It was facing away from the site, the trailer in the back with a lowered ramp to give the flippies easy access. She climbed into the passenger-side seat and placed a call to John.

He opened the line almost immediately. "Hey, what's up?" He sounded like he was chewing on something.

"What are you eating?" she asked.

"Soy burger," he said, munching into the food. "Don't worry. I'll eat again when you get back."

"Remember, we're limited on supplies."

"I can always run to the commissary."

She laughed. "How's it going back there?"

"Bart and I got the tent up like you wanted. Interesting guy. You know he used to be in the military? Weird career change, huh?"

"He'd rather still be there," she said.

"What do you mean?"

"He was kicked out."

John cocked his brow. "For what?"

"Nothing serious. He aced the physical. He just couldn't hold a rifle steady."

"He got the shakes?"

"I guess so. The doctors called it performance anxiety. I'm not so sure, though. He's the best engineer I've ever met, and he works just fine under pressure."

"Well, good," said John.

"Say, where are the girls?" asked Mei, changing the subject.

"Dunno. I'm still in the middle of this sandwich."

She thumbed the dirt cab's door handle, wrinkling her nose. "Working, probably. Can you see if Zoe needs help with anything, once you're done eating?"

"Yeah, sure thing. Everything going alright down there?"

"The flippies are lugging debris out of the pit, same as usual."

"You talk like I know what that means," said John. He paused. "What the hell's a flippy?"

"A robot, basically."

"Since when do you have robots?"

"They're Travis's, not mine. He uses them to lift heavy things. They're pretty useful."

"You think if I ask him, he'd let me—"

"No, John, they're not for you to play with," said Mei.

"Dammit," he said, sounding defeated. "You never let me have any fun."

"One of us has to be the adult," she said, smiling a little. "Besides, you already get to go play soldier whenever you want. Don't act like your life is so boring."

"Speaking of, I should probably head out soon. Central gave me orders to map the area, and I haven't even started yet."

"Too distracted?"

He snickered, and his voice deepened. "You're the only distraction I *need*, babe."

"Oh, my god," she said, laughing. "I can't believe you just said that."

"What's wrong? Can't handle the corny one-liners? They're pretty classy, I know. It's okay to feel intimidated. Just don't tell anyone about my softer side."

"How embarrassing for you," she said, giggling. "But I promise not to tell."

"That's why I love you," he said. "You know how to keep a secret."

2

Ortego Outpost File Logs
Play Audio File 270
Recorded: April 13, 2350

CURIE: *Excavation is going well. The flippies have removed about two-thirds of the debris. I expect we'll have the rest out of there by the end of the month.*

PRESCOTT: *What about your work on the coil?*

CURIE: *Bartholomew is overseeing the repairs. I've attached his report, along with my own. He's making progress, but there's still more work to be done.*

PRESCOTT: *I'm looking it over as we speak, but it's hardly encouraging. Recovering the coils is your primary objective here. Isn't it the whole reason you're there?*

CURIE: *Actually, sir, the mission I pitched to the board covered a wide range of—*

PRESCOTT: *Yes, yes, of course. Still, the coil was our main concern. We made it clear when we greenlit your project. I hope you are making this a priority.*

CURIE: *It's no less important than anything else we're doing, I assure you.*

PRESCOTT: *It needs to become your primary focus, Doctor Curie. The board keeps badgering me for something more than simple reports. You've been up there for months. It's time to start producing results.*

CURIE: *What about the Ortego Disks we've taken from the ruins? Aren't those worth the board's time?*

PRESCOTT: *Fine work, yes, but nothing matches the potential of a brand new source of energy. You can understand their eagerness, I'm sure.*

CURIE: *Of course I can, but—*

PRESCOTT: *Then I will let the board know you'll have more to show in next week's report. Good luck with your work, Doctor Curie. Please don't let us down.*

End Audio File

Ortego Reconstruction Outpost
April 13, 2350

Mei sat in the conference tent, waiting for the others to arrive. She was fifteen minutes early but didn't mind the quiet solitude.

Sometimes spending a few minutes alone was the best way to work through a problem. In this case, her boss.

Mei hated Prescott. He made her job even more difficult than it should be, which was really saying something.

The last few days had been going so well, too. Travis and his flippies were making noticeable progress clearing the rubble from the Ortego building. Zoe and Sophie had managed to recover and log several dozen Ortego Disks. Bartholomew seemed to be doing well. And John was here. Everything was going so well.

But then she had the conference call with Dr. Prescott, the lowest ranking member of the science division's project oversight board. He wanted her to put all of her people to work on the Framling Coil project, which meant ignoring everything else. Didn't he care about the radiation? They still didn't understand where it was coming from. What about the petabites of information Zoe had found within those Ortego Disks? Weren't they worth something?

Shortsighted as he might be, this wasn't entirely Prescott's fault. When she really sat and thought about it, Mei couldn't help but blame herself.

Truthfully, the Framling Coil had been a key selling point to greenlighting this project. Mei had approached the board with a request to send a team to assess and potentially recover artifacts from the former Ortego headquarters. In response to this, she received a short, albeit polite rejection. According to the board, Central's new focus was the expansion and reconstruction of humanity. An archeological dig in the middle of the desert was simply too difficult to justify.

Mei understood the reasoning, but it didn't stop her from trying again. She reevaluated her proposal and made sure to include some enticing details about the Framling Coils, calling them a significant alternative source of energy, completely independent and self-sustaining. A perfect solution for future outposts.

A few weeks later, she received the authorization she needed. It was a victory.

I guess I should be happy I made it this far, she thought. Indeed, the chance of her returning to these ruins with any kind of research outfit had been thin at best. So why was she so upset? She got what she wanted, and the work was going well, wasn't it?

Because you still don't have any answers, she heard herself say. Despite the past few months and the smorgasbord of information they'd uncovered, she still couldn't find any information on the Second Jolt or why the building had been destroyed. More importantly, she still didn't understand what had happened to Terry. She had so many questions.

If only she could allocate her resources the way she wanted. Why did the board have to micromanage everything?

Maybe if I give them what they want, they'll leave me alone, she thought but knew it was a lie. She kicked the table. As soon as she gave them what they wanted, they'd order her home. She had to find another way.

Zoe entered the tent laughing with Travis and Sophie followed closely behind. "Give me a break," she said. "Mort would kick Jeff's ass, hands down."

Travis rolled his eyes. "Yeah, right! Jefferson has a quarter more load capacity, plus his casing is newer. Mortimer wouldn't stand a chance."

"Dr. Curie, what do you think? Mortimer or Jefferson, who would win in a fight to the death?"

It took Mei a second to realize what they were talking about. "You mean the flippies?" she asked. "Where did this come from?"

Sophie took a seat across from Mei. "Don't ask me."

Travis motioned at Sophie before answering. "Zoe here threatened to reprogram the flippies to fight each other. I was against it at first, but she's got me half-convinced. The only problem is her top pick." He shook his head at Zoe. "I'm so disappointed in you."

"We'll see who's disappointed when Mort kicks the crap out of Jeff. Give me two days with the little guy. You won't even recognize him."

Travis scoffed. "Oh, I see. So you're going to modify him? Tack on a saw, maybe a flame thrower? You can't go changing the rules."

Mei motioned for the two of them to sit. "Is everyone ready to get started? Where's Bartholomew?"

The flap to the tent opened and Bart walked in. "Over here, boss." John was right behind him. Mei waited for them to take their seats before she began.

"I received a call this morning from Prescott," she said.

"What did the little weasel want?" asked Zoe.

Mei went through the entire call, beat for beat, detailing everything Prescott had said.

"Sounds like they're getting impatient," said Travis.

"No surprise there," said Zoe.

"I might have something soon, but I can't make any promises," said Bart.

"I need a more concrete answer," said Mei.

"I get that, but there's so many problems, big and small. I'm doing everything I can to get one of these buckets up and running. It's not easy. Tell them we need more time."

"I already did," said Mei. She bit the inside of her lip, breaking the skin. She already hated herself for what she was about to ask. "What if I relocate a few people to help?"

He shook his head. "I'm the only one here who knows the first thing about the coils."

"Except me," said Travis. "But you need me for the dig."

"Right," said Bart.

"Not true," said Zoe, raising her finger. "Travis has been teaching me how to use the flippies. They're mostly automated, so all it takes is knowing how to boot them on and shut them down. I can handle it."

Mei shot a glance at Travis, arching her brow. "When did you have time to teach her about the flippies?"

"The last few times you sent us to the site by ourselves," said Zoe.

John grinned. "You two were down there alone? My, my." Mei gave him stern look that said to shut up. He frowned and stared at the table.

"Bart, are you fine with Travis helping you out?" asked Mei.

He shrugged. "We all have to make sacrifices sometimes."

"You make it sound like I'm a burden," said Travis.

"Hey, you said it, not me."

Mei ignored them and glanced at Zoe. "Are you absolutely certain you can handle the flippies?"

"Better than this guy," she said, thumbing at Travis and grinning. "But yeah, I can do it."

"Great. We're settled. Zoe's on flippie duty while Travis helps Bart with the Framling Coil."

"For how long?" asked Travis.

"However long it takes to get one of those machines partially functional. I don't care if it's the coil itself or the power supply. We just need something to show the board. We need to give them a distraction."

Unknown Location
April 14, 2350

Today was Terry's eighteenth birthday. It was also the third year he'd spent on this strange new planet so very far from home.

In the early days, he didn't move around much, staying close to the spot where the portal had dropped him. The world was unfamiliar, so it was better to stay where he knew it was safe. But when he found there wasn't a lot of food or resources there, he began to explore further, migrating away. He found better sources of food, better places to camp.

Over the years, he had returned there, but it had become

increasingly rare. For the last two years, he only went there on his birthday. An annual pilgrimage.

In those early days and much to his surprise, he'd found a cluster of ancient ruins, seemingly advanced, built and shaped by what he assumed must be an intelligent race of beings, though they had long since vanished. Only their architecture remained—little dome houses overgrown with weeds.

Had the Variant atmosphere killed them, too? The gas had obliterated most of the human race, spreading across the globe and consuming everything. Perhaps these forgotten aliens created it here. For several months, Terry tried to understand who they were, searching through the buildings for answers. But he never found anything substantial. He couldn't read their language. He couldn't find any evidence of why they were gone. He had nothing.

The ruins were where the portal left him, so he only saw them when he returned on his birthday. Today he would see them again, the same as he had the year before. It was something to look forward to.

He traveled for half a day through valley and jungle until at last he came upon them, these decrepit, ancient buildings. Vines encased most of the domes, while thick weeds littered much of the ground. Given enough time, he wondered, would the planet take it back? Would it be as though nothing had ever existed here?

Where did all the people go? asked Janice, the voice in his head.

"I don't know," he muttered, passing by a door with a circular window nearby. He glanced inside, spotting an empty room with rotting furniture. He remembered exploring a home like this and pressing his foot against what must have been a couch, only to see it crumble to pieces.

I bet they hated it here and left, said Janice.

"Could be," he said.

Maybe they died, she said. *Maybe you killed them when you came here, just like you killed your friends on the other side.*

He didn't answer.

Yes, she said matter-of-factly. *Yes, I'm sure you did.*

Terry walked through the center of town, toward what he believed to be the southern end, though of course he couldn't say if this was true. He had no idea how directions worked on this new world, but he looked at where the suns rose and called it east, because there was no other way. And who would tell him he was wrong?

Beyond the final stretch of buildings sat a forest, the threshold demarcated by a massive tree with thick branches which bent so far they touched the ground. A carpet of red flowers covered the dirt near its roots, fighting with the weeds for dominance. Terry passed under the arch of a branch, picking leaves from it and flicking them away.

The air was thick with moisture as storm clouds gathered overhead, darkening the forest and dampening the sky. It took him an hour to reach his old campsite—a small cave buried in a grassy hillside—and by then, a shower of rain had begun to fall, soft and steady. The cavern was fairly shallow, only about three meters of space between the rocks, but the overhang was enough to give him some reprieve. He had liked it well enough when he lived here. If the food in this area had been more plentiful, he might've even stayed.

Terry sat against the wall of the cave, resting at the edge of the shade and listening to the rhythm of drops as they pattered against the leaves, running off in rivulets before swelling and falling into the mud below. From his bag, he retrieved a piece of fruit and his machete, a slab of metal he'd taken from the Ortego building's debris when he first arrived. Over time, he managed to sharpen the edge into a weapon. It made traveling through the jungle significantly easier.

He set the blade against the wall of the cave in case he needed it later.

Terry sighed and bit into the ripened skin of the fruit. Pink juices slid down his cheeks and dripped onto his thighs. Against his better judgment, he ate a second helping, savoring the taste.

It was his birthday, after all. He might as well indulge.

Terry awoke to the sound of animals whining. He stretched his arms and moaned. Another day in paradise.

The dawn clouds were mostly parted, soon to be replaced by a vast and open firmament, and one of the twin suns rose brightly on the horizon's edge. The Variant air always smelled so clean and sweet after the rain. It would be a good day.

He grabbed his pack and emerged from the cave, leaving the hole in the earth behind and continuing along his way. His destination lay on a cliff overlooking the forest near the abandoned city. The trek required another hour's hike through the forest and then a river-crossing, not to mention the eventual climb.

Late in the morning, he emerged from beneath the trees and found himself on the bank of the river, which was swollen by the storm and diluted with fallen leaves. Several trees littered the riverside, their rotting trunks drowning in the stream. He walked along the northern bank of red clay, leaving a series of footprints behind, a trail for no one to follow.

A cry rang out somewhere close by, identical to the one that woke him. It came from the east.

What do you think it is? asked Janice.

"Could be a bird," he muttered.

More like lunch, she said. *You should check. I'm hungry.*

He nodded and headed into the forest. A few minutes later, he heard another cry, except it was louder. He was getting close.

A short time later, he found an opening in the trees, revealing a small glade filled with boulders and broken twigs. Stepping between the rocks, he tried to stay as quiet as possible. As he approached a few of the larger stones, he heard a whimpering groan, light and nasally. Terry leaned against the side of the boulder in order to see the source of the crying.

The animals were lying on a pile of twigs, huddled together like balls of fur, their eyes still sealed. They appeared to be newborns.

It was a nest.

Each of the animals had gray hair all over its body. He recognized the species, which typically carried horns on their foreheads, although this particular feature was noticeably absent on the offspring. The animals had strong back legs with shorter arms in the front, each with six thin claws. Dangerous when fully grown.

Food is food, said Janice. *Grab one, and let's go.*

Terry hesitated. He didn't want to kill a helpless infant, not even for food. He still had fruit. He'd be alright.

Don't be a coward.

Terry stepped away from the nest. He'd made a mistake coming here. The mother wasn't around right now, but she might be soon, and he didn't feel like introducing himself.

As he moved, one of the animals yelped, causing the others to do the same. Somehow, he'd disturbed them. *Better get out of here quick,* he thought.

He leapt over one of the rocks, grabbing the branch of a nearby tree and pulling himself onto it. He took a moment to look at the nest, but immediately regretted it.

Two meters from the infants, staring at him from the grass, a hulking beast stood breathing, slime dripping from its mouth and nose.

Terry maintained eye contact, not quite knowing what to do. The animal growled, opening its jaws to reveal an unpleasantly large set of teeth.

This isn't good, said Janice.

Terry turned and bolted, leaping from the tree and out of the glade. He curved around a stump, kicking up dirt and switching directions. The animal was fast and growing closer with every step. He reached to his side for the machete. He'd never killed anything larger than a small bird with it, so there was no way of knowing how effective it would be against an animal this size. The idea of orphaning the newborns wasn't appealing, but he'd do what he had to.

He left the forest and saw the river. The beast emerged soon after, enraged and snarling. Terry saw no other option but to run headlong into the current, hoping the beast would know better than to follow. It didn't and plunged into the water behind him.

The riverbed was riddled with pebbles, making it difficult to stand. He lost his footing a few times to the pressure of the rapids, falling into the water as he struggled to regain his composure. He gripped the sunken earth, caking his hands in red mud, cutting his palms and feet. After a frantic shuffle through the water, he finally reached the other side.

He struggled out of the water, drenched and dripping. Glancing over his shoulder, he saw the creature swimming toward him, shrieking as it tried to stay afloat. But the rapids were strong and powerful, slowing the beast significantly.

Terry ran into the tree line, paying no mind to his direction. He'd find his way out eventually. For now, he was more concerned with getting some distance between himself and the raging mother of three.

Several minutes into the woods, he realized he could no longer hear the animal's wailing. Maybe she abandoned her chase or was swept away by the river. Either one was a relief.

He considered going back the way he came, but he wasn't eager for a repeat encounter with the den mother. The trees were thinner ahead, which could mean a clearing. He decided to investigate. If anything, he'd find a spot to rest.

A short walk later, he discovered a break in the trees, revealing a massive valley. Not only that, but another dome like the ones in the city. This one seemed to be much larger, though—at least twice the size of the others. He'd never known this place existed, despite all his time exploring the nearby countryside. Why would they build such a thing so far from the other buildings?

Lots of reasons, said Janice.

He nodded. Humans often had remote installations far away from their cities and towns. Maybe it was for a specific resource. Maybe there was a mine nearby. He'd never found one before, but it didn't mean they didn't exist.

Terry descended into the valley toward the building. Standing before it, he stared through the windows but saw nothing. A door was ajar, pushed open by a patch of overgrown weeds.

He went inside, minding the corpse of a small rat-like animal near the entrance. Stepping beside the body, he winced at the smell. The dome was sectioned off into different floors, unlike most of the others he'd seen previously. Attached to the foyer where he stood, there was a long hallway leading to several rooms.

The nearest didn't have much, except for a pile of metal tiles near the corner. A quick glance showed the floor was only half completed. Had the builders been in the process of constructing this place when they abandoned it? There certainly wasn't much furniture to speak of, unlike the other buildings.

He left to check the next room. This one was empty, too, but there were no piles of building supplies this time. It was simply vacant. He moved on, but found the same thing in each of the other rooms. At the far end of the hall, there was a staircase, which he decided to climb, but with dwindling expectations. This place was proving such a disappointment, just like everything else on this planet.

He touched the railing of the staircase, stirring dust into the air. He took a step and a soft creak echoed through the dome, followed by another as he pressed his foot against the step and continued. He wondered how sturdy the material was or if he should be concerned with the noise, but quickly put it out of his mind.

As he emerged from the stairs, he found the second story to be much like the first, with the exception of the distant window overlooking the valley. As before, Terry checked each of the rooms, only to discover they'd yet to have their tiles installed. Again, he wondered what happened to cause them to stop construction so abruptly.

Terry went to the back of the hall and stood at the window, staring into the blue valley. Perhaps he would stay the night here. He considered camping in the city once when he first discovered it, but each of those buildings looked lived in, like memorials or graves. Not like this one, which remained untouched.

The twin suns set in the late evening, replaced with the beautiful night sky. The arm of a galaxy spread across the darkness, engulfed by millions of flickering dots of light. Somewhere in that chaos was the world he had come from, though it was lost to him.

On the second floor of the alien dome, using his pack as a

pillow, he lay against the cold metal tiles, staring through the window and longing for sleep.

Brother, said the girl in his mind. *Why are you so scared?*

The voice startled him. He turned on his side and closed his eyes.

None of them loved you. Not like I do. You know it's true.

He buried his face in his pack, squeezing the straps, trying to shut out the words.

You're scared, she said. *You're afraid.*

He began to shake.

You're going to die alone.

3

Ortego Outpost File Logs

Play Audio File 281

Recorded: April 15, 2350

THISTLE: *Some of these readings are a bit confusing, Sergeant.*

FINN: *Sorry, sir. I ran into a hitch on the road.*

THISTLE: *Rabs?*

FINN: *Flat tire. Had to swap it with a spare.*

THISTLE: *Why didn't you finish the run?*

FINN: *And risk another one going out on me? I'd be stranded.*

THISTLE: *Fair enough. So when you going back?*

FINN: *I'll make a second pass tomorrow, but so far I'm not seeing any nests or hazardous wildlife. Seems pretty clean.*

THISTLE: *Remember, Colonel Ross wants a full sweep. No exceptions.*

FINN: *Come on, Cap. I'll do the full job. You know me. I'm not lazy.*

THISTLE: *Is this the part where I bring up the time you left your weapon behind?*

FINN: *Hey, I went back for it.*

THISTLE: *Not before we were halfway to the nest.*

FINN: *I made it back in time for the fight, didn't I?*

THISTLE: *Hmph. I suppose you did.*

FINN: *Apology accepted, boss.*

THISTLE: *Alright Johnny, there's one last thing I'm supposed to tell you, before I forget.*

FINN: *Yes, sir?*

THISTLE: *The outpost you're staying at…how's it looking? Are those scientists doing alright?*

FINN: *Seems like it. Why?*

THISTLE: *Central's worried about their prolonged isolation. They've been there for months now.*

FINN: *There's nothing to worry about. Besides, I'm keeping things lively.*

THISTLE: *Good to hear, Finn. But make sure you report anything out of the ordinary. We need to keep our people safe.*

End Audio File

Unknown Location
April 15, 2350

Terry bent to the left and cracked his spine as soon as he woke up. Several clicks followed as he stretched the rest of his body.

The soft hue of morning light had hit him through the window, waking him. He reached into his pack and grabbed a piece of fruit for breakfast. He noted there were only three left after this. He'd have to go foraging today.

After Terry swallowed the last of the fruit, he headed downstairs and set about exploring. Since he had come from the east and found nothing, he decided to start north and work his way to the west. He'd heard birds chirping in the night, which meant a viable source of protein. He'd look for them later, once he had a chance to scout the area.

He searched for an hour before discovering a nest of tiny rodent-like creatures, which he'd previously named beavermites. The animals were scrawny and yellow, their eyes pure white. Using two large teeth, which together were the size equivalent of one of their heads, they carved nests inside their chosen trees, sucking moisture and nutrients out of the bark. Terry had actually tried to eat one a few years back, unsuccessfully. Aside from there being almost no meat on the bones, it actually made him sick. For nearly two days, he couldn't stop vomiting.

Terry kept walking, eventually happening upon a field overgrown with grass and tangled weeds and littered with strange trees unlike any others he'd found in the forest so far. A quick examination showed them to have fruit on their branches but quite different from the kind in his pack. The fruit—yellow with a coat of blue fuzz—grew twice as thick, and upon examination had a smell resembling strawberries.

With his bone knife, he split one in half to reveal a juicy interior. He debated eating it, then shrugged and did it anyway. As the juice hit his lips and tongue, its powerful flavor overtook him, and he smiled. Delicious.

This single tree alone had over a dozen pieces of fruit. As he scanned the field, he spotted at least twenty other trees, each exactly like this one. Had he somehow stumbled upon the remnants of an orchard? Was he truly so lucky? In all his time on this planet, he'd never found food as plentiful as this.

A cloud passed overhead and Terry looked to see the twin suns descending from their zenith, marking the afternoon's approach. He had several hours' worth of light left, and he still had things to do.

Ortego Reconstruction Outpost
April 15, 2350

THE FLIPPY TENT was crowded with parts and supplies. Mei sat on the table swinging her short legs while Zoe fiddled with the controls, trying to power on little Mortimer. Two of the other robots, Jefferson and Stanley, were already outside moving debris from the pit and making good time.

"Looks like the system stopped cooling," said Zoe. She had

Mortimer's back panel open. "Give me a sec." She got to her feet and retrieved a new unit from the nearby bin.

Mei was surprised at how adept Zoe was at handling the flippies. A few problems arose now and again, but for the most part she handled her new role well. It must've been a nice change of pace after decoding and cataloguing Ortego Disks for so many months, but Zoe never complained one way or the other, making it difficult to tell if she actually enjoyed the change. Regardless, Mei was relieved to see her adapting so well.

Travis was a different story. Both he and Bart were exceptionally gifted engineers, but they preferred working alone. Mei understood their perspective, but the reality simply didn't allow for any alternative. Luckily, both men seemed to understand what was at stake. They dealt with the situation like professionals, albeit reluctantly.

"Here we go," said Zoe, hitting the power switch and shutting the panel. Her voice had a hint of uncertainty in it. The flippy hummed as the system rebooted, its eyes turning blue once the process was complete. "Diagnostic check," said Zoe, glancing at the pad in her hand. "Looks like Morty's back to normal. Let's try some exercises." She tapped the screen, and the flippy raised its tentacles, then dropped them to the side.

"Can he get to work now?" asked Mei.

"Looks like it." Zoe typed a command, and Mortimer waddled out of the tent to join his two brothers.

"Great job," said Mei. The sooner the flippies did their work, the better. It wouldn't be much longer before they cleared enough rubble to access the basement level. In fact, if the scan she performed an hour ago was any indication, they were nearly there already. A few days, in fact, if things went smoothly.

Zoe approached Mei and leaned against the side of the table she was sitting on. "So you really think we'll find anything underneath all those rocks?"

"I'm hoping," said Mei.

"I have to be honest," she said. "I don't get it."

"Don't get what?"

Zoe hesitated but went on. "It's no big secret what happened to you and your boyfriend," she said, catching Mei a little off guard. None of her staff had referred to John in such a way since he arrived, although it wasn't like she'd been keeping their relationship a secret. But still, she didn't expect it. "You and him… those other kids. We all know the story."

Not the full story, thought Mei. She and her friends had left out the part about Alex's homicidal breakdown. "What's your point, Zoe?"

"Why would you want to come back here? Why go through all the political hoops? I know it wasn't easy for you to convince your boss." She beamed a knowing smile at Mei. "You could have given them the idea and stepped aside. Why'd you ask to come here?"

Mei briefly considered admitting the truth. It would be so easy. *I'm here to find out what happened to Terry. I need answers.* But she couldn't risk it. If anyone reported her true motives, they might shut the project down. The board had already indicated their concern over whether or not Mei could remain impartial due to her experiences on the surface. Ultimately, they allowed it, but only because it was her project, and she knew more about this place than anyone. If they discovered what she was really after, they'd call her objectivity into question. Maybe they'd assign someone new to oversee the team. Zoe and the others might be allowed to stay. But not Mei. She'd be recalled immediately, made to work a meager lab job until some undisclosed time had passed. She couldn't bear the thought. "Honestly? You really want to know?"

Zoe's eyes lit up. "Yeah, of course."

Mei leaned towards her. "I don't trust anyone else."

"Huh?"

Mei grinned. "The work's too important to let some idiot handle it. This is the place where Variant came from, right? And it was brought here because of a machine. We shut it down, but all it did was thin the gas, not get rid of it. If we can find more information about how they built the portal, we might be able to find a way to clean the rest of the air." It was the same pitch she'd originally given her superiors before including the part about the coils. It was a good lie, the kind with a sliver of truth in it.

"So you're here because you don't trust anyone else?" asked Zoe.

"Precisely," nodded Mei. "People are stupid. They would've turned this mission into a salvage operation just like the board's trying to do now with the coil. None of them have their priorities right."

"You might have a point with people being idiots," said Zoe. "I get what you're saying."

"Good," said Mei and was thankful for it. No one needed to

know what she was really doing here. Not the board or her team…not even John. There was no reason to tell any of them. "I believe in what we're doing here. If I didn't, I never would've come."

"I'm glad to be here, too," said Zoe.

"I couldn't ask for a better team," she said, smiling, and it really was the truth.

Unknown
April 16, 2350

TERRY SPENT the bulk of his morning exploring the orchard he'd previously discovered in the woods. Afterwards, once he'd collected more than enough fruit to last him the week, he returned to the glade. From there, he set off to scout the eastern woods, taking note of the position of the suns. It was slightly before noon, which gave him plenty of time to explore.

After an hour or so of hiking, he came upon a small pond. The water was so thick with mud and grime, it was difficult to see more than a few centimeters. Clumps of blue weeds littered the surface, occasionally moving when a small breeze blew through the trees. *There might be one of those animals in there*, suggested Janice. She was of course referencing the Mudsnakes, annoying vermin Terry had taken to avoiding. The last thing he needed was an infestation migrating into his new camp. He'd better find out now in case he had to get rid of them.

He snagged some rocks and tossed one into the pond.

Plop.

He circled to the other side, throwing the rest, one at a time.

Plop. Plop. Plop.

Half a dozen ripples grew until they merged with the surrounding earth. A small knot of weeds rustled in the water, shaking generously. From between the stalks, a thin set of blue eyes emerged, surrounded by black, slimy skin. The animal stared at him, blinking. Terry met its gaze and watched as it slowly submerged.

He was afraid of this. Mudsnakes were the worst kind of pests. They slept underwater during the day only to spend their nights scavenging on land. He'd chosen his last camp because it was next to a running stream too small for a mudsnake to swim through. Did he have to worry now about his new camp and his food supply? The pond was a good long walk from the dome, but was it far enough? He didn't know if he should take the risk or try exterminating them while he still had some daylight.

Not now, suggested Janice. *We still have to explore. Come back later.*

Right. He could wait. Return with some proper tools.

Let's go! Time's wasting, said Janice.

Terry nodded his agreement. The day was fading, and he still had plenty of ground to cover. Who knew what he'd discover? He might get lucky and run into another orchard. Maybe this whole area had once been a massive farm. Wouldn't that be something? He'd never have to worry about food again.

A short walk later, he found the edge of the woods. As he entered yet another clearing, he came face to face with a ridge no larger than a dozen meters. He followed it around, and it only grew in size. In the far distance, he spotted several small domes resting adjacent to the rockface. They almost looked strategic. But why here?

He ran to them, then stopped when he saw what they were guarding—a large artificial cave with flattened stone walls inside. As he approached, he could see a set of descending stairs.

Looks dangerous, said Janice. *We should leave.*

"I wanna check it out," he said, peering into the cave.

Fine, but be careful, she said.

The air inside the cave was thick and full of dust. The deeper he went, the colder it grew. Like every other structure he'd found on this world, this one felt like a tomb. After a few minutes when the light had gone completely out, his hybrid eyes adjusted, allowing him to see clearly. To his surprise, the stairs went on and on, deep into the cavern. A hundred meters, perhaps, but he kept going.

Where are we going? Asked Janice.

He shrugged. "Nowhere." The echo of his voice surprised him.

Monsters live in caves, she said. *Big monsters with shiny claws and scary faces. You remember. They'll kill us both.*

An image of a razorback flashed in his mind. He froze instantly. The animal's body had been covered in silver quills, which fluttered and moved depending on what it was doing. He imagined those empty eyes staring at him, seemingly devoid of thought. A creature bred on instinct. He remembered the fight in the tunnel, back when Roland was killed by one of the monsters. Terry had tried to stop it, but he was too late.

What if there's one down here? Asked Janice.

"There won't be," he said, softly.

You don't know.

He found the base of the stairs and discovered a vast opening. What he'd assumed was a cave appeared to be a tunnel, expertly carved, stretching far into the earth. From what he could tell, it went on for at least a kilometer before curving to the north. Dozens of other paths branched off to unknown areas.

Scary, said Janice. *What do you think this is?*

"I don't know," he muttered. "Could be anything."

We should go. It's getting late.

He nodded. He'd return later when he had more time to explore. Besides, his stomach was growling.

Terry left the cave and entered the light of the two setting suns. He had about forty five minutes before nightfall. Plenty of time to get home, back to his shack in the glade.

Marching briskly through the woods, he found the abandoned dome with several minutes to spare. Upstairs, he took out several pieces of the fruit he'd found at the orchard and ate them freely. Since his arrival on this planet, his belly had never been full, but today would be different. With so much food in the orchard, he could afford to live a little, even if only for a day.

Afterwards, he took his knife and carved a map into the wall near where he slept. He marked the glade, the orchard, the pond, and the ridge. He also included the cave and the two huts outside, lingering on them for longer than he cared to admit. What was the point of this place? Had it been a mine of some kind? He'd never seen any machinery or carts, nor did the walls look like they'd been worked. In fact, they seemed more like the walls of the city back home, designed like the inside of a building. Did people once live down there?

He went to the other side of the room and carved the opening of the cave on the wall. He followed it with some stairs and the first major tunnel. Staring at it, he could not help but contemplate how deep the passages stretched. There must be something there, he knew.

A secret in the dark.

4

Ortego Outpost File Logs
Play Audio File 289
Recorded: April 17, 2350

THISTLE: *Anything to report, Sergeant? How'd the run go?*

FINN: *I spotted a few tracks to the north, about four kilometers out. Could be rabs, but I doubt it.*

THISTLE*: Any signs of a nest?*

FINN*: Not as far as I can tell. There's no buildings or caves. It's all just leveled plains.*

THISTLE*: And the tracks? What are they?*

FINN*: If I had to guess, I'd say we're dealing with a heard of kits. They like to migrate this way during the early summer.*

THISTLE*: Kits?*

***FINN**: Kitoboras, sir. They're like goats, but uglier. I think these are the ones we usually see near Salamander Outpost.*

***THISTLE**: Kits, eh? First time I've heard the nickname. Cost of working behind a desk, I guess. You miss out on the field slang.*

***FINN**: Anytime you wanna suit up and join the squad, we're always glad to have you, sir. As far as I'm concerned, it's still your detachment.*

***THISTLE**: Nice try, but you're not pawning your responsibilities off on me. Besides, Central has other plans for my corpse.*

***FINN**: You're not that old, sir.*

***THISTLE**: Enjoy the outdoors while you can, Johnny. Before you know it, you'll be stuck in an office, same as me. You'll hate every second of it, and it'll take everything you've got not to scream or punch the idiot secretary they give you.*

***FINN**: Aw, don't punch Jerry. He makes good coffee.*

***THISTLE**: Unless you want another promotion, I'd stow the sarcasm. I can make you a paper pusher this time tomorrow.*

***FINN**: Whoa! Boss, you win. Let's not do anything drastic.*

End Audio File

Unknown

April 17, 2350

Terry planned on spending most of the day exploring the tunnel. He packed several pieces of fruit, knowing he had a long task ahead of him. As he hiked there, he contemplated which passageway he'd search first. There were so many, he recalled, going out in every direction. He didn't know where to start.

When he arrived, he descended into the cavern below, following the main path about fifty meters. From there, he was able to get a clearer view of the various branching passages. He couldn't tell how deep each one went, but some appeared to be fairly small, opening into larger chambers or connecting with other paths. He saw himself spending days or even weeks exploring these ruins. He decided to follow the first tunnel from the entrance and each subsequent one he encountered afterwards. It wouldn't be long before he had the entire facility explored.

Terry followed the first path to a room filled with a slew of crates and bags. He had seen similar storage containers in the domes, but usually their contents had rotted beyond recognition. He didn't expect to find anything different here, but it was worth checking. Many of the crates were already lodged open and apparently empty, but he spotted a few still closed, with thick metal lids sealed firmly across their tops. Terry tried to pry one open, but found it unusually difficult. After several futile pulls on the lid, he opted for the more aggressive approach and kicked it, knocking the box on its side.

The crate's top came undone and its guts spilled onto the floor. Several metallic objects crashed against each other, echoing loudly. He ran to examine them. The objects were heavier than they looked, each one of a different shape and design. One appeared to have vents on its side, with buttons on the other. It looked like some kind of computer, but he couldn't be sure. He'd never found anything like this in any of the domes, nor did he expect to. As far as he could tell, this civilization had never progressed beyond the bronze age, or so he'd previously believed. *Maybe it's time to revise that theory*, he thought.

He grabbed the smallest of the devices and stowed it in his pack. He'd study it more in depth once he got home. In the meantime, he might as well check the rest of the crates, then scout a few more rooms.

Most of the containers broke apart the same as the first. A few had similar devices of the kind he'd found in the first box, while several others only spilled piles of dust into the air. Terry covered his face with a rag, but it was no use. He couldn't keep the musky smell out, and he gagged, taking a few steps back as he waited for it to settle.

Once it had, he examined the pile of filth more closely. There was something buried in it, which he uncovered with the toe of his boot. The objects were round and fairly brittle. They cracked and disintegrated when he applied pressure. Food, maybe? If this was a storage area, it made sense for them to hold food and other essentials, but why so much? And why underground? He had so many questions.

After leaving the storage bins, if that's what they were, Terry walked through the halls, exploring several other rooms identical to the first. He ignored them for the most part and continued his search, hoping for answers.

At the end of another hall lay a set of stairs, which descended into a vast chamber filled with hundreds of other crates, most of which were sealed shut. Terry stood at the center of the warehouse. There didn't seem to be any vehicles or machines to move the objects. How did these people manage to lift such heavy crates without assistance?

What was all of this for? Clearly, these aliens had been preparing for something, perhaps some kind of long term settlement. It reminded him of the history of his own people and how they'd left the surface behind to live underground. They'd done it out of necessity, because the outside world was no longer suitable for human survival. Had the same thing happened here? Did the gas kill them off the way it had his own people?

He went home with more questions than answers, but it didn't matter. He wanted to know as much as possible about these people and where they came from. More importantly, he wanted to know where they went.

He sat in his new house, chewing on a piece of fruit and fumbling with the ancient device he'd stumbled upon. Using his machete, he pried open the side, revealing a slab of bronzed electronics. Was it a computer? He wished Mei were here to guide him, because he didn't know the first thing about computers or engineering.

He put the machine away and ate his dinner. The weeks ahead would be filled with exploration, with plenty of time to find his answers. He didn't know what to expect from any of this, but it was something to do. It was a way to stay busy.

Unknown

April 18, 2350

When Terry awoke, he reached into his bag and inhaled four pieces of fruit. Afterwards, he left for the cave, eager to continue his work.

This time he tried the opposite side of the main passageway. As he did, he discovered several bays as large as the cargo holds, many of which contained hundreds of bunks. It seemed as though he'd finally found the sleeping quarters.

Most of the beds were in the bays, lined symmetrically along the walls, but a few smaller rooms contained one or two bunks to themselves, possibly reserved for someone with authority. The mattresses were similar to the kind he'd seen in the domes on the surface—large, but flat, with no sheets or blankets to cover them. Was this some kind of military instillation? Perhaps they were planning for an attack of some kind.

At any moment, Terry expected to find the mummified remains of an alien being (or worse, dozens of them) lying somewhere in the dark, huddled in the position they'd died in, similar to the stories he'd read about Pompeii. He recalled standing in the Ortego building, stepping over two hundred year old corpses, gagging at the stink of rotting meat. Shouldn't these ancient catacombs be ripe with the skeletons of the dead if they had, in fact, expired here? Yet there was nothing, no hint of struggle or panic. It was like the people here were suddenly swept away, their bodies taken to some far off place. Only their technology remained.

Only their ghosts.

Ortego Reconstruction Outpost
April 18, 2350

"What's it called again?" whispered Mei, squatting next to John and Travis near the dirt cab. She was sitting at the edge of a lush field of blue grass, staring at an animal she'd never seen before. It was large, roughly the size of a small buffalo, though it looked strong enough to still be dangerous. Its red skin had patches of black hair, mostly along the spine and thighs. A long, jagged bone protruded from its forehead, reminding Mei of a rhinoceros or perhaps an ugly unicorn.

"A kitobora," said John. "We call them kits for short. The herd's nearby. I found them this morning."

"Are they dangerous?" she asked.

"Not really," he said.

Travis nodded. "I've heard of these. There's a biologist at Salamander who's trying to study them. He's only been messing with them for a few months, but he says they're pretty tame."

"Seems like we're discovering new animals all the time," said Mei.

"The more we explore, the more we uncover," said Travis. "There's a whole world out there."

"You'd be amazed what I've seen," said John, sounding prideful.

"He likes to brag," said Mei.

John grinned. "I'll share a few stories with you sometime, Trav. I've got tons."

"Can't wait," said Travis.

"So this animal," said Mei, getting back to the matter at hand. "Should we be worried?"

"Why would you be?" asked John.

"What if they come into camp looking for food?" she asked.

"They're herbivores," said Travis, motioning to the nearby grass. "Look at this field compared to the camp. Pretty sure we're safe."

"Fair point," said Mei.

Travis got to his feet. "Zoe would love this," he said, looking at the animal.

"Too bad she left for Komodo this morning," said John.

"She's missing all the fun," said Mei.

Travis sighed. "Yeah, it's a shame. Maybe I'll bring her here tomorrow when she gets back."

"I wouldn't count on it," said John.

Travis looked at him. "Why?"

"From what I've seen, they're heading east. Yesterday they were a kilometer west of here. They move pretty fast when they're not stuffing their ugly faces."

"How'd you find them if they're constantly on the run?" asked Travis.

"Part of my mission here is to scout the region and plant sensors. I spotted these guys using some I already set up, but pretty soon they'll be out of range. By this time tomorrow, I won't have eyes on them."

Travis looked at the kit and frowned. "Damn."

"Take a picture for her," suggested Mei. "She'll appreciate it."

He scoffed. "A picture would only make it worse. She'd be mad she missed out."

"Man, you're really into this girl, huh?" snickered John.

"Don't tease him," said Mei.

"Why not? You do it to me all the time."

"I'm allowed to make fun of you when you're being all cliché and lame. It's different."

John clutched his chest. "Why can't you let me love you?"

She grinned. "If it wasn't a challenge, you'd get bored."

"So true," he said with a sigh. "What can I say? I'm a hunter. I must conquer."

Mei rolled her eyes. "Yeah, okay. You couldn't hunt a tree."

"Don't listen to her, Travis. Mei wouldn't know romance if..." He paused. "Hey, where'd he go?"

Mei glanced around, but spotted him four meters behind John, creeping slowly toward the kitobora. He had a tuft of grass in his hand. "There he is," said Mei, pointing.

"Hey!" called John. "What are you doing, man? Are you stupid?"

Travis shushed him. "Give me a sec," he whispered.

Mei edged forward, but John grabbed her wrist. She looked at him, but he shook his head. Did John actually intend on letting Travis go through with this? It was a wild animal, completely unpredictable. Maybe it wasn't carnivorous, but that didn't mean it wasn't violent. He was going to get himself killed.

Travis calmly approached the kit, reached with his hand and presented the food. Until now, the kitobora had been strangely oblivious to their presence, but only because John insisted they keep a dozen meters between them.

"Have you ever seen them attack someone?" asked Mei.

John kept his eyes on Travis. "No."

It sounded like a lie, but Mei couldn't be certain. She fought the urge to argue and instead kept quiet and waited.

The kit raised its head and blinked at the grass in Travis's palm. Its little black eyes reflected the light of the sun as it set along the horizon. It sniffed at Travis, flaring its large nostrils and tilting its head slightly. "Hey," whispered Travis. "Hey, boy, look what I got here."

The animal took a step toward him, pausing to look around, and finally moved in to snag the food. It nibbled on his palm, snagging the grass with its tongue and grinding its large, flat teeth together as it ate. Travis touched the kit's neck, flattening his hand and gliding it across the animal's fur. He did this several times, whispering to it. "There you go," he said. "Good boy. There you go."

"Holy crap," said John. "He's actually doing it."

"But why? Doesn't he understand it's dangerous?" asked Mei.

Travis stepped to the side of the kit and continued to pet it. Despite the attention, the animal bent down and took another bite of grass. Travis gave the signal for the others to approach.

Mei hesitated. "This is a bad idea."

"Come on. I'll protect you," teased John.

Travis ran his fingers along the kit's neck to its forehead. "He's not so bad," he said.

"Okay, but I'm not touching it," she said, and finally joined them.

"I've never done anything like this," said Travis, brushing the kitobora with his fingers.

"None of us have," said John.

"What a weird animal," said Mei.

The kitobora raised its head at this, grass hanging from its mouth. It stared at Mei, almost curiously.

She returned the glance. "What?" she asked it.

The kitobora said nothing.

"He wants you to pet him," said Travis.

"How the hell do you know?" asked John.

Travis shrugged.

Mei held out her hand, reluctantly. She rubbed the kit's neck. It dropped its head and continued eating. "You know, we might be the first people to ever touch one of these," said Mei. "Have you thought about that? No one else in the world has ever done what we're doing right now."

Travis smiled and nodded. "Which is why we should absolutely take it home with us."

John arched his brow. "Come again?"

"Travis, don't be ridiculous," said Mei.

"Why not? We know he's docile. Look at his face."

She did and saw a vacant expression and a mouthful of grass. "I don't think so. We have enough to worry about without having to take care of a wild animal."

John scoffed. "Besides, you're only doing this because you wanna impress your girlfriend."

Travis ignored the jab. "Doctor Curie, think about this for a second. We're doing all this work with the coil and the excavation, but the board is still on your ass to deliver more research. I could send an invitation to the biologist at Salamander to see if he's still interested in these animals. If he is, our outpost suddenly gains an extra project and an added scientist, one with some weight behind his name. It isn't much, but it could help in the long run."

"What's this biologist's name?" asked John.

Travis snagged his pad from his pack. "Hang on," he said, searching. "Doctor Christopher Tabata. He's a medical doctor…volunteered to work in the slums for…geez, twelve years. Did that until he got reassigned to Central where he…"

"What?" asked Mei.

"It says he got offered a job on the board," said Travis.

"There's no one on the board named Tabata," said Mei.

"Yeah, he turned it down. It doesn't say why. But this was before the Second Jolt. As soon as the outposts went up, he moved to Salamander. It says he's the resident physician there."

"Tabata," muttered Mei. "And you think he'd say yes?"

Travis shrugged. "It couldn't hurt to ask him."

Mei knew Travis was only trying to do this in order to impress Zoe, but in doing so, he'd brought up a good point about Tabata. If the board liked this guy enough to offer him a seat, he could prove to be a valuable asset, even an ally. Mei would have to do her own research first, but she could certainly see the value in Travis's proposition.

"Ma'am? How about it?" asked Travis.

"If you do this, you have to take care of it," said Mei. "I'm talking about building a pen, feeding it, cleaning up after it. Do you understand?"

"Sure, I can do that."

Mei held up her finger. "I'm serious, Travis."

"Okay, I promise," he said.

John laughed. "Looks like your mom said you can keep it. Isn't that awesome?" He gave Travis a pat on the back. "Congrats, buddy. You deserve it."

Ortego Reconstruction Outpost
April 21, 2350

"WHAT DO WE HAVE?" asked Mei, staring at Zoe in anticipation. "Did they find anything? Is it stable?"

Zoe took a moment to answer. She was busy monitoring the flippies' feeds as they traversed the newly uncovered sub-basement of the former Ortego building. "One sec."

Mei fidgeted, tapping her thigh as she waited for answers. The flippies found the path to the basement less than an hour ago. This was expected, given the daily scans and a fundamental understanding of the building's architecture, but there was no telling what awaited them beyond this point. Mei's scans were limited in range to twenty meters, making them useless for anything long range, given how the basement actually extended several hundred meters below the surface.

She tried to manage her expectations. There was a solid chance most of the underground compartments were crushed or destroyed, which might mean weeks of tedious work clearing the path even more than they already had. For all she knew, this could be the end of her mission altogether. Only Zoe and the flippies could reveal the truth.

"It's so dark under there," said Zoe. "I had to turn their night vision on."

"So you can see now?" asked Mei.

"Sort of. There's still stuff in the way. Morty's doing a scan right now to see how bad it is."

After a few minutes, the monitor dinged, and Zoe read the report. "Okay, looks like five meters of collapsed hallway directly ahead."

"Anything else?" asked Mei.

"Not yet, but we won't know until we're farther in."

"How far can the flippies go before you have to pull them out?" asked Mei.

"You mean before the signal fades and I can't reach them anymore? Not much longer. The piles of FlexCrete between us and the flippies doesn't make it easy."

"Start clearing the hall, then. We need to be able to walk down there."

Zoe nodded. "You got it."

"How long will it take?" asked Mei.

Zoe mouthed some numbers as she did the math in her head. "Two hours. Probably."

"You don't sound very sure."

"Two hours," she repeated, this time with more confidence. "No worries."

"Okay."

"You might wanna call Travis, too. He should probably be here in case there's a problem with the flippies."

Mei nodded. "Alright, if you think we need him."

"I'm adequate at this, but Travis is the one who built the little bastards. If anything goes wrong down there, we'll need him nearby."

Mei agreed and made the call. When Travis answered, he was already talking to somebody else. "Go right ahead and see what happens," he barked. "But I'm telling you, if you don't use a better coolant, the coil's gonna fry itself. Hey! You listening to me?"

"Don't you have a goat to feed?" asked Bart.

"He's a kitobora, not a goat!" yelled Travis.

"Looks like one to me."

"Because you're an idiot!"

"Hey!" shouted Mei. "Will you two stop bickering like a couple of children? You're giving me a headache."

"Oh, uh, sorry, Doctor Curie. I thought it was Zoe calling."

"Nope, just me. I need you to drive here immediately. We accessed the basement and you need to be around in case the flippies get crushed by a collapsed wall and need fixing."

"Whoa, seriously?" The frustration in his voice was instantly gone. "When did you guys reach the basement? Did you find anything yet? What's the scoop?"

"What's up? Did they hit the bottom level?" asked Bart.

"Hang on. I'm asking," said Travis.

"Tell her I wanna go with you," said Bart.

"Stop nagging me,"

Mei sighed. "Both of you can come, but you need to get moving. I'd like to start as soon as the flippies clear a hallway."

"We'll leave right away," said Travis, frantically. "Hurry, Bart. We gotta go."

"Fine, but I'm driving," he said.

Unknown
April 21, 2350

Terry managed in a matter of days to map dozens of tunnels near the opening passage in the underground complex. Since his discovery of the bunks and the storage rooms, he'd also found many empty ones, a few half-completed tunnels, and what he could only assume was a mess hall.

Today Terry was going to travel farther through the main tunnel. He'd ignore the side passages for a while. He needed to know precisely how deep this particular rabbit hole went.

It became clear the tunnel was long, branching into hundreds of smaller paths along the way. It must lead somewhere, surely. Why else would they have built it? Terry could only guess.

He followed the path for hours. It curved and bent multiple times, pulling him deeper into the earth. How far would he go before turning back? It wasn't as though he had anywhere to be, but spending a few days underground didn't sound very appealing.

Late into the afternoon, right before he was about to head home, the massive tunnel opened into a large and daunting auditorium filled with dozens of round and rectangular tables, as well as hundreds of chairs.

"I guess this is it," he said, casually moving between two of the larger countertops. There was a tall metallic door at the other end of the room, sitting atop a raised platform. The foundation appeared to be made of a different metal than the rest of the floor. As he stepped onto it, he heard a loud thud, as though the platform were hollow.

The actual door had several symbols carved into it, though Terry couldn't make out what they were. He thought maybe they were a kind of writing, like Egyptian hieroglyphics. He touched the images, feeling the depth of the curves.

He'd never found anything like this in the domes. Whatever this was, it seemed to be unique.

Terry felt for the crack between the metal and stone, bent his knees and pulled.

It didn't move. He'd have to concentrate for this one. Call on his strength.

Time to shine, big brother, said Janice. A light giggle echoed through his mind.

He closed his eyes and quickened his breathing to get his

heart to beat faster. A short moment later, the heat in his chest swelled, as though his blood was boiling. When he opened his eyes, the room was slightly brighter, and he felt the urge to move.

Terry gripped the side of the door again, but this time when he tugged, it opened. He slid the block of metal like a piece of hollow wood. Once the door was wide enough to enter, he closed his eyes and calmed himself.

Don't overdo it, said Janice.

Terry stepped through the massive doorway into the next room. The place was at least three times as wide as the tunnel had been, and twice as tall. There were machines nearby, covered in dust but largely untouched. He slid his finger along the casing of the nearest one, which he assumed must be some kind of computer, and found it to be quite cold. The consoles were littered with buttons and panels.

Looking around the facility, he spotted another archway, although it had no door. He walked through, more curious by the second. Inside were several more machines, many of which were double the size of the rest. His eyes passed over them, following the path of the room, and he saw it.

To his surprise, a tall circular object loomed near the far end, dwarfing everything nearby. Mostly hollow, a thick outer layer of black metal enveloped a raised platform. It looked like a giant ring.

What is it? asked Janice.

Terry's first reaction was to say he didn't know, but a thought occurred. *Could this be another gate?* The facility certainly reminded him of the one Ortego had built. Was it possible they'd made another?

No. He'd seen the vid where the scientists turned the machine on. They all died immediately, completely unaware of what they created. This world had Variant in it, so there was no way they could have come here themselves. It had to be someone else.

Maybe the aliens did it, said Janice.

Terry ignored her. The domes he'd found before had all been simple buildings with crude furniture in them. There were no signs of advanced technology at all. No electronics, vehicles, or anything to indicate these people knew how to build a bridge between worlds.

None of it made any sense.

He walked along the ramp leading to the empty ring, passing through to the other side of the platform. If this really was a gate, maybe he could discover how to use it.

Terry set his pack by the room's entrance and went to the largest console he could find. He sat in the chair behind it and swept the dust with the heel of his palm, gathering a coat of grime and wiping it on the side of his seat. It could take him a lifetime to figure out this technology, maybe longer. Where would he even start? He doubted the computers were anything like the kind back home. Where was Mei when he needed her?

Terry stared at the console, debating whether to press the buttons or to leave well enough alone. After several minutes of sitting in the dark, he shrugged. "What the hell?" he whispered. "Can't hurt."

He flipped one of the dongle switches and waited. Nothing happened.

Do it again, said Janice.

He did, but got no reaction. He pressed several buttons on the machine, flipped every switch he could find, and went to the next one and tried again. "Nothing," he said. "The power must be dead."

Stupid aliens, said Janice.

A loud bang rang through the walls, vibrating the floor. Terry flinched and quickly turned around. He shot a look at the gate, uncertain. It didn't move. Right then, another bang ran through the tunnel, only this time Terry could tell it was coming from the other end, somewhere back the way he came.

He could feel his heart racing. Something was happening outside. He'd have to leave for now…go check out this new disturbance. Could it be a lightning storm? Maybe an animal accidentally wandered into the cave. Either way, he had to make sure the door to this place was sealed. He couldn't have a flood or a wild animal destroying anything, not so soon after he'd found it.

Terry ran through the first room and back into the hall. He turned and grabbed the side of the metal door, gathering his strength and pulling. The barrier slid along the floor, filling the ancient tunnel with a horrible, heavy noise before finally locking into place.

Wiping his dirty hands on his thighs, he paused and cursed. He'd forgotten his pack inside. "Dammit!" he snapped. He felt his side for the machete, letting out a sigh of relief when he found it. At least he didn't have to worry about going out there unarmed.

Terry jogged through the empty tunnel. There was another explosive crackle, filling the space around him. Several others soon followed. Much to his surprise, each one was louder and more startling than the last.

It sounded like the end of the world.

5

Ortego Outpost File Logs
Play Audio File 302
To: Mei_Curie
From: Christopher_Tabata
Recorded: April 21, 2350

TABATA: *Dr. Curie, thank you very much for your letter regarding the kitobora you have in your possession. Rest assured I am very interested in visiting your facility.*

It will take me a day or two to get approval from my superiors, but I expect no objections. My faculty here is more than capable without me, barring some disaster.

As for the trip itself, I'll be staying a week with the possibility of an extension based on my findings. I trust you can make the living arrangements before I arrive.

In the meantime, I believe congratulations are in order. You and your team are the first people to tame a living animal in over two centuries. It's quite the accomplishment.

You should be very proud.

End Audio File

Ortego Reconstruction Outpost
April 21, 2350

Travis and Bartholomew arrived shortly before the flippies finished their excavation of the tunnel, much to Mei's annoyance.

"What took you so long?" she asked.

The two engineers entered the tent fully dressed in radiation suits and hurried to the monitor. "Did we miss anything?" asked Travis.

"I asked you a question," said Mei.

Bartholomew bit the side of his lip. "Sorry, but we had to grab a few things before we left."

"What things?"

"They're outside," said Travis, hunched over Zoe's shoulder and staring at the monitor. "Looks like my boys are making good time. Not bad, kiddo."

Zoe pursed her lips. "I take it you want to be smacked."

He grinned. "Aha! You can't do any smacking while we're in these suits. Too dangerous."

She shrugged. "You gotta sleep sometime."

Mei looked at Bart. "What does he mean *they're outside*?"

"Don't get mad, but they kind of insisted," said Bart.

"We sure did!" roared John as he opened the flap of the tent and stepped inside. Sophie followed closely behind. "Took me a while to get this stupid suit on, but here we are."

Mei glared at Bartholomew. "Why would you bring him? Do you have any idea how dangerous this is? Sergeant Finn isn't trained to wear a radiation suit. What if he didn't seal it correctly?" She shuffled to John's side and examined him. "How do you feel? Any dizziness or fatigue? Nausea?"

"Easy, spaz," said John. "Sophie checked me before we left."

Mei almost forgot about her assistant. "So what's your excuse? You know policy states we can't all be here at the same time."

"Sorry, ma'am," said Sophie. "I was curious."

"It's not a big deal, is it?" asked Bart.

Travis poked his head up from the display. "I can take her back, but since she's already here…"

Mei sighed. "Fine, stay. Watch the show."

John clapped his gloves together. "Awesome! Glad you're on board."

It took another twelve minutes for the flippies to finish their work, but the "all clear" icon finally flashed to tell them it was over. Zoe pulled Jefferson and Stanley out of the hall before sending Mortimer ahead to scout.

The monitor to Mortimer's feed showed an open room.

"There's some debris," said Zoe. "A few computer consoles. It's a small room, but I see a door. Hang on."

Mortimer latched onto the handle with his tentacle and turned it, pulling the door open and leaving it cracked behind him. A second later, the flippy came to a stop, and Zoe turned to look at Mei. "Can't go any farther. We could lose the signal."

"Alright. Stay put for now, but try to look around. Can you see anything?"

"It's a little fuzzy," she said, messing with the controls.

Travis gave her a nudge. "You can focus the camera here."

"Thanks," she said under her breath. The camera focused immediately, and Zoe looked it over. There were several large black boxes ahead of the flippy, taller than the little robot, lining the walls of a surprisingly large room. It was a server farm.

"Jackpot," muttered Travis.

"Did the blueprints show this?" asked Bart.

"They don't go into detail," said Mei. "The projects were all classified, so the best I have is a basic layout design."

"Better than nothing," said John.

"What's the plan now?" asked Travis. "We can't take Mortimer any farther."

John clasped his gloves together. "We going in?"

Mei scoffed. "Don't be ridiculous. I called for Travis because I want him to install a repeater for the drones. We need to stretch the signal."

John looked disappointed.

"Not a problem," said Travis. "I've got one made already. We only need to get it set up."

"Let's see it," said Mei.

Travis nodded and went to a nearby crate. He popped the lid and searched, pulling parts out, discarding most of them. After a short while, he uncovered a tiny box and presented it to Mei. "I've got a dozen more of these at home in my tent if we need them."

Mei nodded. "Alright. How long do you need to get this working?"

"Not long. We can place it right where Mortimer is now."

"I'll bring Stanley up," said Zoe. "He can handle it."

"Do it," said Mei.

Zoe called the little robot to the surface. Travis gave him the repeater and took the controls. Stanley descended into the basement and as directed, made his way through the tunnel in Mortimer's location.

"Be careful placing it," said Mei. "I don't feel like waiting for another repeater to get here."

"No problem," said Travis. He had Stanley set the repeater on the floor. It was already on, so nothing else had to be done. "Now we can take multiple flippies through there, and it shouldn't be an issue."

"Take whichever flippies you want, but leave one at the door where Mortimer is. We need at least one on this side in case something goes wrong."

"What could go wrong?" asked John.

"She's being safe in case Travis screwed up the repeater," said Sophie.

"Gee, thanks," said Travis.

"The plan for today is to observe," said Mei. "Send the flippies everywhere and record what you find. Don't touch anything. If it looks safe, I'll send a team to retrieve whatever we can, like the data in those servers."

"Got it," said Zoe.

"Alright," said Mei. "Let's get to work."

Unknown

April 21, 2350

Terry ran through the subterranean hallways as if racing for his life. The sounds overhead were unlike anything he'd ever heard. The bangs and cracks were like thunder but heavier and more frequent, shaking his chest and echoing in his ears. He had to know what they were.

It took over an hour to reach the mouth of the cave, and by then, the noise had dissipated. He climbed the stairs quickly, sweat pouring off him. He wiped his eyes, ignoring the sting and burn of the sweat as it slid along his pores.

He flinched as he emerged into the light. Once his eyes adjusted, the chaos before him took shape. There on the ground, a massive creature lay covered in blood, surrounded by several others of varying sizes. None of them seemed to be moving. As Terry approached the first corpse, he saw it was the very same species he'd encountered several days ago in the forest, the mother protecting her nest. He never expected to run into one of them all the way out here.

There were at least a dozen of them. An entire herd wiped out.

In the distance, he heard shallow breaths and wheezing. It was coming from a smaller animal near the tree line. Its chest rose and fell steadily, as though it were asleep. But its eyes were wide open, twitching like a fish on dry land. The creature didn't seem to notice him, or if it did, it didn't care. Terry kept his distance. What could have done this? Terry stared into the eyes of the dying thing, trying to understand. Several streams of blood gushed out of its thick hide. The holes didn't look like teeth marks, but it was difficult to tell with so much blood. None of the flesh had been torn or ripped out. It was clean, as if the animal had been stabbed…or shot.

There was a loud pop in the distance, and the beast flinched. Terry snapped around, facing the woods. It had come from the direction of his glade.

He ran, wild and furious.

He passed the pond on his way, spotting several tracks in the mud around the water. They were average-sized, about the same as his own. If he didn't know better, he'd think they were human.

When he made it to the glade, he didn't enter. Instead, he climbed one of the trees to get a better view. For several minutes, he saw nothing—no signs of movement, no invading monster hordes. Then he closed his eyes and concentrated, opening his senses to the world around him, and he listened.

The jungle behind him erupted into a living orchestra of

insects, animal calls, and a hundred thousand rustling leaves. He filtered them out immediately, focusing on the field before him. There was the grass, sweeping in the wind, the chirping of several birds on the other side of the glade, and a plethora of bugs along the ground and in the air, their wings humming and buzzing. One at a time, he let them go, searching for whatever felt out of place.

Finally he found it. A chuckling voice, cackling in a stutter of what must be—

"Fe fe fe! Naav fisi. Gast, naav fisi! Rii shar?"

Language! These noises, they sounded like words. Real and beautiful words.

"Rajiali er nekelp fisi." A different voice this time. Deeper and calmer.

"Riotf shi fayri!"

"Uir, res!" Several voices at once, nearly in unison.

I have to get a better look, thought Terry. He got down from the tree and hurried to get closer. He kept close to the trees, never leaving the shade of their branches. He advanced to the rear of the dome, watching for any signs of movement. The voices quickly became clearer. He barely had to concentrate.

"Haylq raji faaq elreqi."

"Faaq? Fe! Shiu jyrc wi osaylq fisi."

He watched the side of the dome, hoping to catch a glimpse of the speakers, but still he couldn't see them. Were they inside or simply standing together in the front, out of sight? He debated briefly with rushing toward the building for a better view, but immediately rejected the notion. Those animals had died, he was certain, from some kind of weapon. He'd better play it safe.

Careful big brother, said Janice.

A shadow stepped out from the other side of the building, startling him. A dark figure with charred black skin, white hair, and purple eyes. These remarkable features were attached to a bipedal body with a nose, a mouth, a chest, two legs, and two arms—the makings of a human being. But they couldn't be human, Terry knew. That was impossible.

Wasn't it?

The man's ears were long and pointed, stretching well above his head. He had a remarkably normal face, except for the nose, which was flat and long.

Terry backed away. He needed to find a better vantage point. Somewhere he could see these people clearly…maybe track them afterwards, too. He took several steps to his right, losing sight of the stranger in the process. As Terry came around to the other side of the dome, however, he caught a glimpse of someone else's backside.

This one was shorter, thicker and had a blend of red and blond hair instead of white. He wore a piece of gray cloth around his waist, and above it on his naked back, a brown holster holding a long piece of metal tube with a wooden grip. It looked like a gun.

Terry tried to rationalize how primitive looking humans could have access to weapons like this but remembered the advanced technology in the underground city. Surely, whoever built such a place was capable of making something as trivial as a gun. If so, perhaps the men standing before him now were their descendants. Maybe they didn't need to build their own weapons because their ancestors had done it for them.

It seemed the wounds in the animals had indeed been bullet holes. *I should be careful.*

We need to leave, said Janice.

A twig cracked behind him. He flinched and heard some heavy breathing. He turned, expecting to see one of the tribesmen, thinking he'd been found. Instead, sitting atop a fallen stump, he found a beavermite staring at him with an open mouth.

A sigh of relief overtook him. He edged his way toward a nearby tree and grabbed the branch. Beavermites were harmless, so long as he didn't eat them. What to do now, though? He could either climb or run. Stay or go.

A soft moan came from under the branch he was holding. He peered down to see another, even smaller beavermite poke its head out of a hole. It held a piece of fruit in its tiny paws. The larger one on the ground behind him made a similar noise, though it was more like a chirp. Terry raised his brow. *Maybe this wasn't such a good idea*, he thought.

A third beavermite appeared, joining the others, tilting its head to look at him. Then another. Suddenly, there were half a dozen of them, chirping and moaning, all of their eyes fixated on him. He let go of the branch and crept away from them. The big one let out a noise like a scream. *Crap.*

The voice of one of the men shouted. "B'foc bor shoc?"

"Shi Hassirc!"

The beavermites continued to scream. Terry felt a rush in his chest. He looked at the dome, only to see several men emerging from the other side. He counted four of them altogether, but who knew how many others there might be? There could be more inside. Maybe upstairs. What was he going to do?

Run, whispered Janice.

I can't, he thought. This might be his only chance to talk to these people. He'd spent three years in the wilderness alone. What if he never saw another person for the rest of his life?

The man with the white hair took the weapon and readied it in his arms.

Run, repeated Janice.

Terry took a step back but paused. The man with the white hair scanned the edge of the forest with his violet eyes, finding Terry in the trees at last. The man stared at him, opening his mouth to smile. With a crooked finger, he pointed, calling to the rest.

Run! Screamed Janice for the third and final time.

And finally he obeyed.

Ortego Reconstruction Outpost
April 21, 2350

It was the late evening. Despite the excitement of today's discovery in the Ortego ruins, Mei had told most of her staff, excluding Travis, to head home. Reluctantly, they agreed. From now on, everything else was on hold. They'd work in shifts with the flippies until such a time as Mei saw fit. Bartholomew was the exception, because the board would still want their coils.

"Anything yet?" Mei asked Travis.

"Not really. I'm still extracting data from those servers with Morty and Stan. I'm using Jeff to map the rest of the floor."

"Keep working. We need as much as we can get from those systems." Mei had no intention of establishing a long term twenty-four hour schedule, but she also wanted to have something significant to present to the board before her next conference call with Prescott. She took a seat on the table next to Travis. "How many Ortego Disks have we found so far?"

"Thirty-two, by my count," he answered.

She smiled. "Fantastic."

"What do you think we'll get out of them?"

"Hard to say. It could be nothing more than personnel data. Employee history. Backlogs of email with nothing but gossip. A lot of what we've uncovered before now has been useless. But…" She raised a brow at him and smiled.

"This time could be different," he said, grinning back.

"Exactly. There's no telling what's down there."

Travis nodded slowly, turning to the monitor. "Makes you wonder."

It sure does, she thought. "I need to lie down for a few minutes. Let me know if anything happens."

"Will do, Doc."

Mei stood and left, heading to the dirt cab. She opened the door and sat in the passenger's side, stretching her legs out on the cushions. The rad suit was flexible, but not very comfortable. Still, she found lying in the vehicle to be slightly more tolerable than standing or sitting in the tent.

A light on her visor sparked, indicating a call. She accepted it, but before she could say anything, a deep voice boomed into her helmet. "Mei, this is God. Please respond. I have to talk to you about your personal life choices."

She snickered. "Sorry, Mister Deity. I have work to do."

"Don't make me smite you."

She rolled her eyes. "Are you lonely, John?"

"Bored, maybe," he said. "Why couldn't you take the day shift?"

"I will after tomorrow. I wanted to stay here until the flippies mapped the rest of the ruins, just in case."

"In case of what?"

She took a few seconds. "You remember when we were here? The things we saw?"

"Sure I do."

"We found other things we never expected to find. The same could be true of the lower levels. There could be something special just waiting for us."

"Okay, but there was also a doomsday device."

"I know, I know. That's why I have to be here…to make sure whatever's there gets handled with absolute care."

"I get it, believe me," he said.

"I know you do," she said softly.

There was a long pause. "On the bright side, Bart says he's making progress."

"Good. I have a call to make in two days. If he doesn't have something to present, we could be in trouble."

"I wouldn't worry. Bart's a smart guy. You got a good team, Mei."

She smiled. "Thanks."

"I'm leaving tomorrow for a bit," he said suddenly.

"Where to this time?" she asked, trying not to sound surprised.

"South."

"The fourth leg of your mission. You're nearly done."

"I told you I'm taking some leave afterwards. I'll stick around here for another month. Central's already cleared it."

"You don't have to, but I certainly won't object if you—"

A red light blinked in the corner of her visor, followed by a series of long beeps. It was the emergency channel. "Hold on a sec," said Mei quickly.

"What did you say?" asked John. "I can't hear you over this beeping thing on my screen—"

John's voice cut off, replaced with an image in the upper right corner of her screen. It was black at first, but quickly faded into a pair of gloves resting on a metal desk. They were twitching and squeezing, light moans coming from somewhere nearby. The camera, which was attached to someone else's helmet, tilted as the person struggled to move. There was a monitor nearby, displaying one of the video feeds from the flippies. "Travis," muttered Mei.

She leapt out of the dirt cab, getting to the tent in time to see one of the flippies emerge from the crater, a box of artifacts in its tentacles.

Mei stepped inside and found Travis hunched over the desk, barely able to move. She lifted him by his chest, trying to see inside his visor. Vomit covered half his screen, sloshing around as she moved him. She gagged at the sight of it.

Grabbing his arm and shoulder, she signaled John. He answered right away.

"What's going on?" His voice was a frantic. "Are you okay?"

"I'm fine. Travis is sick. I'm taking him home."

"You gonna be able to carry him?"

She lifted Travis over her shoulder. She wasn't as strong as John, but her genes gave her the strength of a grown man twice her size. "I've got him."

"Should I get the others?" he asked.

"Tell Sophie to grab a med kit and a radiation monitor," said Mei.

"I'm going right now."

One of the flippies—Stanley, by the look of it—was outside loading material into the back of the dirt cab. She latched Travis into the passenger side, then hit the gas. The flippy fell off the ramp and landed on its side, attempting to right itself but failing miserably. As Mei sped away from the Ortego work site, she kept glancing at Travis, yelling his name. He wasn't moving.

When she arrived at the outpost, John and Sophie were already there, waiting. Zoe and Bartholomew came running out of their designated tents in a wild panic.

Mei brought the cab to a quick and violent stop with the ramp still dragging behind. John opened the passenger door and grabbed Travis, pulling him to the ground. Mei took off her helmet and watched from the other side of the vehicle as Sophie attempted CPR.

What the hell was happening? Was he okay? It was Mei's job to keep her team safe. *Oh, my god,* she thought. *It's happening again. I have to—*

A sudden pain hit her in the temple, and she wavered. She felt a weakness in her legs, so she grabbed the side of the cab to right herself. Staring at her hand, everything began to blur. What was going on?

"Mei?" John was standing now, watching as she tried to keep her composure. "Are you okay?"

She opened her mouth to say she was fine, but it was too late. Her legs went numb, and she collapsed, kicking up a swirl of dust and knocking the wind from her lungs. In less than a second, John's arms were around her shoulders. His lips moved, but he wasn't saying anything. The entire world had gone quiet, and the light quickly faded into dark.

Soon she was alone, drifting in a sea of empty thought, surrounded by nothing.

6

Ortego Outpost File Logs
Play Audio File 333
Recorded: April 23, 2350

ROSS*: Still no word on how the boy died?*

THISTLE*: They're saying it was radiation poisoning.*

ROSS*: How? I thought Curie's team had precautions in place.*

THISTLE*: They did.*

ROSS*: So what happened?*

THISTLE*: We aren't sure. The labs say it could've been a breach in the suits, but the chance of it happening to both of them at the same time is pretty low.*

ROSS*: Maybe we should order them home. Is the girl stable enough to transport?*

THISTLE*: Sergeant Finn doesn't seem to think so.*

ROSS: *He's not exactly unbiased.*

THISTLE: *Maybe not, but he's trustworthy. He tells me no one else is sick. They might be fine if they stay in the camp.*

ROSS: *I'm concerned this may get out of hand. The last thing we need is an entire outpost dying of radiation poisoning.*

THISTLE: *Moving the girl right now could be dangerous, or so I'm told.*

ROSS: *By whom?*

THISTLE: *I think his name is Tabata. He arrived there yesterday.*

ROSS: *For what purpose?*

THISTLE: *Something to do with an animal they captured there. In addition to being a doctor, he's also some kind of wildlife expert.*

ROSS: *Sounds like we're lucky he arrived when did.*

THISTLE: *Yes, ma'am. Should I keep you updated? I've ordered Finn to report in daily until this gets resolved. He's volunteered to stick around if we need him.*

ROSS: *Keep him there. We could use the extra set of eyes. But as far as the rest of it goes, I trust you to handle things, Captain. All I ask is you let me know if the situation takes a turn for the worse.*

THISTLE: *Of course, Colonel.*

End Audio File

Unknown

April 23, 2350

Terry wanted nothing more than to sleep. Two days running in the wild was almost too much to bear, even for a genetically engineered hybrid.

But he could not rest, not yet. Throughout both nights he could hear the faint rumblings of something in the distance, following him, shuffling through dirt and fallen leaves, spouting nonsense in a language he would never understand. The strangers with the metal barrels on their backs, tracking him like prey.

They aimed to kill him. He was certain of that.

He had considered going to his old home on the cliff, but decided to wait a few more days. If he was lucky, he'd lose them before much longer and finally get a chance to rest. Only when he was certain no one was after him would he make an attempt at returning to the cave.

Twin suns drifted through the morning as heavy clouds passed overhead, darkening the sky with threats of rain. Welcomed threats, since a shower right now might do him some good—not only to dampen his stench, which he could barely stand, but to drown his trail and put an end to this game once and for all.

He waited for a storm to ride in, but despite the hard winds, nothing came until the early evening when both suns were halfway through their descent.

Thunder cackled in the distance. Had he not been running for his life, he might have found it comforting.

Before the day was gone, a soft shower veiled the land,

covering as far as the sky could stretch. The water dripped against his skin, waking him from his zombie state.

He tried listening for his pursuers but heard nothing. It was difficult with the rain, but after constantly running for so long, Terry was sure he'd put enough distance between them to make a difference. Maybe now he could finally stop and rest.

Keep going, said the little girl's voice in the back of his mind. *You can't stop yet. The monsters will get you if you do.*

"I need to rest," he said. Rain drizzled down his cheeks and filled his mouth with the salty taste of his sweat.

It's dangerous, she told him.

"I have to sleep."

You'll die if you do.

"I don't care."

He cut through the field and entered a forest, taking refuge under the shade of a larger tree. He collapsed against its trunk, letting out a long and gentle sigh as he closed his eyes.

The rain grew louder over the next several minutes as the storm came into its own. Thick, swollen drops fell through the leaves high above his head, occasionally landing on his chest and legs.

But for most of the night he slept, and there in the dark, closed off from the world, deep in his tattered mind, he heard a voice, saying, "Come and see."

Terry found himself walking along an empty road, searching for the source. He passed through a wasteland as vast as a continent, moving through ancient and long forgotten cities, belonging only to the dead. Despite this, he continued, always to the east. He went toward the echoing voice, which sounded like a flowing river, flowing rapidly to some unknown end.

"Come and see."

He walked through stone and mud, until the ground ensnared him, and he could no longer move. He became a statue, frozen and still, waiting, until at last the dirt swelled and expanded, dragging him into itself and burying his body, consuming him entirely. He fell, far and away, deep into the bowels of the earth.

He emerged in a glistening city, standing on the corner of a street, watching as a crowd passed. A familiar woman tugged a child along, their voices garbled, their faces shrouded. They faded before his eyes, disintegrating into dust. Piles of ashes.

Now he stood in a classroom, children all around him. He was a child, too. There was a man with one arm, their teacher. The man smiled with empty eyes. Dead eyes. He opened his mouth, and with a voice identical to the last, he said, "Come and see."

The world faded, replaced by a cave, dark and cold as the night. But he could still see. He could always see. It was a large room, a place he'd been before, with dusty computers scattered everywhere. No regard for upkeep. Where were the workers? Why did they leave? Didn't they care about their work?

There was a pack in the corner. His bag. He'd left it there.

In the back, far removed from the rest of the consoles and their blackened screens, a massive circle stood forgotten, silent as the dead.

Light filled the place, spooling in from nowhere, taking the grime and dust away, making the machines look new again. They glistened, spotless and clean.

He looked at the metal circle standing before him, brilliant and real. It called to him. Not with words but with gravity. With force.

He walked forward and onto the ramp which extended through the center of the object. The metal of the ring trembled and quaked with each step he took.

The circle moved, spinning around repeatedly and with increasing speed. A black pool of liquid appeared. Terry took another step, and the void before him changed. It morphed chaotically, bending and pulling, until finally it came to a stop in the shape of something else. A living, pulsating void.

"Come…" whispered the voice from within.

Amid the darkness, a slit appeared, peeling back to white and then…purple. An iris. An eye.

And it blinked.

Terry stared into it, transfixed, unable to move. "What is this?" he finally asked.

But the eye of the void only answered, "Come and see."

Ortego Reconstruction Outpost
April 24, 2350

Mei opened her eyes to see an old man staring down at her,

scratching his cheek. She tried to move but felt a tug on her left arm. It was an I.V.

"Good morning, Doctor Curie. I apologize for intruding on you like this, but it was urgent I speak with you. My name is Christopher Tabata. I'm a physician."

Mei thought for a minute. She'd heard the name before. But from where? She felt so dizzy. "Where did you come from?"

"Salamander. One of your people sent a letter asking me to take a look at the animal you captured. I replied directly to you several days ago."

"Oh," she whispered, remembering the kitobora. "Right, sorry." She tried to sit up in the bed, but her arms were too weak and she collapsed. John rushed to her side and helped her to a sitting position. She moaned and it hurt. "Are you the one who did this?" she asked, nodding at the I.V. tube coming out of her arm.

"I'm assisting in your recovery, yes."

She coughed and swallowed. "Thanks, but you can take it out now. I need to talk to my staff."

"Actually, they've already brought me up to speed with what's going on. I can fill you in now if you'd prefer."

Mei stared at him, incredulously. Who did this person think he was? "They're my people. I need to speak with them myself."

Tabata held up his hand. "Before you do, let me brief you on your condition, will you?"

"Fine, but please hurry."

He nodded. "I came here two days ago. You've been asleep for three. Since then, I've been monitoring your vitals consistently every few hours. As you may have guessed, you're improving, but it will take time to fully recover. You need to take it easy."

Three days? She could hardly believe it.

"You probably guessed it was radiation poisoning. But the suits didn't fail."

"What do you mean? If it wasn't the suits, then how—"

"Because it's increasing, Doctor Curie. Your team figured it out yesterday. The radiation levels are rising steadily, and it won't be long before they overtake this entire area."

Mei's eyes widened. "How's that possible?"

"One of your assistants—Miss Mitchell I believe—she's working on it as we speak."

Sophie? She was capable enough, but she couldn't do this on her own. She needed Mei's help. "Has she made any progress?"

"Not enough, I'm afraid. She's tracking the radiation spikes, but she doesn't know why they're happening or where they're coming from."

Mei shot a glance at John, who was sitting in the back of the tent, staying uncharacteristically silent. "John, I need you to do something."

"What's up?" he asked.

"I'm sure Travis is still sick, but tell him he needs to show Zoe how to use the flippies to set up some sensors in the irradiated areas. We need as much data as possible if we're going to solve this."

John looked at the floor.

"John?"

"Doctor Curie," interrupted Tabata. "I'm afraid I have some

unfortunate news. The man you're asking about—Travis Scott? I'm sorry to tell you he passed away."

A sudden wave of panic swept over her, a cold chill in her arms and chest. "I don't understand. I got him back here right away. I'm not that sick. How could he—in such a short amount of time—it's not…"

John shook his head. "You're not the same, Mei. You know you aren't."

"But…" Her voice trailed off. She didn't know what to say. Travis was dead. He was part of her team. How could this happen?

"Doctor Curie, I'd like to run a few more tests on you, if you don't mind."

Her eyes darted around the tent. She had to do something.

"Doctor Curie," repeated Tabata.

She looked at him. "What?" she snapped.

"Please, I need to examine you. It is important."

She cringed, tightening her fists. "Why? Travis is dead. What good will it do?"

"You survived because—"

"Because of what I am," she said.

Tabata nodded. "Yes. It may help us in some way. At the very least it will allow me to understand how to treat you more effectively."

Her eyes drifted to her lap. There was a long pause before she answered. "Fine. Do whatever you want. But as soon as you're done, I'm going back to work."

"I'd advise taking it slow," he said. "If not, you might—"

She snapped around to look at him. "If those radiation levels don't stop rising, this project is over. You said it yourself. It won't take long for it to reach us all the way out here. I didn't work three years to get here only to give up and go home." She motioned to John. "Tell the others to be ready. We'll meet in a few hours."

"You won't be able to leave your bed for at least a few more days," said Tabata.

She didn't bother answering. "Forget the conference room. Bring them here instead. We need to get ahead of this thing before it gets worse."

"You got it," said John. He squeezed her hand, got to his feet, and left.

"Doctor, I'm sorry to be a pain, but would you mind if I slept for a while?" she asked.

"I was about to suggest you rest," he said, standing. "I'll be back to check on you in an hour." He grabbed his bag, a gray satchel he carried on his shoulder, and left the tent.

Mei turned on her side and stared vacantly at the tent wall beside the bed. Her arm itched, and she scratched it.

Thoughts and images ran through her like an old movie. She pictured the look on Travis' face when she'd found him, how she dragged him to the truck and watched as he lay there, motionless.

She continued to scratch her arm, harder and harder, until there was a sudden pinch of pain, and she flinched. A thin line of blood streamed out of the cut, gliding along her arm and into the bed. She pressed the cut against the blanket and tried to ignore the irritating itch as it ran along her arm, chest, and finally her scalp, like an insect moving below her epidermis, wriggling and squirming, gnawing from within. She pressed her fingers to the side of her head to scratch, but stopped when several stands of hair fell onto the bed. Mei stared at them in silence. She tugged her hair, barely feeling the pressure. Threads fluttered through the air and onto the sheet. In her palm she held the bulk of it.

A clump so large it could fill a child's hand.

7

Ortego Outpost File Logs
Play Audio File 340
Recorded: April 24, 2350

THISTLE*: I'll need some time with this, Colonel.*

ROSS*: How long?*

THISTLE*: A few weeks. Curie's team is hard at work coming up with viable solutions, though to be honest, I'm more concerned about her than I am this outpost.*

ROSS*: How is she?*

THISTLE*: The girl is something else. She's crazy strong, and I don't mean her body. That kid's got more drive in her than half of Central combined. If she weren't already famous, she'd find a way to get there eventually.*

ROSS*: You won't hear any disagreements from me.*

THISTLE: *Finn says she's improving lightning fast. Doctor Tabata from Salamander Outpost arrived a few days ago, and he's been looking after her. We already knew those kids had tough immune systems and some top notch regenerative abilities, but I don't think anyone expected this. According to Tabata, the radiation she was exposed to should have killed her.*

ROSS: *You mean like it did the Scott boy.*

THISTLE: *Travis Scott, yes, ma'am. He died in minutes. Curie on the other hand…her fortitude is damned impressive.*

ROSS: *Those children are full of surprises.*

THISTLE: *We wouldn't be able to survive on the surface without them. Their blood's like a cure all. There's no telling what else we can learn from them. Sorta makes you wonder if we should've made more of them.*

ROSS: *You think so, do you? Let's not forget the reality behind their conception, Captain. All those other children...*

THISTLE: *Apologies, ma'am. I meant no disrespect.*

ROSS: *Relax. I won't pretend those children haven't helped us. We'd still be locked underground if it weren't for them. I'm in no denial about that…but what Archer and Bishop did to those kids was unforgiveable.*

THISTLE: *Still, it brought us closer than we've been in two hundred years.*

ROSS: *Yes. They were right, in a way. Maybe in a century or two, professors and historians can sit around debating whether those decisions were justified. Who knows? It's a lot easier to judge these things in hindsight.*

THISTLE: *So you believe you made the right call by shutting down the Amber Project?*

ROSS: *Make no mistake, Captain. I don't doubt my actions for a second. My only regret was not doing it sooner. Maybe if I had, the other children we lost from those godawful experiments might still be alive.*

End Audio File

Unknown
April 24, 2350

Terry awoke to the sounds of laughter.

He opened his eyes and saw four men towering over him, their rifles cradled in their arms, snickering as he lay against a tree.

“Naav oc ec,” said the one with the red and blond hair.

“Ec er ra r’jonn!” laughed another, who had a hair color that was something between teal and brown. There was a large scar along his neck.

“Fi jyrc wi o jycolc,” said the redhead.

There were two others standing close. One with solid black hair, grinning slightly, and another which Terry recognized as the purple-eyed man from before.

The one with the scar tapped Terry’s leg with the barrel of his gun. “Yg!” he yelled.

Terry held up his hands.

“Yg!” the man repeated.

The redhead pointed at Terry and raised his finger, motioning to the sky. “Yg.” He aimed his rifle at Terry’s face. “Yg.”

Yg, thought Terry. Did that mean *up*? He got to his feet, keeping his arms raised.

The scarred guy laughed. "Fi'r o jasal!"

The man with the purple eyes motioned to the others. The two who had been laughing grabbed Terry and pulled his hands around his back while the third kept a weapon on him. They wrapped his wrists in some kind of rope and pushed him a few steps forward. "Pa," said the redhead.

"What?" asked Terry. Did *pa* mean *move* or *go*? "I don't—"

"Pa, pa, pa!" shouted the man. He pushed him again, and Terry stumbled forward.

"Okay! *Pa*. I got it. Relax."

The man chuckled.

Terry walked beside one with the rest behind him. He had to find a way out of this. He could probably fight them, maybe run for it. Given his superior strength and speed, he'd have a fair shot at getting away. The guns were the real problem. If they'd been carrying spears, he might be able to dodge a few of those, but not bullets. He wasn't invincible. Before they got to wherever it was they were going, he'd have to find a low risk opportunity to escape. If the chance never came, well…he didn't come halfway across the universe to be somebody else's prisoner.

He gave them names to pass the time. The first three were easy. Red, Scar, and Purple Eyes. The fourth was a little more difficult, however.

Call him Charlie, suggested Janice, and so it was decided.

They led him through the woods toward the field he passed on the way here. There was still water on the grass, and it smelled like nature, clean and filthy. It was hard to believe they could track him in this mess.

Terry stomped through the muddy countryside, and his feet sank into the mud with every step. It felt like he was being pulled into the dirt…as though he were being swallowed.

The image of the room with the ring flashed in his mind, and suddenly he remembered the dream. No, the nightmare. The desolate wasteland, empty cities, the rotting earth pulling him under…and the void. The Eye.

Come and see.

Red shoved Terry's back, and he nearly stumbled. "Horcis!" he snapped. "Horcis!"

"Okay, man," said Terry. "Whatever horcis means."

Red yelled more gibberish and poked Terry hard in the side with his gun.

He didn't flinch. The pain wasn't much of a bother. It was more annoying than anything. He couldn't help but wonder what it might feel like if he wasn't genetically modified. Would it have broken a bone or two?

The strangers led him through the field toward the south. Terry had fled from the east, crossing the field to the western forest, but apparently the meadow went on for quite a distance, separating the two forests like a river of grass.

After a few hours, the group came upon a large stone where they stopped to sit and eat. Scar lifted a sack and distributed various pieces of what Terry assumed must be vegetables. They also lit a small fire and roasted an animal. The corpse reminded him of a fox, except it was bald and had no eyes.

He sat against the rock, which towered over them all. It was more of a boulder, fat and out of place. The black haired man, whose name was now Charlie, unbound Terry's hands, then tossed him a piece of meat. "Ioc," he said, putting his fingers to his own mouth.

Terry nodded. *Ioc*, he thought, repeating the word in his head. *Eat.*

So he did, chewing the flesh in his mouth and ignoring the dry, flavorless taste of the meat. When he was done, they gave him a sack made from animal skin. "Qselv." *Drink.*

The hour passed as the group replenished their calories. They sat together, laughing and occasionally pointing at Terry throughout the conversation. All the while, the man with the white hair remained silent, sitting peacefully behind the others, observing the scene, and occasionally chewing on a piece of grass. His purple eyes blinked, and he watched Terry with a curious and unfiltered gaze.

You are not like us, the eyes seemed to whisper. *Everything about you is wrong.*

Ortego Reconstruction Outpost
April 24, 2350

Mei was going to miss her hair. The radiation poisoning would claim it all, Tabata said. But she wouldn't let some stupid sickness take it. She'd see to it herself.

John stood over her with a buzzer, his image reflected in the mirror before them. "Are you sure about this?" he asked.

"Don't ask dumb questions," she said.

He pressed the tip of the clippers to her scalp. They were cold and sent a chill down her neck. He gulped. "Here we go."

The buzzer ran along her skin, and a shower of hair fell to the floor. Mei watched as the reflection in the mirror transformed, and she saw a girl she didn't know.

"All done," said John after a few minutes.

Mei's eyes widened as she stared at herself. *Is that me?* "I look like a doorknob."

"It's not so bad," said John.

"You wouldn't say that if it was you." She got up and went to the other end of the tent. She hated everything about the last few days. This illness, the work problems, and Travis. What else did the universe have in store for her before the week was out?

A soft hum came from behind. John must have turned the clippers on again, probably to clean them. The noise made her uneasy. She turned to look at him. Ask him to stop. But there, grinning like a child, stood John, holding the clippers clumsily in his hands, pressing them against his head.

"What are you doing?" she asked quickly.

"Hang on," he told her. He swiped his scalp and clumps of charcoal hair glided down. "I'm almost done."

She watched in awe as he ran the clippers side to side, front to back, until there was nothing left. He set the device aside and swept his hand across his skull, a look of satisfaction on his face.

She ran to him, touching his head. "You're crazy! Why would you do that?"

"You know why," he said. "We're in this together, the same as we've always been."

"You're an idiot." She punched him in the arm, then hugged him.

"Maybe so," he said, kissing her forehead. "But now we're both doorknobs."

Unknown
April 24, 2350

TERRY WATCHED as his captors built a fire, preparing to camp for the night. They re-tied the rope binding his wrists and attached the other end to a nearby tree. He couldn't help but think they were right for taking such precautions. Too bad for them it wouldn't do any good.

Throughout the day, Terry toyed with the idea of escaping, but chose to stay patient instead. The chance to run would come when most of them slept.

He watched them each lie on the ground, their backs on the dirt with only their clothes to cover them. Over the next hour, they each fell asleep, one after the other. Only one remained awake to guard him. Scar, who seemed less interested in making conversation or doing much of anything. Instead, he chose to sit in the darkness, staring into the wild valley before them, saying nothing.

Terry pretended to sleep, waiting for the right opportunity. A short time later, he opened his eyes, afraid he would pass out if he wasn't careful, only to see the man still there, motionless. Terry's eyes drifted to the sky. Based on the moon's position, he gathered it must be close to midnight. Maybe now was a good time to—

They found you before, said the voice in his head. *They'll find you again.*

No, not this time. He'd find a way to stop them if they came after him a second time. He could fight them if he had to… maybe set a trap. He'd head in the opposite direction they were going now. If he kept a good pace, they would have to give up eventually.

Wouldn't they?

Terry fidgeted with the rope, nudging it loose. The knot was firm, but he eventually managed. Several minutes later he had one hand free, followed by the next.

He stared at Scar, who seemed to be ignoring him. The man only sat there staring, his eyes distant and empty. What could he be doing? Earlier in the day, this man and his friends had been so loud and energetic, ready to kick Terry's face in. Here in the dark, however, he'd changed. He was like a stone, still and quiet, as though his soul had gone away, leaving only the body behind like some kind of hollow shell.

Terry shook his head. None of it mattered. He was about to leave, and he'd hopefully never see these people again. He'd have to pull on his power in order to make the run, but he could do it.

He closed his eyes and slowed his breathing, and in a moment, he felt the change take him. The world seemed to slow around him, and suddenly the darkness turned to light, brightening as it had deep in those underground tunnels. He heard the other men's breathing, listening to them suck the air in and finally release it, louder than if they were next to him. He looked at Scar and waited but was surprised to hear nothing coming from him. No breathing. No heartbeat. Nothing to indicate he was alive.

What the hell were these guys?

There was no time to delay, though. He couldn't keep the focus for longer than a few minutes. He'd have to hurry.

Terry leapt to his feet and took a deep breath. He placed his heel against the tree behind him. With a burst of strength, he pushed himself off the trunk and dashed as fast as his legs could carry him.

Scar looked at him, suddenly alive. He snapped to his feet, calling to the others.

With each step, Terry ran faster. He turned to see the guard readying his weapon, while the other three stirred.

A bang went off behind him. The bullet whizzed by. He dashed into the nearby woods.

Another bullet exploded from the gun, striking a nearby tree, splintering chunks of bark into the air.

Terry didn't slow down. He ran as fast as he possibly could. He knew those men would follow immediately, and they wouldn't stop until they had no other choice. He'd have to push himself, summon every ounce of strength he had.

It was time to put his abilities to the test.

Ortego Reconstruction Outpost
April 24, 2350

THE AIR FELT cold against Mei's scalp. It had only been a few hours since John had buzzed her hair. Did she make a mistake? *Doesn't matter*, she thought as she made her way toward Bartholomew's work tent. *I made the decision, and it's done. Time to move on.*

Today, Zoe was driving to Komodo to unload a cab full of research materials. Normally this only happened once a month, but thanks to recent developments, the process had to be accelerated. They didn't have much time to get everything out, and Mei wanted to be prepared to leave at a moment's notice.

There was also the matter of Travis's body, which had to be shipped all the way to Central so there could be a proper funeral. Mei didn't like the idea of stuffing him inside a box and sending him away, but they didn't give her much of a choice. The labs insisted on doing an autopsy. Tabata assured her it was necessary, saying they needed as much information about the radiation as possible, but none of it made her feel any better.

As she reached Bart's tent, she could hear metal hitting metal as the engineer performed his work. Unzipping and opening the flap, she saw Bart standing there holding what appeared to be a section of a Fever Killer. The hulking object was nearly as tall as Mei, but in Bart's arms it looked much smaller. He wheezed, hefting it onto the table and letting it slam down. "Oops," he said, gasping. "Sorry, Doctor Curie."

"No, no, it's my fault," she answered. "I should have called ahead."

He wiped the sweat from his forehead with his shoulder. "What can I do for you?"

"Zoe's about to take off for Komodo. Did you want her to pick up anything?"

"Some potatoes would be nice," he said, reaching for the toolbox at the other end of the table. He grabbed a Philips and spun it around in his hand like a fan blade. "Any reason she's got you asking me? Seems like you should be in bed."

Mei waved her hand at him. "I volunteered. Tabata says I need to exercise."

"As long as you don't overdo it."

"So potatoes?"

He nodded. "A few dozen, if she doesn't mind."

"Why so many?"

"I've had a craving for some diced potato bits, maybe grilled and seasoned. If she gets enough, I'll fix a plate for everyone."

Mei smiled. "Sounds pretty good. I'm not too sure if Komodo has any, but I'll ask her to look. We might get lucky."

"We could do with some luck if you ask me," he said, unscrewing a piece of the Fever Killer.

"I noticed you didn't have any shipments to send home."

"Still in the process," he said, pointing to the other end of the tent with his screwdriver. Several crates were resting in the corner. "Filled half of them last night. I'll have something ready next time."

"Not this piece?" she asked, motioning to the machine on the table.

"I'm getting ready to test something."

"Sure."

"This'll be the twenty-sixth try. Can't say I'm expecting much, though. Backward engineering is one thing, but reassembling a hundred pieces and *then* doing it is slightly more complicated."

"Keep me posted," she said, getting ready to leave. She had no qualms with listening to Bart, but standing was proving difficult the longer she stayed. "I'll see you at the meeting in a few hours."

He didn't answer.

She left the tent and went to the edge of the camp near the fence. Zoe was there, hanging on the door of the dirt cab, one arm dangling through the window frame. She was talking with John.

"So you think you can get it for me?" he asked.

"Pineapple? I'll see what I can do," she said.

"Remember, it spoils pretty fast once it's exposed to Variant. After that, you only get a few hours to eat it, so don't break the seal."

"Yeah, yeah, okay. I got it."

Mei made her way to the dirt cab, trying her best not to look too exhausted. "Do you have everything you need, Zoe?"

"Packed and loaded, ma'am."

Mei looked at the tail of the vehicle, at the box with Travis inside. "And the extra cargo?"

Zoe's face sunk. "Safe," she said after a short pause. "I've got him."

"Are you sure you don't need me to go with you?" asked John.

"I might not look like much, but I make these trips every month. I know how to take care of myself. Besides," she said, motioning toward Mei. "Your girlfriend looks like she might pass out any second now."

"I'm fine," said Mei. But she wasn't. The energy in her legs had nearly given out. Her head was growing foggy. All she wanted to do was sleep.

"Uh huh," said Zoe, unconvinced.

"Before I forget, Bart wants potatoes," said Mei.

"Potatoes, got it," she said.

John walked over to Mei and wrapped one of his arms around her shoulders. "See you when you get back, Zoe."

Zoe nodded before climbing into the cab. A second later, the engines roared to life, and she drove off, kicking a small cloud of dust into the air.

John and Mei watched her leave. When she was far enough away, Mei let herself sink into John's arms, relinquishing support. "I need to lie down," she finally said.

John didn't say a word. He simply swept her up and carried her into the tent.

Lying in her bed at last, Mei held his wrist, exhausted. "Wake me in a few hours."

"I will," he answered, stroking her arm. He smiled warmly at her.

A fog formed in her mind, pulling her to rest. She thought of

Travis, imagining him standing beside her. She wished she could talk to him. Hear his voice. If only she'd paid more attention. If only...

"Mei, what's wrong?" asked John.

She looked at him. "Nothing…" she whispered.

John tilted his head. "Are you sure?"

It's all my fault. I killed him, the same as…

"Mei?"

…the same as Terry, all those years ago. Couldn't see the answers. I'm always too late to see…

"Are you okay?" He felt her forehead. "You feel warm…"

…to see the truth…but I'm a fool, a stupid little girl trying to pretend, trying to be something I'm not…

"Can you hear me, Mei?" asked John.

…and it's my fault…it's all my fault…everything…because of me…

"Someone help!" shouted John. "Doctor Tabata? Somebody get in here!"

…my fault…

8

Ortego Outpost File Logs
Play Audio File 347
Recorded: April 25, 2350

PRESCOTT: *I'm sorry, but what did you say your name was?*

MITCHELL: *Sophie Mitchell, sir. I'm Doctor Curie's apprentice.*

PRESCOTT: *Why am I talking to you instead of your mentor?*

MITCHELL: *It's as I've said, sir. She is currently occupied.*

PRESCOTT: *Occupied with what, exactly? She'd better have a good excuse for missing this call.*

MITCHELL: *As you are aware, sir, the recent tragedy involving Travis Scott has left a gap in work performance. Doctor Curie is busy overseeing the transfer of responsibilities. She has authorized me to speak with you on her behalf.*

PRESCOTT: *This is absurd. Doesn't she know how important these* *assessment calls are? If I deliver a poor review to the board, she could lose funding.*

MITCHELL*: I assure you, sir, I am fully capable of delivering the report to you. Being Doctor Curie's apprentice requires me to understand each and every facet of the project, regardless of—*

PRESCOTT*: Fine, Ms. Mitchell. Go ahead and give your report. Let's get this over with.*

MITCHELL*: Thank you, sir. As you know, the subsections of the former Ortego compound have been uncovered. Upon excavation, the team discovered several intact rooms filled with servers, terminals, and other resources. Dozens of disks have been collected and are awaiting analysis as we speak.*

PRESCOTT*: And the radiation?*

MITCHELL*: Still spreading, unfortunately. It seems the radius of exposure is expanding, though the rate is slow.*

PRESCOTT*: How long before it reaches the outpost?*

MITCHELL*: A little under two weeks. Doctor Curie is actively working on a solution for containment and remains hopeful—*

PRESCOTT*: The board wants solutions, Ms. Mitchell. I have orders directly from Doctor Tremaine stating that if your team can't figure something out by the seventh day, you're to be pulled and relocated. Do you understand?*

MITCHELL*: Yes, sir.*

PRESCOTT*: What about the Framling Coil? Anything to share?*

MITCHELL*: I've attached the report from our specialist, Bartholomew Higgs. He has made significant progress since the last update.*

PRESCOTT*: The board will decide what is significant.*

MITCHELL*: Yes, sir. Do you have any other questions for me today?*

PRESCOTT*: No. Please inform Doctor Curie I'll be contacting her in* *two days for another update. In the meantime, I hope you'll express to her the importance of these calls.*

***MITCHELL**: Of course, Doctor. You have my word.*

End Audio File

Ortego Reconstruction Outpost
April 25, 2350

John watched as Mei stared vacantly at the wall of the tent, dazed from the drugs circulating through her bloodstream. Doctor Tabata had given her some painkillers in addition to the usual radiation treatment. This made her sleep often and without provocation, allowing only a few moments of lucid consciousness. When she *was* awake, her words barely made sense. Half the time, all she could do was moan.

John sat beside her, tending like a nurse to her bodily needs. He didn't mind. Besides, better him than someone else. Her team didn't need to see her like this.

She seemed to come and go, and so did the chills, the fevers, and the sweats. She vomited often, sometimes until nothing came. Until the dry heaves made her cry.

John rubbed her back and smiled. "Easy," he whispered.

Her face was wet and pink, and her lip trembled below her runny nose. "W-Where am I?" she asked, darting her eyes around.

"It's okay, Mei," he answered, trying his best to stay calm. "You're with me. We're in our tent. Everything's going to be fine."

She looked into his eyes for a brief moment, a look of realization in her eyes. She nodded, lying on the bed and sleeping once more.

The whole thing terrified him.

John retrieved his pad from the floor nearby and called Doctor Tabata. "Where are you?" he asked.

"I'm tending to the kitobora," said the doctor.

"I need you here," said John, rather insistently. "She's getting worse."

"It's the fever," said Tabata. "She'll be fine. I checked her vitals a few hours ago."

"Come on, Doc. Can you please get over here and take a look at her so I can relax? She's been acting really strange."

There was a short pause. "Very well, Sergeant Finn. Give me ten minutes to finish what I'm doing."

John sighed. "Thank you."

He ended the call and sat there, staring, watching her sleep. He'd only been here for a few weeks, but already he wanted to go home. Take her in his arms and leave for Central.

But he knew he couldn't. Mei would never give up. She would never stop trying.

What can I do? He asked her silently. *Tell me what I'm supposed to do.*

Tabata arrived soon and checked Mei's vitals, taking her temperature and giving her another injection. John wanted to ask how the old man could be so confident. But Bart had said he was one of the best physicians around, so certainly he had to know a thing or two.

"How is she?" asked John, once the doctor was finished.

"The delirium you've seen is from the fever and the drugs," he explained. "I've given her something to help her sleep. You were right to call me."

John frowned. "She seemed fine before, walking around the camp until she just fell over. I don't get it."

"Her body is still reacting to the radiation poisoning. She was never fully recovered, despite being able to function and talk coherently. The fever could be a late symptom."

"What if it's an infection? Maybe she picked up a bug," said John, who thought he knew a thing or two about that.

"Interesting," said the doctor, tapping his chin. "It's not unheard of for a patient who's been exposed to radiation to develop an autoimmune disease. You could be right."

"Can you test for it?"

"Not without a lab. We'd have to transport her to another outpost."

"Isn't there something we can do here?" asked John.

Tabata's eyes dropped to the floor and stayed there for a while. "Do you know when she was last ill?"

John tried to remember, but couldn't place it. He'd known Mei all her life or most of it, and aside from their exposures in the Chamber when they were children, he'd never seen her sick or displaying any symptoms. In fact, neither of them had. "No, she's always been healthy, I think."

"Interesting," muttered Tabata.

"Why?"

The old man scratched his chin. "Apologies, I should be clearer. Neither of you have been ill, correct?"

John nodded. "Right."

"I'm no William Archer, but if I had to guess I'd attribute this to your remarkable genes."

"What are you getting at?"

"Normally, in response to radiation poisoning, one of the procedures is to perform a blood transfusion, which is typically done with Oxyblood, a synthetic blood replacement. They make it in the labs and store it at the various hospitals around the city as well as the outposts in case of emergencies. We have some here, actually, but I've been reluctant to use it."

"Why?" asked John.

Tabata paused. "Because of what she is, frankly. The two of you…your bodies aren't normal. There's a fair chance a procedure like this could do more harm than good."

John imagined Mei's reaction to hearing this. She'd be annoyed as hell, probably insulted. She hated the idea of them being different from anyone else—of being nonhuman. It was a separation both she and John had largely chosen to ignore, but it was nonetheless true. Fundamentally, genetically, biologically, they were different. "So what do we do?"

Tabata thought for a moment. "Sergeant, do you mind if I ask what blood type you have?"

John shrugged. "No one's ever told me."

Tabata pulled out his pad. "Don't worry. It's no matter. I can pull it up on the medical database. All citizen files include blood type."

"Oh, boy," said John.

"Ah, here we are," exclaimed Tabata. "Type O. You're a universal donor."

"What about Mei?"

He tapped the screen a few times. "Seems she's AB positive."

Are those good things?" asked John.

"Good enough for our situation," he said, smiling a little. "It means you can make a donation."

John cocked his brow. "What?"

"Like I said before, one of the treatments for radiation poisoning is a blood transfusion, but since Oxyblood is specifically made for regular humans, we have no idea how someone like Doctor Curie would react to it. As such, it would be safer to perform a traditional transfusion with a compatible donor such as yourself."

"But what if she has an infection, too?" asked John.

"If she has one, getting rid of the radiation will help her body fight the infection. Additionally, you each possess genetic qualities allowing you to heal faster. There is an added chance the healthy blood you donate could improve her recovery rate even more."

"So no matter what, this will help her?"

"Probably," said Tabata. "But there's always a chance it might not do anything. Your bodies are uncharted territory as far as medical science goes."

John didn't even have to think about it. "I'm in," he said with absolute certainty.

Tabata nodded. "Very well. I'll get my tools and we can begin."

JOHN SAT IN HIS CHAIR, watching the blood drain out of his arm and into a small box. A tube ran from the box into Mei's arm. Imagining his blood circulating through her veins was a strange thought, but if this could help her, he didn't mind. He only wanted her to be safe.

"The regulations on this say you shouldn't do more than a single pint," explained Tabata. "But we don't have any other source to draw from, so if you think you can handle it afterwards, I'd like to try for two. Let me know if you feel sick or lightheaded."

John nodded. The doctor had given him a sleeve of cookies and told him to eat. He was surprised, but didn't ask questions. Food was food, and he wouldn't complain, especially not about free cookies.

The transfusion was supposed to take approximately two hours. Tabata repeatedly checked Mei's vitals and asked John how he felt. He said he was fine each time, but the words were slowly becoming a lie.

He decided it was better not to mention the fog forming in his head. He was no stranger to blood loss. He'd been stabbed and injured in the field several times, so he knew perfectly well how far his body could go before it gave out. Tabata was a doctor, though, and he'd probably stop the procedure if he suspected

John felt sour. *Better to shut up and deal,* thought John, remembering the phrase Captain Thistle had often used. Shut up and deal, son. Ain't no sense in complaining when the world's all gone to Hell.

Ain't that the truth? You always know what to say, boss.

Strap on your stick, and let's go a-killin'. Hooah?

Hooah, boss.

John glanced at Mei. She was fast asleep, completely unaware of what he was doing. It was probably for the best. She'd call him an idiot for this and say he was being reckless.

Maybe she'd be right. *Good thing I'm too dumb to know better.*

His tongue felt numb, and he smacked his lips. He took one of the cookies and bit into it, chewing for a few seconds before the crumbs fell out of his mouth.

Tabata noticed his sloppiness and spoke up. "Sergeant Finn?"

John didn't answer. He was getting sleepy.

The doctor snapped his fingers in front of John's face. "Sergeant? Can you hear me? I'm disconnecting you from the device."

John tried to tell him not to do it, to keep this ride going because it was important. He knew where his limits were. But when he tried to say it, the only thing he could do was moan.

Then he passed out.

JOHN AWOKE in the back of Mei's tent, an I.V. in his arm. When everything came into focus, he saw Bart, Zoe, and Doctor Tabata staring at him.

"You moron," said Zoe.

John blinked a few times, opening and popping his jaw. "What did I do?"

"What was your big plan?" she asked. "You give all your moron blood to Doctor Curie so she gets as stupid as you?"

"Wouldn't be my worst idea," he said, trying to force a smile.

Zoe threw her hands up, exasperated, and went to Mei's bedside.

"Don't mind her," said Bart. "She's upset for other reasons."

John understood. Travis hadn't been dead for more than a few days, so she was bound to be a little on edge. "What's the diagnosis?" he asked.

"You'll be fine," said Tabata.

"I meant Mei," he said.

"We won't know for a while, but I'll tell you when I do."

"Thanks, Doc. You're a lifesaver. Literally."

Tabata nodded and walked away, taking a seat next to Mei's bed.

"How you feeling?" asked Bart.

"Like someone hit me in the head with a pipe," said John.

"Yeah, you look like it."

"Thanks, buddy. Don't you have some work to do?"

Bart shrugged. "I'm taking a break."

"Sounds like slacking to me."

"Says the guy in the bed." Bart leaned in. "Seriously, you okay?"

"No need to worry."

"Good," said Bart, smiling. "On the plus side, I'm making

some solid progress with those coils. By the time Curie gets back on her feet, I might have something to show her."

"What about the radiation?" asked John.

"Oh, uh, Sophie's in charge of the radiation problem."

"Right, sorry," said John. "I forgot."

"No problem. Your head must still be fogged up."

"Yeah."

"Alright," said Bart. "I gotta get back. Feel better." He left the tent, and Zoe followed him. John turned to his side and closed his eyes. When he opened them, the daylight was gone and the tent was completely dark. Everyone had left.

Except Mei. She was still in the bed on the other side of the room. John sat up and twisted his feet around, touching the floor. He clumsily pushed himself off the bed and stumbled toward Mei's side. When he found her bed, he eased himself onto it, sitting beside her waist.

She was fast asleep and breathing steadily. He watched silently, expecting her to open those gorgeous brown eyes at any moment and tell him everything was fine. She'd call him an idiot for the blood thing and he'd say she was a dork, and then they'd lie together and laugh about how silly the world could be.

He smiled and brushed her palm. She was so beautiful, but not for the usual reasons. She would never look like the girls in those old movies, covered in glamour and defined by her curves. Instead, it was her mind, her ideas, and her strength that set her apart. She was the girl who never gave up, who always had to understand the truth and get to the heart of things. She never asked for his protection, never cared for girly things. There was no shame in her, not for who she was or where she came from. She was beautiful for her brilliance, for the way she saw the world.

She was beautiful because she loved him.

He wondered when she would wake. Perhaps tomorrow? The day after? If things didn't improve, would they have to move her to Komodo? Was she ever going to get out of this bed? He didn't know if he could do this without her.

He trembled at the very idea, and after a moment, his face grew warm, and he wept. The tears dripped onto Mei's waist, and he tried fruitlessly to wipe them from her sheet with his hands.

She was his best friend and the love of his life, and while he'd told her as much on multiple occasions, it never felt like enough.

9

Ortego Outpost File Logs
Play Audio File 351
Recorded: April 26, 2350

THISTLE: *Thanks for getting back to me, Doc.*

TABATA: *Certainly, Captain. What can I do for you?*

THISTLE: *I need you to update me with the status of the Ortego Research Outpost and its crew. We've been receiving conflicting reports.*

TABATA: *Wouldn't you prefer to speak with Sergeant Finn? He's been here longer than I have. Besides, I understand you know him.*

THISTLE: *I had a call with Finn this morning. He's mentally fried. Kid tells me it's nothing, but I'm no idiot. I know my man well enough to see when something's got him by the ear.*

TABATA: *And the other researchers? I imagine one of them would—*

***THISTLE**: You said it yourself. You're new, and you don't know these people. It makes you more impartial to what's going on.*

***TABATA**: I see. Alright, how can I assist you?*

***THISTLE**: First, what's happening with Doctor Curie? No one's been able to reach her, but everyone's saying she's fine.*

***TABATA**: I'm afraid the young woman has taken ill. Rest assured, though, it is nothing serious.*

***THISTLE**: You mean she's sick? That's all?*

***TABATA**: A slight flu. She's prone to overworking herself, so I've restricted her from making any calls or performing any stressful tasks. I apologize for the confusion.*

***THISTLE**: Why didn't anyone report this?*

***TABATA**: From what I have seen, Doctor Curie elicits a great deal of respect from her subordinates. They likely didn't want to arouse any concern.*

***THISTLE**: I understand, but they need to stick to protocol. It's there for a reason.*

***TABATA**: Certainly.*

***THISTLE**: Is this why Finn's so out of it? His girlfriend's sick?*

***TABATA**: I'm afraid I wouldn't know anything about that. I spend the bulk of my time studying animals and reading medical papers. I've hardly the time for gossip.*

End Audio File

Unknown
April 26, 2350

Terry was relieved and exhausted all at once. On one hand, he no longer heard the sounds of his pursuers trailing behind him. On the other, he could barely keep his eyes open, and half of his body felt numb.

He'd been running for nearly two days toward the north. Along the way he passed through three forests and five fields without any sign of his former captors. As far as he could tell, they'd long since stopped looking for him.

He let himself rest. Hopefully, this time he wouldn't wake to find a bunch of aliens laughing and poking him. Fingers crossed.

After four or five hours—he wasn't quite sure—he opened his eyes and felt a swell of relief when he saw no one there. He concentrated and listened, waiting for any indication of the strange men, but he could only hear the forest. At last, he was finally safe.

He got to his feet and continued walking, not knowing what to do next. If he returned to the glade with the dome, he might get caught again. If he abandoned his new home, it would mean losing an easy source of food. Would he have to go back to sleeping in caves or the dirt while trying to survive? He'd almost starved a few times before, and he wasn't apt to repeat the experience.

There was also the underground city and the ring inside. If he walked away, he'd have to give up on discovering its secrets.

Don't do it, said Janice, deep in the back of his mind. She'd been quiet for so long he'd almost forgotten she was there. *They'll catch you, big brother. They'll catch you, and you'll die.*

He ignored her, though she had a point. Maybe it was better

to keep going north. Find some food, rest a few days. After a while, he could always return. They'd only spotted him because of the beavermites. The next time he'd stay hidden. Maybe live in the tunnels instead of the dome. They'd never find him there.

In the meantime, he could explore more of the countryside and hopefully get some food along the way. Maybe even a bath. Terry had never traveled more than a few days in any direction. He had no idea what to expect.

The possibility of danger and death were suddenly so very real. For the first time in three years, he had discovered a threat beyond any animal.

He had found intelligent life.

Unknown
April 27, 2350

IN THE AFTERNOON of the third day of his aimless journey, Terry came upon a path deep in the heart of the woods.

The winding trail came from the northeast and continued southwest. His first thought was to leave it altogether. If those strangers were any indication of what the people on this planet were like, he wasn't sure he wanted to meet any others. At the same time, following this path might reveal something important, like the location of a town. If he knew where it was, he could avoid it in the future.

Bad idea, said Janice.

Terry didn't think so. He could follow the path from a distance. Stay hidden in the woods. If anyone were nearby, he'd hear them coming and hide. He'd be fine.

Terry put about two hundred meters between himself and the road. This seemed like enough space in case something happened, and he had to run.

He walked carefully through the woods, minding the direction of the path and keeping his distance. Over the next several hours, Terry noticed a change in the air, a different smell beneath the Variant. Almost like saltwater.

The winding road led him out of the forest and into a valley, a wide alluvial plain stretching several kilometers. On the other side, tall cliffs surrounded the expanse. Between the ridges, far to the north, Terry saw an ocean, thousands of waves dancing to the direction of the wind. He could hear them crashing on the shore.

He never dreamed of seeing such a thing.

He heard a sudden laugh, and his eyes receded from the water to the vale. He looked toward the sound and saw what lay at the end of the road. A large building, surrounded by a fence and fields of agriculture—tall plants, lined like the orchard from before, maintained and organized.

Near the fence, a child threw rocks into the air and giggled. He had the face of a boy.

Terry stared toward the farm with anxious curiosity. He was also starving. It had been days since he last ate. If he could sneak in during the night, he might be able to steal some food.

The child raised his head and looked in Terry's direction. He stood there, gawking and unmoving. Then he waved.

He wants to play, said Janice.

Dammit. He was spotted. The parents wouldn't take kindly to a stranger near their home. They might see him as a threat. He had already experienced the pain and frustration of dealing with the natives on this planet. He could do without a repeat encounter.

But the boy was smiling now and calling to him. He wasn't hostile or screaming. There was no indication of fear or rage. But he was only a kid. Adults were always different.

Adults did terrible things to children.

No, he wouldn't trust them. He'd leave and not come back. There had to be food elsewhere. The cliffs in the distance were another option, but they were at least an hour's hike from the farm. Could he make it there without being caught?

Terry ran back inside the forest behind him, hiding under a large tree. He shot another glance at the farm, looking for the boy. He was gone, but to where? Was he getting his parents?

The door to the house swung open, and a thick man appeared wearing a set of brick red clothes. His hair was black and fell well below his shoulders close to his waist and tied in a series of knots, laced with intricate design patterns. He left the house and stepped into the meters, scanning the fields. His eyes found Terry almost immediately.

Shit, he thought. Hiding behind the tree had done nothing. These people must have incredible eyesight. *Just like me.*

The man walked briskly toward him, waving an arm and

smiling as he did. It would take some time before he arrived. The farm was over half a kilometer away. Terry could run and get away. He still had time.

Leave, whispered Janice. *Leave. Leave. Leave.*

He looked at the ocean, considering his options. He took a step back toward the woods, wavering a moment. The stranger's eyes arched. He began to jog, waving his arm in the air. "Boec!" shouted the stranger. "Boec o jajilc!"

He's going to kill us, whispered the girl in his brain.

Terry shook his head. *There's only one of him.*

It's too risky, she argued.

He knew she was right. Terry barely understood anything about this planet or its native people. So far he'd seen their violence and temperament. Staying here was risking more of the same. But if he ran, it would mean living alone in the wilderness, living in a state of—

Freedom, said Janice.

Isolation, he corrected, and he knew it was true. If he ran now, he'd never stop. He'd die in the woods or on a mountain, alone or with a dozen voices screaming in his head. He wouldn't last, not for long, and in the end, he'd crack and do the thing he said he'd never do.

Or he could stay…try the other path. What if—

A loud roar erupted behind him, filling the silent field and shaking his chest. Terry twisted around, but found nothing there. He stepped from the tree and into the glade. "What the hell was that?" he asked.

"Boec!" yelled the man, who was now running in a full sprint. "Boec! Boec!"

Another roar this time, high-pitched and violent. In the forest, a tree suddenly twitched. A moment later, a second one shook, and another. *Something must be moving between the branches*, he thought.

Terry felt for his knife but cursed when he remembered how the four men had taken it.

Whatever the hell was in those trees let out another cry, and Terry took another step into the field. He searched the branches for the animal, but found only a vague fluttering of leaves. He watched as the shaking grew closer, one tree at a time.

Terry concentrated and squeezed his hands, breathing rapidly. His chest grew warm as his heartbeat skyrocketed. The muscles in his arms and legs tensed. The man behind him continued screaming, but Terry ignored him. Instead, he focused on the leaves, slowing them in his mind and waiting for whatever came.

He blinked.

The leaves burst open, scattering in the air, and a pair of white claws shot toward him with the speed of a bullet.

He dove to one side, barely escaping the attack. The animal hit the ground on its hind legs and bounced a few times, finally digging its massive claws into the dirt to right itself.

The creature was nearly two meters tall, a coat of white encasing most of its body, with a thick tail as long as the distance between its face and hips. It snarled at him, revealing a set of yellow, jagged teeth.

Great, thought Terry.

The beast leapt at him, claws outstretched like daggers. Terry ducked and fell on his back, kicking the monster in the stomach and knocking it off balance. The animal let out a sharp yelp and landed a few meters away, tumbling in the grass. It wheezed, staring at Terry, drool leaking from its mouth. Sawing its claws against one another, the animal planted its heels and sprang into the air.

Terry slowed his perception and slid to the side. The beast's claws came within a few centimeters of his chest. Terry kicked the beast in its ribs, knocking it to the side. He watched as the animal hit the grass and slid, squealing as the impact took the air out of its lungs.

The beast struggled to stand, but kept its eyes on Terry. With a snap of its jaw, the animal roared, pressing its hind legs into the dirt, preparing for another go.

As its feet left the ground, a small shard of metal pierced the monster's neck, causing a spurt of blood into its white coat. The animal gasped for air, drowning in garbled screams before collapsing on its side, no longer moving.

The stranger from the farm stood several meters away, another knife in hand, breathing heavily to catch his breath. He leaned on his knees, looked at the animal, and smiled. "Jaak," he said after a few more heavy breaths.

Terry gave a slow nod, staring at the blade in the man's hand.

The stranger seemed to notice his concern and tucked the knife in a scabbard on his thigh. He held both his hands in the air. "Wnaaq," he said, pointing at Terry.

"Right," muttered Terry. "Thanks for the help."

The stranger tilted his head, a confused look on his face. "Bfec?" He pointed at his own chest and again at Terry. "Wnaaq!"

Terry opened his mouth to say he didn't understand, but paused when he felt something warm sliding down his chest. He glanced down and saw a patch of blood expanding beneath his shirt. He covered the gash with his hand, trying to put pressure on it. But the blood washed over his fingers, dripping to the ground.

Suddenly, he was dizzy. He wanted to lie down. The light of the valley was growing darker, as if a thick cloud had passed overhead, blocking out the suns. He stumbled back, then fell on his side.

The man in red rushed to him. He muttered more nonsense before reaching into his pocket and pulling out a small vial of purple liquid. He showed it to Terry and pointed at his chest. Terry nodded, and the man poured half the bottle on his wound and motioned for him to drink the rest. Terry did, and it tasted like fire, burning his chest and igniting his throat. He coughed and screamed. The pain filled every piece of him. This wasn't medicine. It was poison. He should have listened to Janice when he had the chance.

Terry gripped the man's sleeve and pulled him close. "What did you do?" he yelled at the top of his lungs. "You bastard! You're killing me!"

Ortego Reconstruction Outpost
April 27, 2350

MEI DRIFTED in the night like a ship lost at sea, immersed in the void for what felt like an eternity.

She wandered in it for a while, alone. There was a fog there, too, invisible, but thick and choking the air from her lungs. She cried desperately for some relief, feeling for a hand but never finding one.

Buried in the night, however, she thought she saw a figure, always at the edge of her sight. He eluded her, a child with a shrouded face. "Abandoner," he said with a voice like running water. "You killed me in that tower. Left me there to die."

"No…" she said, knowing it was a lie.

The figure appeared before her now, a blurry face in an old school uniform. Next to him, another child, this one with blood on his chest, oozing out and dripping on the ground. "Mei the Killer," they said together. "Murdered us both and now we're dead."

She ran toward them, but no matter how fast she went, she never got any closer. "I can save you," she said, trying to scream.

The boy with the blood in his chest laughed. "Bullet for the bitch," he cackled. "Stabbed me in the chest and threw me off a rafter."

Alex, she thought, but before she could say his name, he disappeared, leaving the other boy alone. "Who are you?" she begged to know.

The boy with the blurry face laughed, and suddenly the

darkness behind him opened, and the machine from the Ortego building appeared. "I have to go away," he told her. He walked to the console at the base of the machine and flipped the switch.

Mei's eyes widened. She screamed at him to stop. "I can fix it," she cried. "Terry, wait!"

But it was no use. The rift expanded and consumed him, filling the sky and eating the world. She had killed them all.

Mei awoke, drenched in sweat. The blanket and the bed were soaked, and it smelled foul and sour. She looked down to see a puddle of urine in her lap. Fantastic.

She climbed out of the sheets and gathered them together, along with the clothes she was wearing. She hadn't peed the bed since she was six.

How embarrassing.

But at least she felt better now. She rolled the sheets and blankets along with her clothes, then placed them in a laundry bag. She'd wash them after she showered. Hopefully no one would find out about this.

She slipped on some fresh clothes and flipped the mattress to hide the stains. First stop was the latrine tent. She couldn't wait.

With a robe on and a towel in her hand, she walked briskly across the camp to the showers. As she approached the tent, however, Sophie emerged.

"Doctor Curie!" exclaimed her assistant. "When did you wake up? Doctor Tabata was supposed to keep me updated."

Mei stopped cold in her tracks. "I'm okay, thanks," she said quickly.

Sophie examined her. "You look much better, ma'am. I'm so relieved."

"Thank you," said Mei, trying to keep her answers short and to the point. *Let me by, Sophie, please.*

"We were about to have a meeting, actually. I was getting ready to head there now. Did you want to join us?"

"Go ahead without me. You and I can go over the details later. Right now I need to shower and use the bathroom."

"Oh," said Sophie, looking her over. "I apologize for keeping you. Please go ahead, ma'am."

"Thank you," said Mei, sliding past her. "We'll talk later."

Mei ran into the shower and turned the water on. She didn't bother waiting for it to heat up all the way. The sooner she got rid of this filthy stench, the better. She pressed the soap dispenser button and a small glob eased onto her palm. She clasped her hands and scrubbed her body. Consumption policy stated each person was only supposed to consume an ounce of soap per shower, but Mei didn't care right now. She used the dispenser half a dozen more times before she was finished. Even then, she didn't feel clean.

After the shower, Mei grabbed her towel and returned to her tent. She dried and dressed herself, then sat in the chair facing her bed. She could still smell the piss. It filled the entire room with its pungent musk, a persisting reminder of what she'd done.

She grabbed her pad and called Sophie. It only rang twice before her assistant answered. "Ma'am, is everything alright?"

"Fine," said Mei. "What time are we meeting to go over everything?"

"How does 1700 sound?"

Mei glanced at the clock in the upper right-hand corner of the screen. It currently read 12:57. "Make it 1330. I'll meet you in the conference room." She ended the call before Sophie could answer, placed the pad on the small table nearby, and covered her face with her hands.

A brief moment later, John came running into the room. "Mei?" he said, barreling in. He spotted her in the bed. "It's true! You're awake!"

He ran to her side and embraced her tight, squeezing her so hard she could barely breathe. She patted his back. "Okay, okay," she managed to say.

He released her, but kept his hands on her shoulders. "I'm so glad you're okay!" He had the widest smile she'd ever seen on his face.

It made her laugh. "Thanks, dear."

He hugged her again.

"What's the deal with everybody today? You're acting like I disappeared."

He frowned. "You were sick. You had a fever, and it got kind of bad."

This was news to her. "How long was I asleep?"

"A few days," he said.

Her mouth fell open. "Seriously?"

He nodded. "Tabata suggested a blood transfusion, but he wasn't sure if it would work, but it looks like he was right. You seem great!"

A blood transfusion? Had it really been so serious? Mei

grabbed her pad and looked at the date. April 24, 2350. She could hardly believe it.

"One sec," said John, still grinning. He ran outside and returned a few moments later with Doctor Tabata. "Check it out, Doc."

Tabata nodded. "Good. Let's have a look at you, Doctor Curie." He retrieve a digital thermometer. "Open wide."

She grabbed the thermometer out of his hand. "I'll do it, thanks," she said, placing it under her tongue. A few seconds later it beeped. She handed it back to him.

"Ninety-eight degrees. Looks good. I'll have to run a few tests on the rest of you, but overall you seem to be doing much better."

"I should think so, since I'm no longer in a coma," she said.

"It was hardly a coma," said Tabata.

A loud thunderous *boom* shook the ground, startling everyone.

"What was that?" asked Mei.

Another identical sound followed. Mei nearly fell out of her bed.

"What the hell is going on?" she yelled, getting to her feet.

She and John ran outside, and there was another sound, which shook the ground. It seemed to be coming from Bart's workshop. Sophie soon emerged from the conference tent, where she had presumably been waiting for Mei to arrive. "What was…" said Sophie, but her words were drowned out by further noise.

"Sounds familiar!" yelled John. "Don't you think?"

"Huh?" she asked.

"Listen to it! Don't you remember?"

Mei tilted her head, trying to think. *Thump. Thump. Thump. Ksst.* The noise had a rhythm to it, like a machine. Yes, of course. It was the same sound she and John had heard when they first discovered this field all those years ago. "It's a Fever Killer!"

John nodded. "Come on!" He grabbed her hand and led her to the back of Bart's tent. Sophie followed behind them, a clueless look on her face.

They found Bart standing before the Fever Killer. It stood several meters tall, lording over them, pounding repeatedly into the ground. Bart kept his distance, wearing a pair of protective goggles. He didn't seem to notice the others' arrival.

"Bart!" yelled John.

He flinched at the sound of his own name before turning to see them. Clenching his teeth and clearly embarrassed, he grabbed his pad and powered off the machine. "Sorry! I didn't think it would be this loud."

"You nearly gave us all a heart attack," said Sophie.

Doctor Tabata came jogging toward them. "Is everything alright?" he asked.

"Everyone's fine, slow poke," said John.

"I'm not as spry as you kids," said Tabata.

"Always full of excuses," said John. "Tsk tsk."

"Are you sure it works now?" asked Mei.

Bart shrugged. "Maybe. It was only on for about thirty seconds."

"Thirty seconds too long if you ask me," muttered Tabata.

Mei examined the Fever Killer. Standing about four meters

tall and towering above her, she could see how the rough metal casing was still worn from the events of three years ago. The coils themselves looked fairly new, which wasn't surprising. She'd seen the originals shatter into pieces. Bart had scavenged what he could, but some parts had to be built from scratch.

This device had been the perfect excuse Mei needed to convince the board to let her bring a team here. Did this mean her work was finished? The mission certainly had other goals besides the Fever Killer.

Mei touched the device, sliding her hand against its rough surface. The radiation levels were rising, and they would soon swallow this entire area. With such a risk in sight and with the coil now secure and operational, the board might decide to recall her team sooner than expected. There was a very good chance she'd be on her way home tomorrow, all because of this machine.

"What is it, Mei?" asked John.

Sophie pointed to the coil. "She's worried we're going home early, because of this."

Bart removed his protective goggles. "Hey, don't blame the machine. It's not the coil's fault."

"Yes, but the Framling Coil was the main reason Central greenlit the mission," said Sophie. "With the rising risk of radiation, they'll undoubtedly call us home."

Bart frowned. "I worked really hard on this, and now you're making me regret it."

John put his arm around Bart's shoulder. "It's okay, buddy. I can break it if you want. We can throw it on the ground and smash it together."

"Or wait a few more days to tell them about it," suggested Sophie.

John nodded. "Sure, sure," he said, agreeably. He looked at Bart again. "Think about my offer and get back to me."

"I'm confused," said Tabata. "Has anyone solved the radiation problem? Because if not, there's not much use in stalling the board."

"We're delaying in order to find a solution, sir," said Sophie.

The doctor stroked his chin stubble. "My point is that even if you somehow manage to find one, you still need to implement it, which takes time. How long until the radiation reaches this campsite?"

Sophie pursed her lips. "Another ten days, maybe."

"He's right," muttered Bart. "There's not enough time."

Nobody said anything for a few seconds. No doubt, their brains were hard at work trying to come up with an answer. Mei couldn't help but do the same. *Stalling. Maybe he's right. Maybe there's not enough time*, she thought. The words swirled around in her mind. There was never enough time. If only she had a way to slow it down. If only she could halt the spread of the radiation for a while. She glanced at the coil again, saying nothing. The Fever Killer was a marvel of technology, capable of absorbing and redistributing energy more efficiently than anything to date. All it needed was heat energy and—

Her mouth fell open. Heat was part of the electromagnetic scale, just like gamma radiation. Depending on how the machine worked, it might actually be possible to…

John nudged her side. "Hey," he whispered. "Got anything?"

"I can't believe I didn't think of this before," she muttered.

"Ma'am?" said Bart.

She cast a sideways look at him. "Tell me, would it be possible to reconfigure this device to absorb something other than heat?"

He seemed confused. "I don't know what you..." He paused, a look of realization overcoming him. "Yes...yes, I think so. It only depends what kind of energy we're dealing with."

"Would high frequency electromagnetism work?" she asked.

He thought for a moment. "Yeah, it should," he said.

"What the hell are we talking about right now?" asked John.

"The solution we've been looking for," said Mei. "Only it's been here the whole time, staring at me and my big, stupid face."

She flicked the case of Fever Killer, and it dinged.

10

Doctor Mei Curie's Personal Logs
Play Audio File 145
Recorded: April 27, 2350

CURIE: *After hashing out the details, Bartholomew thinks my plan to use the Framling Coil to absorb gamma radiation instead of thermal may actually be sound. Given how they're both electromagnetic energy, albeit on completely different ends of the spectrum, I'm honestly surprised I didn't think of it sooner. I guess I've been a little distracted with everything that's happened lately.*

Regardless, Bart seems confident enough. I'm a little worried he'll have trouble getting the coil to go from absorbing non-ionizing to ionizing radiation, but it might not matter at all. Right now it's unclear whether this difference will affect how the coil operates. For all I know, it might not do anything at all.

I've asked the entire team to assist with the project. We only have a few more days before the board pulls us, and we're forced to vacate the camp. We don't have a lot of time here, which makes this our only shot.

End Audio File

Unknown
April 27, 2350

Terry awoke in the dark, tucked in a bed and unable to move. The pain was gone, but he could barely move his arms and legs. Sweat covered his forehead and cheeks, but it was somehow freezing cold.

He scanned the area and found he was indoors, alone in a small room with only a bed, a stool, and a window. Where the door should be, there was nothing but an open hallway.

He tried to speak, but coughed instead as he struggled to catch his breath. He cleared his throat and swallowed. "Hello?" he asked in a raw, hoarse voice that surprised him.

A small light appeared far in the distance. It moved along the hallway walls, bouncing and flickering while drawing closer to his room. "Who's there?" he asked as the figure approached the archway.

The light bent and reflected off its wielder's face, revealing the curves of a woman. She appeared to be bald.

"Where am I?" asked Terry.

She didn't answer. Instead, she took a piece of dripping wet cloth from under Terry's bed and dabbed his forehead. She worked her way along his neck and pulled the blanket down. There was a bandage covering the wound, which she avoided with the cloth, wiping the skin around it and returning the blanket to where it was before. She avoided looking at him, so he stared at her scalp. To his surprise, there were markings all over—tattoos by the look of them. None of the men had anything remotely similar, nor were any of them bald, so why this woman? Was it customary for the females of this world to shave their heads and wear such elaborate markings? The more he learned about these people, the stranger they seemed.

Once the woman finished cleaning him, she grabbed the small pail from under his bed and left him alone. Terry watched her go, not knowing what to say. He had to find a way to communicate with her, with all of them.

He closed his eyes, inviting sleep. It was the first time he'd been in a bed in three years. He might as well enjoy the experience while it lasted.

Unknown
April 28, 2350

Terry slept late into the morning. The light from the open window struck him hard as he opened his eyes. He squinted and flinched, turning on his side toward the wall next to the bed. He could hear what sounded like dishes clanking in the room down the hall, and amid the noise, a man's voice speaking nonsense.

He planted his feet on the floor. He expected his chest to hurt from the wound when he moved, but nothing happened. Not even numbness from the medicine. When he touched the bandage around his wound, he felt it. Only the pain was gone. Remarkable.

He already knew his body could heal rather quickly, but it usually took a few days, and the pain always lingered for a while. A wound this size never healed overnight. Whatever the Man in Red had given him must have really done the trick. What else could it have been?

A burly laugh filled the hall and echoed into Terry's room, followed shortly by the stomping of someone coming his way. He watched the archway as the Man in Red popped his head through the gap and gasped delightfully upon seeing him. "Obovi!" shouted the stranger, chuckling. "Obovi oc norc!"

Terry stared blankly, saying nothing. Didn't he realize Terry couldn't understand him?

The man pulled the stool close to the bed and plopped down, sending a loud thud throughout the house. "Bfa?" He pointed at Terry.

"Bfa?"

The man slapped his chest. "Ludo."

"What?"

"Lu-do!" he bellowed, hitting himself a second time. "Ju loji er Ludo." He grinned.

Terry paused. "Is Ludo your name?" He pointed to him. "Ludo?"

The Man in Red chuckled and smacked his chest three times.

Okay, so your name is Ludo. Terry pointed at own his face. "Terry."

Ludo repeated the word slowly under his breath with a thoughtful expression. "Terr-ee. Terr-ee. Terry."

Terry stared at Ludo with disbelief. Was this really how first contact with alien life was supposed to happen? He had watched a few science fiction vids as a kid—leftover films from before the Jolt. Some dealt with close encounters, space exploration, making first contact. They made it seem so calculated and methodical, like there was some sort of guidebook for situations like this. Most of them ended with a massive intergalactic war, but a few never made it so far.

"Terry Terry Terry," said Ludo. He laughed and smacked his chest again.

"You got it," said Terry, knowing his words meant nothing.

"Terry," said Ludo. He motioned behind him to the hall. "Hannab."

"Hannab?" asked Terry.

"Terry hannab Ludo." He stood and faced the door, took three steps, and returned to his original position. "Terry hannab Ludo."

"You want me to go with you?"

"Hannab," said Ludo, rather insistently.

"Okay," said Terry.

Despite not knowing English, Ludo seemed to understand.

He led Terry through the hall, passing four other rooms along the way, each with an open doorway. Two of them appeared to be bedrooms—each with a bed, chest, and several mats on the floor. The second bedroom was smaller than the first with a handful of blocks scattered at the base of a much smaller bed.

The third room contained assorted chests. A table stood nearby holding several tools. A few of them had metal tips, but didn't look like weapons. Were they for farming?

In the fourth section, Terry saw a large stone with fire in it, crackling and wheezing behind a thin grate. A boy stood nearby, the same one Terry had seen playing outside before the attack. Next to him, some raised slabs held a variety of plants. The child was smashing one of them with a stone. He looked at Terry for a moment, smiled, and quickly returned to his work.

Ludo brought Terry to the largest room in the house: the foyer. It was similar in design to the other domes he'd explored, but while the others had couches, chairs, tables, and even decorative art, this one only had cushions, rugs, and a small fire pit in the center.

A few meters from the dome's entrance, the woman stood watching them. She had blue eyes and a small nose, with an almost regal composure. She wore a red gown with blue patterns on it, and a metallic headdress which kept her bald head and strange tattoos completely hidden.

Ludo looked at the woman and his voice went surprisingly soft. "Jou bi ioc?" he said to her.

She nodded.

Ludo smiled and went to the fire pit and sat on the rug next to it, motioning to the other side. "Rec," he said.

Terry joined him on the floor. "Does rec mean sit?" he asked.

Ludo grinned. He retrieved the lid of the metal pot and took a large spoonful of the brown liquid inside, pouring it into a bowl and handing it to Terry. He then took a second one and drank from it, letting out a whoop of satisfaction as he smacked his lips.

Terry took the hint and drank from the bowl. It tasted surprisingly similar to eggs with a hint of sweetness—something like apples, perhaps. He wasn't sure.

He lowered the bowl from his face and smiled politely at Ludo. "Thank you," he told him. He drank the rest of the soup, trying not to gulp it down too quickly.

When they were finished, Ludo put the bowl to his side. "Talo!" he yelled.

Terry stiffened at the sudden call, but before he could respond the small boy appeared from behind the back wall. He approached Ludo with his arms extended and his hands flat. In both of his little palms he held a rather large knife. The hilt had several glyphs carved into it, while the blade was littered with specks of glistening stones of various colors.

Ludo took the knife, which looked rather small in his own hand, and showed it to Terry. "Rotsiq," he said in a low, almost respectful voice.

"Rot-siq," muttered Terry.

Ludo handed the knife to the boy and touched his forehead. The child smacked his chest and retreated from the room, passing the woman with the blue eyes as he opened the door and disappeared.

Terry watched as his new friend poured a second bowl of soup for each of them. They drank it together, and this time Terry had no problem drinking slowly. His belly was filling with a warmth he hadn't felt in years. When was the last time he'd had soup? The academy? He could no longer remember.

Ludo's presumed wife left through the door where the boy had disappeared and closed it behind her, saying nothing. Terry wondered if she disapproved of his presence. Was she angry at him for coming into her home? Or was it customary in this society for wives to ignore guests? And what was the deal with the kid and the weird knife? Who were these people and why were they sitting in the middle of nowhere? Terry wished he could speak this stupid language so he could figure out what the hell was going on.

Ludo got to his feet and motioned for Terry to stand. "Hannab," he told him. *Follow.*

He did, and Ludo led him outside. The suns had begun their descent, hovering above the horizon. Ludo led Terry around the side of the house to the edge of one of the fields. The plants reminded him of corn stalks because of how tall they were, but the resemblance ended there. They were blue and contained pieces of red vegetables, though of course he had no idea if they were really vegetables, fruit, or something else altogether. For all he knew, the red things were poison and the only edible part of the plant was the root.

Ludo grabbed a cloth sack near the base of one of the stalks and handed it to Terry. "Fanq," he told him.

Terry looked at the bag, confused.

Ludo grabbed one of the red vegetables from its stem and placed it in Terry's bag. "Holp," he repeated.

"Okay," he said. "Holp."

Ludo took another sack and began filling it with the red vegetables.

Terry did the same. It seemed he'd have to earn his keep here. Not that he minded. It had been a long time since he had the chance to work with someone else. Besides, the bed was nice and the food had been better than raw fruit. He would help however he could.

He took one of the red things and placed it in his bag. He wondered how long he'd be here with these people. Probably no more than a day or two. They didn't know anything about him, and it wasn't like they could communicate properly. If this place proved to be safe, maybe he could set up a camp nearby. He'd have to scout around, make sure he didn't pick an exposed area. He had to be able to run if things went bad.

Terry looked at Ludo, who was nibbling on one of the plants. He might be able to make this work after all.

Ortego Reconstruction Outpost
April 28, 2350

Mei waited patiently for Bartholomew and John to hoist the Fever Killer into place. Tabata, Zoe, and Sophie were all standing nearby, watching in silence. Poor Bart had spent the bulk of two days working on it, only taking a few hours to rest. Mei asked the others to assist where they could, but Bart wasn't having it. He kicked everyone out except Zoe. Mei almost objected but ultimately let it go. She trusted Bart to know what he was doing.

Now came the time to see how good an engineer he truly was.

"Hold it there," shouted Bart.

John gripped the sides of the coil with both of his bulky arms. "Sure," he said. "I'll just be here, hugging this stick."

Bart rushed into his tent. A second later, Mei heard a soft crash from inside. Bart cursed, then reappeared with a drill.

"Everything alright?" asked Mei.

He grunted and went to the coil.

"Now what?" asked John, his arms still wrapped around the device.

"Hang on," said Bart. He used the drill to pull one of the panels off the side of the coil.

"What are you doing?" asked Sophie.

Bart fumbled around with several wires inside the machine, shifting them to the side. He touched the back portion of the outer shell and snapped something into place, then grinned. "Forgot to hook a fuse back in. Close call."

"You idiot," snapped Zoe. "The last thing we need is for the coil to overheat."

"No harm done," said Bart.

Zoe glared at him.

"Alright, John," he said. "Hold it steady."

John nodded with a look of hesitation. "You'd better know what you're doing."

With his pad, Bart called up the control screen for the Fever Killer. He tapped the pad, and the coil let out a loud boom and the ground shook.

John flinched, but held on tight. "When can I let go?" he yelled, his voice distorted by the vibrations.

"Hang on," said Bart. He tapped the pad a few times. The coil let out a loud snap, startling everyone. John seemed especially panicked. "Okay, you can let go!"

John released the machine and scurried back.

"What the hell was that?" asked Tabata. It was the first time he'd spoken in a while. Mei nearly forgot he was there.

Bart tapped the pad again, and the coil powered down. "I activated the locking mechanism for the coil. It shot a rod several meters into the ground, then expanded in nearly every direction, sort of like the roots of a tree."

"Or a bush," added John.

"Which is why he was holding it in place," said Bart.

"Moving on," said Mei. She wanted to get this show on the road. "Can we see if it works?"

Bart nodded. "Give me a second." He tapped the pad once more, turning the coil back on. It was loud for a few seconds, but quickly shifted into a gentle hum.

"Well?" asked Mei.

Bart studied the pad. "As far as I can tell, it's working. I don't think we'll know until the radiation hits it, though."

"So we'll have to move it," said Sophie.

"Right," said Bart. "It won't do us much good sitting in the middle of our camp."

"Why not?" asked John, frowning.

"It has to be within the radiation zone," said Mei. "Once we've got the coil set up, we'll monitor it for a while, see how it does. If we get some worthwhile results, we can put more of them up and gradually push our way forward."

"Like an army moving the front line," said John.

"Something like that," said Mei.

Zoe furrowed her brow. "How are we supposed to transport this thing closer to the radiation, especially after what happened before?"

"It'll work," said Mei. "The radiation isn't very strong until you're in the heart of the Ortego complex, closer to the ruins. We can put it up near the edge of where the radiation is hitting. A normal rad suit should be enough to protect me while I get the coil into place."

John looked at her. "Whoa, whoa, whoa," he said, waving his arms around. "I think you've lost enough hair for one month, lady. Let someone else handle this."

Tabata nodded. "He's right. Your health may have improved since your initial exposure, but your body is still recovering. Another dose of radiation could kill you."

"Good point," said Zoe. "There's no way you'd be able to lift the coil on your own."

Mei hesitated to answer. She knew they were right, but having someone else do the job could result in another accident. It could mean another Travis.

John stepped forward. "I'll do it."

Mei scoffed. "No."

"Hold on," muttered Tabata. "Sergeant Finn's genes are the same as yours, Doctor Curie. He's a hybrid, so his body would be resilient enough to withstand some of the radiation. If anything happens to the suit, he should still survive as long as the exposure is marginal. Having him go makes sense, objectively." He glanced at John. "Though, I imagine it'll hurt, if you actually encounter such a situation."

"I can handle it," said John.

Mei's heart was pounding. She pictured John on the ground, dying the same way Travis had. She didn't know what to do.

John went to her and placed a hand on her shoulder. "Don't worry," he said, as if to answer her concerns. "I risk my life for a living. This won't be any different."

"A gun can't protect you from radiation," she muttered.

Zoe cleared her throat. "I'll monitor his suit. We'll know he's in danger before he does."

John smiled. "You heard the lady. I've got nothing to worry about."

"If you can carry the coil on your own, I can activate it remotely from here," said Bart.

John clasped his hands. "Great."

Bart turned the machine off. "There's still plenty of daylight left. If we hustle, we can get the coil moved in less than two hours."

"Back to work, then," said Zoe, sighing.

Everyone dispersed rather quickly, leaving Bart, John, and Mei behind.

"You gonna be okay?" asked John.

She glared at him. "I didn't need you to step in and save me, John."

"I know."

"Why, then? And don't say you're protecting me."

He considered her question. "Because someone has to, and it couldn't be you. I'm the only one left."

Her gaze fell to the ground. She opened her mouth to respond, but before she could, she felt a pair of thick arms wrap around her, gently squeezing her chest. John nuzzled the top of her bald head, and she felt a gush of relief.

By the time he pulled away, she no longer felt like arguing.

Mei watched through John's eyes as he brought the Fever Killer to its new home, dangerously close to the edge of the irradiated zone.

He'd driven a dirt cab for half an hour, talking with her for most of the way. She considered asking him to come back, tell him to forget about the job, and they'd go home together, but the danger was real, and it wouldn't stop because of her childish fears.

The rain came when he was halfway there, beginning with a soft patter against the cab windshield before turning hard and violent. The wind roared so loudly it sounded like a scream. A few minutes later, the storm had manifested, covering everything from the Ortego site to their camp.

John parked a quarter kilometer from the where the radiation levels were at their weakest, no danger as long as he stayed in the suit.

Or maybe there was. She suddenly wasn't sure. A dozen questions rattled in her head, giving her pause. Had she really sealed his suit properly? What if he accidentally loosened it in the cab or while carrying the coil? John could be clumsy…what if he tripped and fell? A chill ran along the nape of her neck, and her tongue went dry. She smacked her lips, clearing her throat.

John opened the door of the cab and walked to the attached rear trailer. The bed was drenched with rain. He lowered the gate and snagged the coil, sliding it to the end and hoisting the tube on his shoulder.

"Don't drop it," said Bart. He was right behind Mei, peering over her shoulder. "If you do, there's not enough time to make another."

"Relax," said John. "You're acting like I haven't done this before."

"You haven't," said Mei.

He scoffed. "As far as *you* know."

John lugged the Fever Killer several meters from the dirt cab, pausing now and then to reposition himself or switch shoulders. His visor showed the way, indicating which direction to head with a digital green line imposed on the screen. A set of numbers in the bottom right corner counted down the distance to the installation site. Mei had programmed in all of this, hoping to make things as easy as possible for him. Right now, the visor said he was less than a dozen meters from the spot.

He stopped, wavered slightly. A sharp whistle filled his helmet.

"What's wrong?" asked Mei.

"The wind's getting worse," he said, but she could barely hear him.

"You're almost there," she said.

"What?"

"Can you hear me, John?" she yelled.

"Barely. Hang on!" he shouted. The whistle grew until she could no longer understand him.

Instead of talking or screaming, she pulled the keyboard out and typed a message. It appeared a second later on his visor.

KEEP GOING. ALMOST THERE.

If he said anything, she wouldn't know. The counter on the visor indicated he was getting close. Twenty meters. Fifteen. Ten.

He stopped a few more times, moving progressively slower as he neared the goal. The rain fell harder, and the wind blew the drops into his visor so hard they slid sideways.

There was a clap of thunder outside the tent, and several people jumped. Sophie yelped, knocking a few tools off the table she was sitting on. Bart gathered them and motioned for her to stay where she was. She nodded, chewing on a tuft of her hair, an embarrassed look on her face.

Mei kept her eyes on the monitor. John was nearly at the mark. Five meters. Three. Two.

He stopped. He seemed frozen, so she typed a quick message.

SOMETHING WRONG?

He shook his head, and the camera in the visor moved with him. He lifted the coil from his shoulder and set it on the ground. Now came the digging. He unlatched a small shovel from his side and pointed at the dirt directly before him.

YES. RIGHT THERE.

The shovel was barely eight centimeters long, but could be extended with the press of a button near its center. John touched it, but nothing happened. He tried a few more times with no success. At last he clasped both ends and attempted to manually extend it. Nothing worked.

Mei began typing a message to him, but stopped when she saw him drop to his knees and begin digging with the tiny shovel. He flung clumps of soil to his side, one after the next, never slowing. Thunder cackled as the rain beat down on him. Flashes of yellow and white ignited the ground as lightning flashed overhead, reflecting off the hilt of the shovel as well as his silver gloves. Mei fought the urge to close her eyes. *It's okay*, she told herself. *Nothing can hurt him.* She repeated the words in her mind, mouthing them a few times. *Nothing can hurt him. Nothing can hurt him. Nothing can hurt him…*

She didn't care if it was a self-imposed delusion. Sometimes lies were better than the truth.

John dug a hole half a meter deep before stopping. He tossed the little shovel at the freshly made pile of earth and glanced at the coil at his side. Pressing his hand against his knee, he pushed himself to his feet, stumbling a few steps in the process.

He wavered there a moment, doing nothing.

JOHN ARE YOU ALRIGHT?

He raised his hand, giving her a thumb-up. The glove glistened in the rain, shaking slightly as he kept it there. Why was he trembling? Could it be the wind? Maybe the rain was too cold.

John lifted the Fever Killer and set it gently in the ground. Several clumps of mud slid from the peak of the hole like chocolate pudding, dripping into a soup of brown slime and shredded blue grass.

He tossed shovel loads of dirt back into the tiny pit. By the time he had finished, a small puddle was already forming at the base of the coil.

Bart touched Mei on the shoulder. "Don't forget the switch. He needs to activate it."

She nodded, and typed the message to him. John gave her another thumb-up. This time, his hand was noticeably slow. He flipped the coil's latch open, revealing a control pad. Every Framling Coil required a digital numerical code in order to activate. This was a remnant of the original design, created for obvious security purposes that were now obsolete. Bart intended to get rid of them in the future, but right now there was no time.

The activation code was simple. Mei had requested it herself, knowing John would remember it. She watched as he typed the numbers in, nodding each time the glowing green digit appeared on the screen.

04-14-2332

The day they'd been born.

John took a step back, and the Fever Killer rattled with a loud hum as it roared to life. A moment later, the casing shuddered, and the drill inside plummeted into the ground, letting loose a wild *CRACK* and securing its place.

Lightning ignited the northern sky like a spider's web. The flash was so bright it could have been a sunrise.

John turned and headed back toward the dirt cab. When he reached the front of the vehicle, he touched the hood and stopped. He bent forward, bobbing his head, like he was out of breath. Mei was about to ask if something was wrong when he let go and got into the driver's seat.

He pressed the ignition button, and the dashboard lights came on. As he pulled around and began the drive back, Mei noticed his gloves sliding, almost drooping, as he loosely gripped the steering wheel.

When he finally arrived, she was already outside, standing in the rain, dripping wet and waiting to greet him. The cab slowed, but didn't stop. Instead, it plowed directly into the nearby fence, bowling the hood to reveal the engine inside. The metal warped instantly. Steam filled the air around the guts of the cab as the cold rain hit the exposed engine. Mei ran to the door. The rain-water was flowing over the window, too thick for her to see. Panic took hold as she quickly opened the door.

Inside, John was hugging the wheel, his face against the visor. There was a rip in his suit where the shoulder met the neck, and his face had turned a bright red.

Bart and the others came running from the tent. "Holy shit, did he crash the cab?" he asked.

Mei wanted nothing more than to scream, but she tried to stay composed. "John?" She touched his shoulder. "Are you alright?"

He didn't answer.

Her eyes swelled and her throat closed. "John?" She shook him. "Say something, please."

He let out a soft groan. "…Mei?"

"Oh, God!" she shouted, clutching his sleeves with both her hands.

"Sorry." He raised his head, his strained eyes blinking and half-opened. He had the look of exhaustion on him, like he'd been sleeping for days. He smiled, but his lips were shaking. "Hope I didn't worry you."

She hugged him close, wrapping her arms around his chest. "John, you idiot," she said, and all at once she was crying, warm tears mixing with the cold rain.

PART II

Facing it, always facing it,
that's the way to get through.
–Joseph Conrad

Everything is theoretically impossible,
until it is done.
–Robert A. Heinlein

11

Documents of Historical, Scientific, and Cultural Significance

Open Transcript 616

Subtitled: The Memoires of S. E. Pepper – Chapter 5

March 19, 2185

PEPPER: *There is something to be said about the stars, I think, which doesn't get mentioned as much these days. Most of the people living in this city were born sometime after the Great Calamity, but still a few of us attempt to pull the images out whenever the mood strikes, and we surrender ourselves to nostalgia. I often lay awake at night, immersed in mental slideshows, recalling the night sky…twinkling dots amid the dark, begging me to dream. We used to give them stories, playing connect-the-dots with the cosmos.*

"There goes Orion, the hunter, chasing Taurus with his mighty steel. Look at how proudly he stands."

Little did we know how truly mighty our blinking specks could be. If only we could see their true beauty, these mammoth balls of burning plasma a billion times the size of Earth, floating gently in a vacuum, igniting the fabric of existence. Among them, orbiting planets, as varied and complex as any our imaginations could conceive. What would we have said to justify such wonders? This is common knowledge now, of course, but at the time it remained a distant realization.

Studying the stars is a humbling experience, many astronomers used to say. Sadly, they're all dead now. All are gone and forgotten, their collective knowledge a lost and unusable truth. After all, what good are the stars when we cannot even look at them? What's the point?

I do not know the answer to those questions, and I am certain someone will say it is a waste of time…a valid argument, I suppose, when one considers our current predicament.

Still, I know the stars exist. Our ignorance about them will never change this fact. They will go on, regardless of whether or not we acknowledge them. They will live, expand, explode, and shatter across time and space until all the void is black again, and we are nothing but a shadow of a thought.

Perhaps in this sea of endless possibilities there exists another world like ours, capable of supporting life. Such a place may be far removed from us. For all we know, it may very well be outside of what we call existence. But on that rock, wherever it is, floating in the light of another sun, perhaps there is a thinking thing with eyes and wonder in its heart, staring at its own sky, naming dots of lights, and dreaming. Like so many things, I do not know if this is true.

But I hope.

End Audio File

Unknown
October 21, 2350

Terry raised his head from the river, taking a deep breath of the fresh Variant air. The suns drifted high above him, and the midday heat blazed against the cool, rapid water as it collided gently with his cheeks. He took a deep breath and sighed, not to indicate his frustration or boredom but rather his content. He could not imagine himself in any better place. Not on this planet anyway.

It had been six months since Terry found the farm and the family who lived there. Since then, he'd moved into the cliffs beyond the valley and made a home for himself near the place where the river met the sea. With Ludo's help, he'd built a small house into the side of the rock-face, using the flattened stones as the back wall and crafting the rest from the bark of over a dozen trees. As it turned out, Ludo was a man of many talents, including farming, hunting, cooking, and carpentry. He offered these skills freely to Terry, asking nothing in return. The man was the kindest person Terry had ever met, with John perhaps being the rare exception. Someone who gave his devotion freely without reservation. A true friend.

In their eagerness, both Terry and Ludo had made learning the other's language a priority. Much to his disappointment,

Terry quickly discovered he had no talent for linguistics, so his progress was slow and clumsy. He'd managed to learn a great deal, however, fumbling through sentences and conversations, determined to improve. By contrast, Ludo went from knowing nothing of English to speaking with some impressive adequacy. Terry only had to tell him a word once or twice for Ludo to memorize it. Within the first week, he had already mastered basic phrases and most of the common nouns. By the second month, he spoke with the fluency of a small child, knowing many of the words while struggling with proper grammar. After six months, he'd mastered the bulk of the language in the time it took Terry to ask where the bathroom was.

Still, Terry had looked forward to learning how to speak to Ludo and his family in their native language, so he forced himself to work on it and adapt. He'd need the skill if he were to ever encounter more people like this quaint little family, and he imagined he would, given what Ludo had told him. "The world is big," Ludo explained, motioning to the space around him. "Many people live here. You'll see soon. I'll show you."

It was through these conversations that Terry learned a great many things. For starters, the name of the planet was Kant, while the region—or country, depending on how Ludo chose to talk about it—was called Greenwater. Kant rarely came up in conversation, except when Ludo needed to compare Greenwater to something bigger. "Not many live in Greenwater, but it borders Xel and Everlasting."

"Xel and Everlasting?" asked Terry.

"Other countries. Xel is smaller. Everlasting is much bigger." Ludo scratched his ear.

"Who lives there?"

"Xel is a lot like Greenwater, but more villages. The men you saw in the jungle were probably from there. We're close to the border."

The way Ludo had talked about them, the four strangers from the woods had likely been slavers. There was a prison near the Xel border, and they would often send small groups out in search of new people. "And Everlasting?" asked Terry.

Ludo's eyes lit up, and he grinned. "Big place," he said, spreading his arms out. "The people are all beautiful and everyone flies very high. Much higher than us. I've never gone but others says so."

More nonsense about flying, thought Terry. Ludo often talked about people flying, including his own family, but the context never made any sense. None of them had wings. But Terry was still learning the language, and mistranslations were bound to happen. Maybe Ludo was talking about something else, and there simply wasn't a word for it, so he called it flying. There was no way he really believed they all had wings, right?

Terry needed to learn how to communicate better so he could discover more about Kant. It was tempting to leave right now and see what else was out there, but he couldn't go running off, even with an adequate knowledge of the language. There was always time for more adventures later. For now, he was content, perhaps even happy living under a cliff by the sea.

He decided to eat lunch alone today. Ludo had given him

some fishing supplies, which he quickly learned to use in an effort to become as self-sufficient as possible. While he enjoyed the meals he ate on the farm, he always felt like he was imposing. Ludo never seemed to mind. In fact, as far as his friend had explained it, the simple act of eating someone else's food was a sign of great respect, bringing honor to the household. Terry didn't know if the sentiment were true or if Ludo was simply being kind, but he certainly appreciated the gesture.

For the most part, Terry found, the differences in his and Ludo's cultures to be far less than expected, though there were a few things which he found strange and at times truly alien. For example, Ludo's son Talo did most of the cooking and cleaning, which he attended to throughout the afternoon. In the morning, the boy would study under his father's tutelage, though as far as Terry could tell, they mostly focused on family history, botany, and an hour of meditation. The last one appeared to be the same sort of meditation the scarred man had used in the middle of the night while the others slept. Like the other men had done, Ludo and his son sat on the floor with their eyes open, slowing their heart rate as well as their breathing to the point where they hardly seemed alive. The practice must have been a widespread one, probably part of the culture, but he still didn't understand the purpose of it.

Terry remembered learning in history class how some civilizations once used meditation as a form of emotional management or spiritual fulfillment. Those people sought a sense of stillness, humility, and oneness. Throughout the millennia, a variety of groups had adopted the practice and integrated it into their religions, while many more used it as a means of relaxation. Plenty of people back home still used meditation as a relaxation technique. As far as Ludo's people were concerned, this could have gone either way. When Terry had asked his friend about the meditation sessions, the answer only brought more questions. "We do this so we may fly," he had said. "You must touch chakka. Chakka is very important. One day I will show you."

Terry had no idea who or what chakka was, or what flying had to do with any of it. When asked, Ludo simply grinned and said, "Don't worry! I will teach you soon."

Finally, there was Ludo's wife Ysa, who never spoke. For a while, Terry thought this was because she didn't approve of him, but the more time he spent in the house, the more convinced he became that it was part of her demeanor. Aside from this, Terry still didn't understand the meaning of her tattoos or why she was bald, or her complete lack of general responsibilities, but he was certain he would discover those answers in time. What he found truly fascinating was how she appeared to have complete and utter authority over the other two males. Whenever Ludo wished to leave the house, he asked his wife for permission, usually with his head bowed. It was as though she were some kind of farmhouse royalty, worshiped only by her son and husband, never required to lift a finger. When Terry tried to ask why his wife acted in such a fashion, Ludo dropped his head, closed his eyes for a moment, and said, "We do not speak badly of Ysa. She…" he paused, searching for the words. "She flies the highest. Yes! High above to Everlasting." He hugged himself, smiling. "Ysa does so much."

Perhaps what Ludo had said made sense to *him*, but it left Terry with only more questions.

Still, he was certain he'd understand eventually. Given enough time, he *had* to figure it out. For now, he'd try to relax. He'd swim in the river, eat with his new friends, and maybe catch a nap if time allowed.

This place was good for him.

More than anything, however, the voice in his head was gone—the little girl pretending to be his sister. He hadn't heard her in all the time he'd spent with Ludo, and perhaps it was a good thing. She had asked him to run, he remembered, months ago in the field at the edge of the woods. *Leave*, she'd begged, but he refused her, and in an instant she was lost. In exchange, however, he'd found another friend, and surely it was better to talk with someone real, a person made of flesh and bone, than a thing of make-believe trapped inside his brain.

Because Janice wasn't real, he reminded himself.

She never was.

Ludo's Farm, Kant
October 30, 2350

Terry sat between Ludo and Talo, eating dinner after a long day in the fields. Ysa sat across from him, saying nothing. He had tried on several occasions to make conversation with her, but found she wasn't one for small talk. The most he'd ever gotten were short and to the point responses. In the beginning, he'd taken this as a sign of hostility, but after some months had gone by, he came to understand it was simply her way.

Ludo motioned for Talo to retrieve the Sacred Vessel, which he did immediately. Talo handed the box to his father, who opened it and presented the knife to the family. "We ask for protection. We ask for guidance. May the Eye watch over us that we might fly together someday." He put the blade back in the box and handed it to Talo.

It had taken Terry several months to understand the words Ludo spoke each night before dinner, let alone the deeper meaning behind them. From what he'd gleaned, the knife held some sort of religious significance and had been acquired by Ludo in the years before he became a simple farmer, around the time he met his wife. The prayer itself was a request to someone called the Eye, undoubtedly the local god. The Eye watched over every living thing on Kant, according to Ludo, and only through it could a person learn to fly. But of course Terry had never seen anyone flying on this planet, so he took it as a metaphor.

Indeed, Ludo and his family meditated daily, always at the exact same time. This occurred no matter what, even at the cost of other activities, including eating and sleeping. They never missed a session. They often stopped in the middle of a task to go meditate, sometimes without a word. Terry would be standing there with Ludo one moment, only to turn around and find the man gone the next. The meditation hour was the highest priority of their lives, Terry found, but he still barely understood it.

Ludo poured a bowl of soup and handed it to Ysa, Terry,

Talo, and finally himself. The order of delivery had been this way since the week following Terry's arrival. At first, the food had been given to Terry, because at the time he'd been a guest. Since he was now considered a member of the family, according to Ludo, he ate second. Talo was next, because he was the youngest, and finally Ludo, because he was the one preparing the food. Talo usually cooked the meals, but Ludo occasionally stepped into the role of homemaker. He seemed to enjoy taking care of people. Such a ritual was a far cry from the cafeteria line of the academy but not completely dissimilar. People still waited their turns, depending on their positions within the society. The idea of respect, it seemed, was not unique to Earth.

After dinner while Talo cleaned, Terry helped Ludo put together some supplies for the upcoming hunt in a few weeks. This would be the eighth such hunt for Terry, so he was fairly accustomed to the routine.

As Ludo prepared one of the many traps they would be using, Terry stuffed a bag with several small knives and some rope. "Will you join us tonight for meditation?" asked Ludo when he finished wrapping the trap. He often asked this question, never deterred by Terry's repeated declination.

In truth, Terry had been meaning to try the practice out for a while now, but the prospect of getting involved with another culture's religion felt unsettling. He didn't want to offend his friend by doing something wrong or expressing his lack of faith. But he also didn't want to keep declining him. "I don't know, Ludo," said Terry at last. "I've never done it before. I wouldn't know how."

Ludo smiled. "It's okay! I will show you. It's easy to start."

Terry considered this. It wouldn't kill him to give it a shot, he supposed. And after everything Ludo and his family had done, he owed it to them. "Alright, I'll try."

Ludo's smile grew wider, and he beat his chest three times. "Wonderful!" he exclaimed. "You will learn to fly very soon, my friend. Wait and see!"

TERRY, Ludo, and Talo sat together, preparing for the meditation.

Ysa had gone to a separate room per usual to carry out her own version of whatever was about to take place.

Terry never had the opportunity to watch them do this, mostly because he didn't want to risk insulting anyone by staring and not participating. He'd seen the practice once before back in the woods when the redheaded man had closed his eyes and stopped breathing. Looked like he was dead.

No way I can do that, he thought.

Terry waited as Ludo lit a small fire in the center of the room. It burned with a blue flame, a result of the type of leaves. The three of them sat close, facing each other, their legs crossed. "The fire is our guide," said Ludo. "Let it lift you. Let the heat carry your wings."

Terry didn't have wings, but he nodded anyway.

"Next we must close our eyes and focus our breaths. Look at how Talo does it. See the way he is calm and still? His breathing is steady; his mind is at peace."

"What's the goal here?" asked Terry. "What are we trying to do?"

"The goal is that there is no goal," explained Ludo, smiling. "When the mind is quieted, we are free of worry, free of anger and fear. Only through peace can we experience true happiness. This is how we fly."

Terry was pretty sure the term flying didn't mean what Ludo thought it did. Oh, well. Chalk it up to translation problems.

Terry followed Talo's lead in the exercises, trying to copy the way he breathed. Occasionally, they would perform soft chants, repeating certain sounds which carried no real meaning.

According to Ludo, the purpose was to clear one's mind of all thought, concern, worry, stress, and emotion. "Be like the tree," said Ludo, his eyes closed. "The tree does not worry, nor does it weep, nor is it quick to anger. Instead, it simply is, and nothing more." He took a deep breath, and exhaled slowly. "Let your skin become your bark so that it might shield you."

Terry spent the rest of the hour copying what he saw, but he found it difficult to remain still. His mind was all over the place, and he wasn't used to sitting in such an awkward position. Whenever he shut his eyes, his thoughts wandered. He pictured his friends and imagined what they might be doing. Whether they were safe. He thought about the men from the woods. The redheaded man and the one with the purple eyes. He thought about the abandoned city under the mountain and the machines still there. He thought about his sister and how old she must be.

In trying not to, he thought about everything.

Ludo's Farm, Kant
November 29, 2350

TERRY SAT with Ludo and Talo, taking breaths and trying his best to focus on the meditation practices. He'd been at this for several weeks but hadn't made much progress.

Ludo spent the hour teaching him a new mantra, which he then recited many times while focusing on his breathing exercises. Terry wondered if he would ever move beyond breathing and chanting. Ludo and Talo could each do the same as the redheaded man, slowing their heartbeats to an almost dead state.

When Terry asked about this, Ludo told him to wait and see. "Soon you will go with us," he told him. "We will build a palace for you, too."

Again, Terry was at a loss. A palace? What was this? They lived on a farm in the middle of a valley. "Wait and see," he told him again. "Soon."

So Terry breathed and chanted, waiting until he saw whatever Ludo saw, waiting for his chance to learn about the palace.

Until today, when he sat there in the meditation room, chanting a phrase for the thousandth time. This was when it happened. The entire world went dark.

An empty sea of thoughtlessness.

In a fraction of a moment, Terry entered the state in which he drew his strength, where time slowed, and his senses were magnified. In each of the other instances where he had done this, he'd felt a thrill of exhilaration, a power so intense it drove him to take action, to nearly want to scream.

Now, it was different. Now, he felt nothing. All of it was gone, replaced by empty stillness, a void of his own making. There were no sounds blaring in the distance, no need to drown them out or pull himself back. He was simply there, quiet and indifferent, trapped inside a sea of nothing, floating gently, and waiting…

Floating…

Floating…

Floating…

Brother…

His eyes snapped open, a surge of energy filled him, and he gasped, falling backward and hitting the wall.

Ludo ran to him, grabbing his shoulders and holding him. "Are you alright?" he asked.

Beads of sweat poured down Terry's face, filling his eyes with a sharp burn. His chest was heaving. His heart felt like it was going to explode. "What the hell was that?" he said quickly.

"What did you see?" asked Ludo.

Terry licked his lips. He was suddenly so thirsty. "It was so quiet. Everything was so…it was like I was empty…"

Ludo nodded. "This is very good!" he exclaimed.

"What?" asked Terry.

"You have cleared your mind. This is the first step to finding chakka. The first step to flying. This is a great moment for you, my friend!" He let out a roar of laughter. "It takes others years, but you have done it so quickly. This is a great day!"

Once Terry was relaxed, Ludo helped him to his feet, and

together they went to the main foyer. There, they feasted in celebration of Terry's accomplishment. Ludo and Talo recounted the experience to Ysa, who smiled and nodded, a rare sign of approval.

But while the night was good and filled with joy, Terry's thoughts circled the few seconds he'd spent in the dark. There had been a moment, right before he woke. He'd heard something, a voice, but he couldn't remember. He couldn't—

A cold chill ran through him, and his stomach turned into a knot. Why did he feel this way? What was he missing?

It's nothing, he told himself, repeating the words like his own personal mantra.

It's nothing.

It's nothing.

It's...

12

Ortego Outpost File Logs
Play Audio File 373
Recorded: January 05, 2351

CURIE: *I'm sorry, Doctor Prescott, but what you're proposing simply isn't possible.*

PRESCOTT: *Of course it is, Curie. Have your mechanic package one of the Framling Coils and send it home to Central. We've given you plenty of time, and the board is tired of waiting.*

CURIE: *In case you haven't noticed, we're dealing with a containment issue at the moment. My entire team is working nonstop to get this taken care of. We don't have time to—*

PRESCOTT: *You'll have to make time. I'm not giving you an option here. This is an order straight from the board, including Doctor Tremaine.*

CURIE: *I'm telling you it's not possible. Didn't you read the reports?*

We're building coils as fast as we can, but we need every single one to keep the radiation in check. If you really want us to work faster, I suggest you send me a few more engineers to assist Bartholomew. Otherwise, you'll just have to wait.

PRESCOTT: *What was that? Are you getting an attitude with me, Curie? Don't forget I'm your superior, and I can—*

CURIE: *Go tell the board. Yeah, I know. Go ahead. Play them this tape. I don't care. I've got more to worry about right now than you getting pissed at me. Or haven't you been paying attention?*

PRESCOTT: *Now, you listen to me, you little—*

CURIE: *I don't have time for this.*

PRESCOTT: *Curie! Don't you hang up on—*

End Audio File

Ortego Reconstruction Outpost
January 05, 2351

Mei and her team sat in the conference tent getting ready to have their evening meeting. Zoe, Bart, Sophie, and John, who had fully recovered by now from his radiation exposure, were all in attendance. Dr. Tabata, as usual, had opted to study the domesticated kitobora instead.

Mei brought up a map of the Ortego site and the surrounding radiation zone. Several dots littered the grid to indicate where each of the Framling Coils had been placed. As of today, they'd managed to construct and install sixteen of them with increasing ease and success. "Before we get into it, can I get a status check on coil three?" she asked.

Sophie nodded. "Up and running, ma'am. We resolved the problem a few hours ago."

"Great. Any updates on your end, Bart?"

"I should be done with coil seventeen tomorrow afternoon," he said. "I'll start the next immediately."

"No hiccups on this one?"

"So far, none, but we're running low on parts. I put in a request to Komodo today for more. Walters told me he'd have what I needed in three days."

"Just in time for Zoe to make her supply run. Perfect."

"Yay," said Zoe, rolling her eyes.

"What about the flippies?" asked Mei.

"They're good. They installed the last coil in under an hour. Can't get much better than that," said Zoe.

John stretched out his arms. "Better not let those little guys break. They're all we got."

"Relax," said Zoe, waving her hand at him. "I check them every night."

Mei was thrilled to have the flippies back. After John successfully installed the first coil, Zoe was able to get close enough to remotely activate a few of the robots and call them home. Unfortunately, not all of them made the trip.

Since the radiation hit Mei and Travis without warning, they didn't get a chance to power any the flippies down. The batteries eventually died, leaving them in their various places, including the underground ruins. Even if Zoe's signal could somehow reach them, the robots couldn't power on, making them little more than fancy hunks of metal until someone could retrieve them.

Thankfully, two rarely used flippies remained in hibernation mode inside the work tent. After activating them and getting the pair back to camp, Zoe repurposed them to carry and install all of the coils. Since the robots took no damage from the radiation, it made the job much easier and far less dangerous. However, these particular flippies were early alpha models and largely incomplete. Unlike Mortimer and Jefferson, Travis had never retrofitted them with FlexCrete, nor had he completed their programming. Zoe spent much of her time working on them, but she wasn't Travis. She ran into problems constantly. Maybe this was why Zoe had chosen to call them Dee and Dum after the famously stupid twins from *Alice in Wonderland*.

Mei turned to her assistant. "Sophie, anything to add?"

Sophie nodded slightly and went to the large map, resting with her hands behind her back. "As you can see, the coils have actively halted the spread of radiation. With the installation of every new device, we reduce the ambient radiation significantly. However, the levels near and inside the Ortego site remain unchanged. I had hoped the flow would slow or stop by now, but it seems the problem only persists. It is entirely possible that the radiation will increase to the point where the coils are no longer adequate enough to stop the flow." She glanced at Mei. "I strongly suggest we begin looking for new solutions, ma'am."

"And I agree," said Mei. She looked around the table. "Any

suggestions?"

Zoe scratched her neck. "If we can get access to the site again, we can reactivate Mortimer and retrieve the rest of those Ortego Disks from the basement. We might find something there."

"How long before we can go there again?" asked Bart.

Sophie checked her pad. "We'll need several more coils. I'd suggest eight. Ten to be safe. We'll probably have to keep erecting new ones as the radiation levels continue to rise."

Mei nodded. "Bart, can you fill the order?"

He took a moment. "It's doable, but I'll need another week."

"Fine," said Mei. "Keep me posted." Mei tapped her pad, and the large screen turned off. "We don't have a lot of time, just so you all know."

"Why?" asked Zoe. "Is the radiation spreading faster than—"

Mei waved her hand. "Nothing like that."

"Then what?"

"I pissed Prescott off pretty bad this morning. There's a good chance he's going to report me. I don't know what will happen, but I thought I should tell you."

"Are you saying you could get kicked off the project?" asked Zoe.

"It's one possibility. I don't know."

"Screw that guy," said Bart. "We'll go above his head if he tries anything."

"I'm already planning on it," said Mei. "I promise. They'll have to drag me kicking and screaming before I abandon this mission."

Ortego Reconstruction Outpost
January 06, 2351

Mei stood with Zoe a quarter kilometer from the Ortego site. They set up a transmitter on the bed of the dirt cab in order to stay in contact with Dee and Dum as the two robots installed another coil. Given their close proximity to the radiation zone, Sophie had insisted they wear rad suits. Neither of them complained.

"Dee's planting the coil now," said Zoe, hovering over her computer.

"Good," said Mei. She leaned against the side of the cab and stared in the direction of the excavation site. It wouldn't be long before she had access to the ruins again, but the radiation would still be there. As Sophie had pointed out at the meeting a few days ago, the coils were only a temporary fix. Since then, she'd spent fruitless hours trying to think of a solution, all without success. The gamma rays seemed to come from nowhere with no clear defining source. If she didn't solve the puzzle soon—

"Done," said Zoe.

"Good work," said Mei.

"Calling the twins back now."

"Hopefully, Bart can have another one ready in a day or two," said Mei.

"With me helping him, he'll get it done," she said, closing the computer case.

An incoming call lit up Mei's visor. "Doctor Curie," erupted a voice in her ear. It sounded like Sophie.

"Yes?" she answered. "We're about to leave. Can this wait?"

"I don't think so, ma'am. There's a call for you from Central."

"Who is it?"

A pause. "It has Prescott's ID attached, but I can't open the channel. Looks like it's restricted to you."

Mei silently cursed. Not Prescott again. She wagered this couldn't be good. "Fine. Put him through."

The line went dead for a few seconds as the call connected. A nervous tickle ran through Mei's stomach as she anticipated the different scenarios she was about to witness. After several seconds, she heard a soft click followed by a swarm of background noise. At its forefront, heavy breathing.

"Hello?" said Mei. "Doctor Prescott?"

The person on the other end smacked their lips together. "Not quite, honey dear." It was a woman. Her voice was scratchy, almost tired.

"Who is this? Where's Doctor Prescott?"

"He's occupied," said the woman. "This is Doctor Abigale Tremaine."

Mei froze in place at the sound of the name. Abigale Tremaine, head of the Science Division. She replaced Doctor Byrne a year ago, but Mei never had the opportunity to meet or talk with her. The woman ran a third of the government, sat at the head of the board, and rarely made public appearances. What on Earth could she possibly want with Mei?

"Young lady, are you there?"

"Yes," said Mei, forcing the word. She suddenly felt like a child preparing for a parental lecture. "I'm sorry. I…I wasn't expecting you."

"Don't worry about it, dear," she said. "You'll pardon me for calling you under Prescott's ID. I'd rather your subordinates not know about this. You don't mind, do you?"

Mei noticed her mouth was hanging open. She closed it promptly. "No, of course not, ma'am."

"Glad to hear it. Now, do you know why I'm calling you today?"

"I assume it's because of my last report," she said.

"You mean the one where you yelled and hung up on poor little Prescott?" she asked. "That certainly has a part to play."

"I'm so sorry, Doctor Tremaine, but I've been under a lot of stress lately and—"

"Oh, honey dear, don't you worry about it. Nobody likes that egotistical ass, anyway. In fact, I've had him reassigned to the Chameleon Outpost until further notice. Poor boy needs a break from all these silly politics before he gives himself a heart attack."

Mei didn't say anything.

"In the meantime," continued Tremaine. "You'll be reporting to me directly. I'll need full disclosure on everything you're doing, and I do mean *everything*. And yes, I'm including your little bout with radiation poisoning and near death experience. Understand?"

Crap. How did the old woman know about that? Mei hadn't filed a report on it. Did someone on the team let it slip? A flutter ran through her chest before landing in her stomach. "How did you—"

"Relax. If I wanted to shut you down, I would have," said Tremaine. "I don't want to get rid of you, and I don't care if you lied to Prescott about being sick. I get why you did it. The man is shortsighted and he probably would've tried to get you transferred. But you're reporting to me now, and I'm no fool. Do you understand?"

"Yes, ma'am. Thank you," said Mei.

"You're quite welcome. Now, let's get down to business," said the old woman, clearing her throat. "You're going to tell me everything from front to back. Don't leave anything out."

Mei sat in her tent after an extended conversation with Doctor Tremaine. The old woman had asked her to call as soon as she returned to camp, and to do so privately. Mei obliged her request and spent a solid hour telling her everything she wanted to hear. Mei explained the entire situation, beginning with her early excavation work, followed by the radiation bloom and Travis's death, and finally the decision to use the coils as a means of controlling the spread. For the most part, Tremaine seemed to already know the bulk of the story, including events Mei neglected to report on, probably by monitoring her team's emails and personal reports. She may have even gone so far as to plant a few bugs around the camp. Such a thing was not unheard of. It didn't matter if spying were illegal. People with power rarely played by the rules.

Thankfully, Mei's true goal remained a secret. She'd never revealed her actual motives or plans to anyone, not even John, for fear of discovery. If the board ever found out that the only reason she'd proposed this project in the first place was to study the original portal in order to find out what happened to Terry, there's absolutely no way they'd let her continue. They'd call it reckless and a waste of resources, say her perspective was warped by her own personal feelings. Hell, maybe they'd be right. But Terry was gone and probably dead, Mei knew. She had to know why.

She wondered what Tremaine would say if she knew the truth. Would she yank Mei from the team and reassign her like she did Prescott? The Science Division favored objectivity, teaching against personal investment, no matter what. The moment someone's individual motivations began affecting the experiment, the results could no longer be trusted.

But department philosophy and practicality were not always parallel. There were instances in the past where noted scientists had acted on behalf of personal motives only to achieve exceptional results. Doctor Archer, for example. He'd single-handedly reshaped the entire division and created the Amber Project, all because of his personal history with Variant. He worked in secret, broke laws, and walked the moral line, because in his mind he knew the end would be justified.

Mei shuddered at the thought of comparing herself to Archer. Was she truly like him? Had she let her personal issues lead her down this path toward some awful conclusion? Was she also on her way to a barred cell, scribbling notes to pass the time as she deluded herself into thinking she was still relevant?

No, of course not. She had no intention of following in *those* footsteps. Archer sacrificed the lives of children to get what he wanted. All Mei needed were answers. She'd never be so cruel.

Her stomach turned at the thought. *Of course you would,* she heard herself say. *You killed Alex with your own hands, drove that piece of metal right through his chest.* She remembered the look on his face and the terror in his eyes as he realized she'd killed him. But that was different. He was trying to hurt her friends. It was self-defense.

She wanted to understand the rift and to find out what happened to Terry, but she wouldn't risk anyone's life to do it. She was trying to save people, to end the threat before it found them in the first place. The radiation problem couldn't be ignored. *I can't stop now*, she thought. *If I do, more people could die.*

The radiation was coming from somewhere, and she had an obligation to fix it, to end the spread and see this mission through to the very end. If she could somehow find a way to fix it, maybe no one else would have to die.

Sky Forest, Kant
January 15, 2351

TERRY SAT ON A THICK BRANCH, perched high in one of the silver-leafed trees deep in the forest. Ludo had asked him to stay there and wait while he set a few traps. It had been an hour, but Terry could hear his friend working and moving in the distance. The man was thick and tall, yet light on his feet and graceful. He hardly rustled the grass when he ran, never broke any twigs or branches. *Useful skill,* thought Terry, and made a note to ask about it later.

Terry held a knife in his hand, small and narrow like the kind Ludo had used to kill the wild animal on the day they first met. Ludo called the blade a Killing Metal, saying they were never to be used for anything but hunting and personal defense. Terry couldn't help but wonder if Ludo had ever used one to defend himself against an actual person. After all, the man was so docile and kind. Was he really capable of such violence? It was hard to imagine.

Ludo arrived after several minutes, clinging to one of the branches of a nearby tree. He swung around and motioned to Terry. He crossed two fingers and displayed them—a sign Terry had learned meant "quiet." Terry returned the sign, and Ludo grinned.

They waited for a while. Terry concentrated on the sounds of the forest, scanning with his ears and eyes for any signs of movement. He filtered out the insects and the birds, focusing on whatever remained.

Ludo seemed to do the same, waiting patiently on his branch. When anything made a noise, Ludo's pointed ears would twitch, almost instinctually, but the man himself would remain unfazed.

After several minutes, two of the traps went off. Ludo checked on them, keeping to the treetops, but returned empty-handed. One had sprung accidentally, while the other had been triggered by a beavermite.

Shortly thereafter, Terry heard stomps coming from the south. He raised his hand to get Ludo's attention, but he was already moving. Terry was amazed by Ludo's hearing at first, but as he quickly discovered, this was not the only trait they shared. Ludo's strength was on par with his own, and he could even see in the dark. Terry suspected the Variant atmosphere had something to do with it, but he didn't know why.

When they arrived at the source of the noise, they found an average-sized creature digging its hooves into the soil, shredding the weeds and sticking its long tongue into the ground. This animal was called a cheche, named for the sound it made as it grazed. The cheche yanked its tongue in and out rapidly, sending little clumps of dirt into the air around its face. It did this in an effort to find and eat insects. Sure enough, a few seconds later, it pulled a fat bug from the soil. Terry watched the process, intrigued at the sight of an animal operating naturally in the wild.

Ludo motioned at Terry, holding one of the knives in his hand and pointing to the creature on the ground. He seemed to be telling him to attack. Terry nodded, grabbing the blade as he prepared to deliver the kill.

He pressed his thumb to the butt of the knife and twisted it in his fingers, staring at the beast. With a flick of his wrist, he threw the blade at the animal, watching as the metal cut through the air like a slow bullet, passing by the beast's leg and plummeting into the ground. The animal flinched, jerking its head up to scan the area. Terry took another knife and aimed a little higher. He threw it again, this time with some success, hitting the creature in the neck and severing an artery. Blood exploded from the wound, spraying and covering the nearby plants with a red blanket.

Ludo launched two other knives, piercing the animal in the belly and ankle, causing it to buckle and fall. Guts spilled from its side, mixing with the shredded grass beneath its hooves. He leapt from the branch, landing a meter from where it lay. He took the scruff of its neck and quickly slit its throat, holding it there to let the blood drain. "We thank you," he told the beast as its breathing came to an end. "Sleep now and be at peace."

Terry jumped from his branch and joined him. There was a large pool of blood surrounding Ludo and the carcass, sinking into the dirt. "Messy," he said in Ludo's native tongue.

"This one was full of life," replied Ludo in English. "We must make good use of its gift."

Terry nodded. Before meeting Ludo, he'd killed a few animals to survive, but this was different. It was almost spiritual in a way.

Ludo tied the animal's feet together and hoisted it on his back, splattering blood on himself. He'd need to bathe in the river once they were finished. "Time to go home. We shall eat well tonight."

Terry beat his chest, a sign of agreement.

Together, they left and found the road—the same one Terry had discovered while wandering aimlessly alone several months ago. They followed it towards the valley.

"Ludo," said Terry, after they had gone a short distance.

Ludo gripped the leg of the dead animal around his neck, repositioning it. "Terry."

"I wanted to ask if I could meditate with you and Talo tonight."

"Truly?" he asked, wide-eyed and smiling.

"Yes, if you don't mind."

Still grinning, Ludo beat his chest. "I am honored."

Terry didn't join them often for the meditations, but he enjoyed the occasional session. He found them relaxing, and the more he practiced, the better he became at calming his mind.

As they neared the edge of the woods, Ludo stopped in his tracks, his eyes distant and focused. His nostrils flared, and he licked the air, something he'd done many times when they were out tracking an animal.

"What is it?" asked Terry.

Ludo didn't answer. He only stood there, facing the direction of the farm, his eyes empty and distant. He was listening to something far away.

Terry closed his eyes and did the same, focusing his attention towards Ludo's home. He heard some crackling sounds, followed by laughing. But not from Talo or Ysa. No, the voices were too deep and masculine.

Ludo dropped the carcass from his shoulders. "Danger," he said before looking at Terry. "We must go!" Suddenly and without warning, Ludo exploded into a dash through the woods.

Terry followed after him, trying his best to match his speed, but never managing to catch up. "What's going on?" he yelled, calling after his friend.

But there was no answer.

A moment later, the two of them broke through the tree line

and into the wide valley. In the distance, like a beacon in the field, a stack of gray smoke rose steadily from a burning farmhouse, the rising cloud blending with the red sky.

Terry arrived shortly after Ludo, but the fight had already begun. The farmer had three men surrounding him, each of whom Terry recognized. They were the same individuals he'd met in the woods on his way to Ludo's farm.

Red aimed his gun at Ludo. "Give us the woman," he said. "You do not have to die today, traitor."

"He is too afraid to speak," said Scar.

Ludo responded by stomping the ground. "This is not your land. Leave here at once!"

Terry rushed the strangers, coming up behind Scar, unleashing one of his knives. But the man turned to see him, lifting his rifle, and deflecting Terry to his side and knocking the blade into the grass. "Look!" Scar shouted to the others. "The foreigner is here, too!"

Their eyes fell on Terry as he tumbled into the grass, righting himself in the process. "Take him if you can," said Red. "But our priority is the priestess. Do not forget!"

Charlie kept his rifle on Ludo while Red and Scar charged at Terry, stopping a few meters from him with their guns raised.

Terry dove forward between them, clutching one of the rifles and swinging it free, smacking the other's gun as he fired. The shot missed, hitting the dirt behind him. With both of his hands on the barrel, Terry hit Scar in the face with the gun, causing him to stumble and almost let go.

Ludo grappled with the man with the black hair, each of them fighting over the rifle above their heads. Ludo seemed to be handling himself, but there was no reason to wait and see how things played out. The last thing Ysa and Talo needed was for Ludo to get himself killed.

Red and Scar tackled Terry together, knocking him down. As his back hit the ground, he pressed his boots into both of their guts and kicked them away. The two men flew several meters to each side, and Terry launched himself to his feet. As Scar hit the dirt, he finally released the rifle, flinging it into the window of the farmhouse, shattering the glass and releasing a cloud of smoke.

With both men still on their backs, Terry dashed at Red, leaping high and crashing down on his chest with both his knees. Several of the man's bones snapped and he let out a mad shriek. Still clasping the gun, Terry slammed the butt of the rifle into the man's face, breaking his nose. Blood gushed as he screamed.

"Stop him!" cried Red.

Before anyone could respond, the door to the house exploded open, shattering to pieces and knocking Terry down.

From the depths of the fire, the man with the purple eyes came flying through the air on his back. The old man twisted so his feet hit the ground first, and he rolled. A second later, he was standing, breathing steadily and waiting.

A loud cry came from inside the house, high-pitched and terrible. A gray cloud burst out of the doorway, and a figure stepped forward, small flames covering her clothes. It was Ysa, holding a staff in her hands and marching toward the purple-eyed man.

Terry gasped as he saw the flames on her body. She didn't seem to notice or care. He ran toward her, hoping to put the fire out, but one of the men tackled him, wrestling him to the ground.

Ysa raised her bo staff at the old man and charged, but he did not flinch. Instead, he held his arm up and touched her bo with his palm, flicking it aside. She slid her hand under his arm and stabbed him in the stomach with her fingers. He exhaled slightly and moved beside her, kicking her in the back of the knee and knocking her down. As she rolled, pieces of her burning clothes fell away, revealing her naked flesh.

Scar threw himself on Terry, pinning him with his knees and hands. Terry squirmed to get free.

A shot rang out from where Ludo had been fighting.

Charlie fell to his knees, a hole in his neck. Ludo stood before him, gun in his hands. He kicked him on his side, sending his face into the mud.

Terry looked at the gun in Ludo's hand, which was now pointed squarely at Scar's face. "Get up," said Ludo.

Scar eased off Terry's chest and took several steps back.

"Ludo, what's going on?" asked Terry, standing at last.

Ysa screamed and brought her staff down on Purple Eyes. He deflected it, thrusting his fist into her chest. She remained unfazed.

"They are here for Ysa!" shouted Ludo. "We must get the sacred Vessel!"

Red struggled to his feet, blood dripping from his broken nose. Terry ran and kicked him in the face, knocking him down.

"Where is it?" asked Terry, looking back at Ludo.

"A box inside," he said.

Terry remembered the day he'd first awoken here at the farm and the jewel-encrusted knife they showed him. He didn't know what it was at the time, nor did he understand its purpose now, but it was the only thing he could think of that might fit the description. "I'll be right back!"

Terry ran to the rear of the house, knocking open the rear door, and heading inside. The fire was largely restricted to the front of the building, but the rest of the house was filled with smoke and heat. He had to be fast.

He went into Ludo's bedroom, scanning for any signs of the box. He found several chests in the corner, far from the bed. He opened them and sorted through the contents. The first chest was mostly clothes, so he tossed it aside, cursing under his breath. The second had a bunch of handcrafted accessories in it. He kicked the chest away and cracked open the next one. More clothes, of course, as well as a few precious stones. "This is crazy," he said.

He moved the chest, hoping to find a smaller one tucked behind it. No such luck. He was about to get out of there when he noticed an indent on the floor, cut into the wood like a handle. He gripped and pulled, and a small hatch lifted.

"Terry!" shouted a voice from under the floorboards. The person screaming lifted the hatch, revealing a hidden storage compartment. It was Talo, covered in dirt and staring up at him. He seemed to be clutching a small box in his hands.

"Hey, what the hell are you doing down there?" asked Terry.

"Mother said to stay here," he said in English.

Terry beat his chest to show he understood. He grabbed the boy's arm, pulling him from the hole. Terry snagged the blanket off Ludo's bed and wrapped it around both of them.

The fire swelled near the room in the hallway. Burning wood screamed as the fire engulfed the home. Terry and Talo rushed out of the master bedroom, shielding themselves from the heat, then flew through the rear door into the open yard. Terry threw the blanket off of them and carried Talo to the fence at the far back of the farm. "Stay here."

Talo beat his chest.

Terry motioned at the box in the boy's hands and Talo gave it to him. Terry opened the lid and found the dagger, jewels and all. He gave the box to Talo and left to return to the battlefield, running hard and fast.

As everything came into view, he saw the fight had changed. Ysa was on her backside with the old man lording over her.

Ludo stood with his knee on Red's back, pinning him. He waved the rifle at Terry. "Use the metal!" he shouted. "Help Ysa!"

Terry glanced at the dagger in his hand, then at Ysa and her attacker as he pressed the heel of his boot against her throat. Purple Eyes stared down at Ysa with a placid look on his face. "You will come with me," the old man said.

Terry dashed toward them, kicking dirt behind him as he moved. When he drew close, he clasped the hilt of the knife with both his hands and raised it high above his head. As the blade was about to make contact, the old man bent slightly to the side, avoiding the jab. His face retained the same, seemingly bored expression.

Terry tumbled forward, landing face-first into the earth. He slid several meters, shredding grass.

Ysa screamed.

Purple Eyes smiled.

Ludo ran to Ysa and aimed the gun at the man with the white hair, shouting words Terry didn't know. Purple Eyes did not bother to look at the weapon.

"Ludo!" shouted Terry as he got to his feet.

Ludo squeezed the trigger, and the muzzle flamed. The bullet hit the old man, deflecting from his temple. The flattened piece of metal landed a few meters from the target, who remained unfazed.

Terry could hardly believe his own eyes. Was this guy bullet-proof? How was it possible?

"Terry!" shouted Ludo, snapping him out of it. "The knife!" He fired a second round, hitting Purple Eyes in the chest and accomplishing nothing.

Terry grasped the dagger. This was it. He ran toward Ysa and Purple Eyes, leaping a second time, but aiming with his whole body rather than the knife alone.

He landed on the old man's back, wrapping his arm around his wrinkled neck. Purple Eyes shook him, stepping off Ysa in the process. He grasped Terry's arm with his own and dug his finger-nails into his skin.

Terry grit his teeth, trying to ignore the pain. He raised the dagger high above them with his other hand.

The dagger came down, its rainbow jewels glistening in the light of the nearby flames. It slid into the old man's chest with ease, tearing his skin and ripping his flesh.

For the first time, Purple Eyes screamed, his face contorting in pain. He staggered, flinging Terry free and backing away, the knife still in his chest.

Ysa and Terry both got to their feet and stood alongside Ludo.

Purple Eyes clutched the dagger and ripped it free. He took several heavy breaths as crimson blood drained from his body, fixing his sight on Terry. He lifted the dagger high into the air. "Occotv!" he shouted. *Attack!*

Terry looked at Ludo. "Now what?" he asked.

Ludo shook his head. "Problem."

A loud hum filled the valley, growing steadily.

Terry gripped Ludo's shoulder. "What is that?"

Before Ludo could answer, a vehicle appeared from behind one of the distant cliffs, heading in their direction. Fighting the pain in his wrist and arm, Terry managed to focus long enough to see a band of men hanging off the sides and riding atop the metal monstrosity. Three of them seemed to be blowing horns, their faces adorned with paint and bones.

Ludo's mouth dropped. "No!"

The vehicle arrived within moments, and half a dozen men unloaded, weapons in hand.

Ysa attacked them immediately. She disarmed two of the men with ease, kicking their weapons to the ground. She planted her fist on another's jaw, shattering bone and teeth. Terry and Ludo joined her, each of them taking on an individual fighter.

Purple Eyes moved in, the dagger in his palm. He clashed with Ysa, pummeling her into the dirt and holding the blade against her neck. She didn't move.

At this, Ludo paused, which gave the man he was fighting the opportunity to knock him in the back and onto the ground. Terry kicked his opponent away and made a break to help his friend. As he did, he felt a sharp pain rip through his leg, and he fell.

A bullet had ripped through his calf, taking a chunk of his flesh with it. The pain filled his body, and suddenly he felt every punch and every wound all at once.

He collided with the yard fence, breaking apart the wood and rolling towards the burning house. He tried to get on his feet, but collapsed immediately, screaming in pain. He looked to see Scar, standing with a gun in his hand.

Terry watched helplessly as the men took Ludo and Ysa into the vehicle, binding their hands.

The flames spread around him, jumping onto the dying earth and broken wood surrounding the house. The heat was almost too much for him to bear as he lay there on his stomach, covered in mud.

What was he supposed to do? How could he be so helpless? He'd searched for years to find a home, and now it had been ripped from his arms. He didn't want to be in pain. He didn't want to die or be alone. Why couldn't he simply be happy for once? Why couldn't he be free?

He turned on his back, staring into the fire. Was this the end?

Would he—

A laugh echoed in the flames, light and sweet.

Terry jerked his head around, but saw no one. "Who's there?" he asked.

Another laugh. It was a girl. *Terry,* she said. *What are you doing, silly?*

"Janice?" He touched the side of his face, shaking his head. "No, not right now. I can't deal with this again!"

Why are you playing in the mud?

The flames crackled, wavering like tides in a yellow sea. A shadow flickered between them, distorted and fanatic.

I told you to run, whispered the voice, and the figure seemed to move with it. *But you didn't listen.*

"Go away," he gasped, breathing in the heat and coughing. "Please."

Not this time, she said. *This time I'll stay. You need me. You always will.*

The cloud of smoke hovered in the midst of the fire and quickly evaporated into the air. As it did, Terry saw the body of a small girl, pristine and untouched by the flames. Her long brown hair fell below her shoulders as she walked through the chaos of the crumbling structure, calmly approaching him with her hand outstretched. Her face was peaceful and full of youth, exactly the way he remembered it.

"Janice," he managed to gasp.

She smiled, reaching out to him. He felt the touch of her fingertips against his skin. "Soon," she told him.

And then the world went black.

13

Ortego Outpost File Logs
Play Audio File 381
Recorded: January 16, 2351

THISTLE: *You ever coming home, kid?*

FINN: *I'm starting to wonder. Seems like we've been here a while.*

THISTLE: *Well, I take responsibility for that. I turned your vacation into an assignment. Now I'm regretting it.*

FINN: *It's okay, boss, really. I like being here. Feels like we're doing something important, you know?*

THISTLE: *You're just saying that because your girl is there.*

FINN: *Heh, maybe I am.*

THISTLE: *No big deal, Finn. I get it. But don't get too comfortable. As soon as the job's done, and those scientists get the radiation fixed, you're heading back out into the field. Your team needs you.*

FINN: *Doesn't sound like them.*

THISTLE: *You know they'd never admit it, but I can tell when they ask about you.*

FINN: *The next time you hear from them, say I'll be back soon.*

THISTLE: *Sure, but until then, don't do anything stupid. We don't need another radiation accident. I don't care if you think you're Superman or not. Don't risk it.*

FINN: *Come on, boss. You know me.*

THISTLE: *That's exactly my point.*

End Audio File

Somewhere on Kant

January 16, 2351

Terry opened his eyes, only to find he was unable to move. He'd been strapped to a bed. He wasn't going anywhere.

Shit.

He tried lifting his head, pressed against the straps but only managing to move a few centimeters. Peering down at himself, he saw a fresh set of clothes beneath the straps. Not his. Someone had dressed him.

He shot a glance to his side, his arm locked in place by a piece of leather. He still ached with pain, but it was much more tolerable now. The broken bone had been set and wrapped in a splint. Whoever his captors were, they didn't want him dead.

Be thankful for the little things.

He scanned what he could of the room, but there was only stone. Tall rock walls and a rough ceiling. Light came from a window somewhere behind him, but it was too far for his neck to bend. If he could only get free, maybe he'd find a way out.

"Don't worry, brother," said a voice.

"Who's there?" he snapped, but he already knew the answer. It was Janice, only her voice was off. She didn't seem to be inside his head anymore. She was…

A flutter of laughter filled the room. Terry struggled to break free of the straps, twisting and turning, left and right, back and forth. As he did, he saw a quick blur, and he stopped.

Rolling to his side, he focused his eyes, staring at the strange distortion. For a moment, it seemed to fade, but quickly came together, materializing before him. It was like watching a rock shatter into dust, but in reverse.

As the figure materialized Terry's eyes went wide, and he held his breath in disbelief.

Janice stood before him, smiling and twirling her chocolate hair. "Why're you in bed?" she asked. "This is no time to be napping."

He tried to speak, but the words wouldn't form. "I…"

Janice pranced around the room, giggling as she skipped and bounced. "What a neat place!" she exclaimed.

This can't be happening, he thought. *This isn't real.*

"Don't be so mean!" said Janice. "I'll tell Mommy. I will!"

What is she talking about? I didn't say anything.

"Yes, you did. You said I'm not real! What a mean thing to do."

"You..." he paused, not knowing if he should answer.

"I am *so* here!" she snapped, stomping her foot. "Stop saying such mean things."

There was no use in arguing with her. Not right now. He had to get out of this place, find Ludo and Ysa. He'd worry about his sanity later. "Okay," he muttered.

She grinned, instantly dropping all apparent signs of anger. "I'm sorry I left, but I had to. I didn't trust that silly old farmer. Not one bit." She shuffled to his bedside and beamed a cheeky smile at him. "I'm here now, though. I knew you needed me."

"Sure," he said.

The door to his room swung open, sending a breeze of hot air toward him, ruffling the edges of his shirt. A man appeared, nearly as tall as the archway and dressed in metal armor.

"You're awake," said the stranger in the alien tongue. "Time to eat."

At least he could understand these people now. Eight months of studying the language, and he was wasting it on a guard. "Okay," said Terry, going along with it.

The man went to Terry's bedside and silently examined the splint. Terry watched him leave, keeping the door wide open. A moment later, he returned, carrying a steaming bowl of what smelled like soup. Terry felt his stomach growl.

The stranger unstrapped Terry's head, then poured the warm liquid into his mouth. "Drink," said the man.

Terry did, ignoring the bitter taste. He drank until it was gone.

The man stood and left again, closing the door.

"Hello?" called Terry, but there was no answer. Was anyone going to tell him what the hell was going on? Not that it'd do him any good, of course. Whoever these people were, they'd abducted him, taken him prisoner. Strapped him in this bed like some kind of animal.

Is that it? He asked himself. *Am I an animal to these people?*

"No way," said his sister's voice.

He turned to look at her, this time with the full range of his neck. The guard had apparently forgotten to strap him back in. Another little victory.

Janice stood once more in the middle of the room, twisting her waist and flailing her hands playfully. "What do we do now?" she asked.

Hell if he knew. What options did he have? He could only move his head, and what good did it do him?

"Good point," she said, tapping her chin with her finger. "Got any bright ideas?"

He grunted.

"Don't be such a stinky-face."

He fidgeted, wriggling beneath the leather. If he could somehow manage to loosen the straps...

Janice scuttled to his side. She tapped his wrist. "Start with this one. It looks the easiest."

He did as she suggested, thumbing the strap and pulling his hand. Much to his surprise, the band was looser than it looked.

After trying a few different angles, he managed to slide most of his wrist through the leather. Almost there.

"You're doing great!" she said.

He jerked his palm the rest of the way through and finally freed it. With an open hand, he made short work of the other strap. In less than two minutes he was out of the bed and limping. His accelerated healing could only do so much. He'd have to wait a few days before he could walk around.

"I knew you could do it," said Janice.

"If you know so much, find me a way out," he muttered.

"Too easy," she said. "Wait for the guard and beat him up!" She playfully jabbed the air with her fists, pretending to fight. "Pow pow pow!"

He ignored her and scanned the room. There was the bed, a small barred window, and the door. No other way out. He'd rather avoid a confrontation, but there might not be any other option.

"Maybe you can bust through," said Janice.

He pressed both his palms against the door and pushed. When nothing happened, he closed his eyes and tried again, pulling from his strength. But nothing happened.

What good was being superhuman if he couldn't even break down a single door?

"I thought for sure you could do it," his sister said, frowning. "Oh, well."

"Leave me alone," he said.

"Don't be so mean!" she snapped.

"I said get away from me!" he yelled. "You're not real. Look at—"

Someone coughed, and the sound pulled Terry out of his delusion. He blinked and found his little sister gone.

The cough came again, this time from the wall near his bed. He leaned against it and listened. Whoever it was, they were sitting less than a few meters away. "Hello?" said Terry in the alien tongue. "Who's there?"

Another cough. "Who is it?" asked the voice.

"My name is Terry. Can you hear me?"

A short pause. "Terry? Is that really you? It's me, Ludo."

"Are you alright?" he asked. "You sound hurt."

"I'm tired. I need to rest." His words were soft and his voice a whisper.

"What did they do to you?" asked Terry. There was a long pause. "Ludo?"

But an answer never came.

Somewhere on Kant
January 17, 2351

TERRY SAT with his back against the wall adjacent to Ludo's cell. A day had gone by without so much as a word from him, and no one had opened the door to Terry's cell. He wondered if anyone ever would. Had they put him here to die? Why not just shoot him and get it over with?

The light coming from the window told him it was midday. Earlier, a man had tossed a piece of rotting fruit through a slit in the door. Terry chose not to eat it, but now he regretted it. His stomach ached, and it made him sick.

I've gone longer than this without food, he reminded himself. But while it was certainly true, his stomach had apparently forgotten. The last several months spent stuffing himself with fresh meals every day on Ludo's farm had spoiled him.

Janice visited him with erratic frequency, appearing and disappearing at random intervals, taunting him with her childishness. He knew she wasn't really there, but sometimes it took a bit of convincing. He could see her now, the body of the girl from his youth. His baby sister.

Damn her.

The afternoon brought a chill as an outside breeze found its way into the cell. If it hadn't been so cold, he might have found it refreshing. Not long afterwards, Terry heard the door of Ludo's cell swing open.

"Is the traitor dead?" came a stranger's voice.

"The wound is wide and deep," said another.

"You will fix him," said the first.

"I will try," agreed the second.

"We need him awake. The Lord has questions."

Terry pressed his ear against the wall. He could hear someone scuffing the floor, bumping into things. After a moment, the door slammed shut and the men made their way down the hall. It was quiet for a long time.

Night came. Terry crawled under the window and stared into

the darkened sky. The clouds were clearing and he managed to catch sight of the stars. Ludo had shown him a few of the constellations during their months together. There was Gorodos the Great Fish, Keeda the Mother, and Talo the Hunter, for which Ludo's son was named. Talo chased an animal called Windu, which as far as Terry could tell was some kind of wolf, but probably not. Windu was from stories, Ludo had said. As for Gorodos, he swam in the eastern sky this time of year, hovering over the horizon. Terry wished he knew about these characters when he was alone in the jungle.

Looking at Windu, Terry closed his eyes and allowed himself to sleep.

In the early hours of the morning, before the first of the two suns had risen, a sound erupted from the other cell, followed by the voices of the guards.

"He almost lost the ghost," said one. "The Lord would have been angry."

"Put him there," said the other.

Terry crept to the wall, waiting for the guards to leave. They slammed the door, shaking the stone floor, and finally left. He listened closely, focusing his mind, filtering out whatever he found unimportant.

After a moment, he heard breathing, slow and steady, fused with the beating of a healthy heart. There was someone there, but was it Ludo?

"Hello?" whispered Terry to the wall. "Ludo, can you hear me?"

No answer.

He raised his voice a little. "It's Terry. Are you there?"

The body on the other side let out a soft moan. He's alive, thought Terry. "Ludo!"

"Terry..." muttered his friend.

"Are you alright?"

"I must..." His voice trailed a bit, like he was about to pass out. "...Ysa..." His breathing slowed again, this time replaced by a light snore. He must have been exhausted.

The night crept by, but Terry couldn't sleep. His thoughts were on his friend, and he burned at the possibility of what those men had done. What reason did they have for doing any of this? What had Ludo ever done to them? Why had they called him a traitor? He was only a simple farmer, living peacefully with his family...wasn't he?

Of course. Anything else was absurd.

Somewhere on Kant

January 18, 2351

MUCH TO TERRY'S RELIEF, Ludo was still alive the next day. He did not wake until the midafternoon, however, and so Terry waited, listening from inside his tiny cell.

When Ludo did awaken, he let loose a series of violent coughs. Between outbursts, Terry asked him questions. "What is this place? Where did those men take you? How do we get out?"

Ludo gave short answers. This was a Xel prison. The men

had taken him to a healer because of his wound. There was no escape. Not yet.

"What do they want with us?" asked Terry.

"They have Ysa," said Ludo, clearing his throat. "They will make us slaves or kill us."

"What about Talo?" asked Terry.

"I don't think they caught him," said Ludo. "I taught him to go to the cliffs behind the valley, to the cave near the water. He will wait for us there."

"How long will he wait?"

"A few weeks. If we do not meet him, he will go to my sister's home in West Lake. She will look after him."

"I don't understand any of this, Ludo. Why did they take Ysa?"

"Ysa is a priestess. She flies higher than most. She is sacred. You saw her in the field. You know."

Terry remembered the fight at the farm between Ysa and the purpled-eyed man. They were unstoppable, the both of them, fast and strong like gods. Each of them put Terry to shame. Was *that* what flying meant? To do what Ysa had? "How do I fly?" asked Terry.

Ludo coughed and spat, gurgling phlegm in a desperate attempt to breathe. It took him a while before he was able to continue, and when he did, his voice was hoarse and dry, cracking between words. "It takes a long time to fly like Ysa," said Ludo. "Many years are needed. Meditation and study. All the days must be filled with study, but most can never achieve it. Ysa was born already flying. This is why she is special."

"But you meditate all the time," said Terry.

"Everyone has it in them to fly. Some are natural fliers, but each of us is capable. Until the ghost is gone, we must try to touch the sky."

Terry thought of the meditation sessions. If only he had more time to study the practice. He was getting so close to understanding.

"Ludo," said Terry, pressing the corner of his forehead to the wall. "I'm sorry we're here. I'm sorry this happened to you and your family."

"Thank you, my friend," said Ludo, and then he was quiet.

A few minutes later, Terry heard snoring from the other side, and he dared not wake him. Ludo deserved his rest.

Terry crossed his legs, put his hands atop his knees, and closed his eyes. He performed the breathing exercises he'd learned from Ludo and Talo, and attempted to clear his thoughts.

He didn't think this would accomplish anything meaningful. After all, sitting quietly with his eyes shut hardly seemed proactive. It was something to do, he figured—better than talking to a make-believe four-year-old. More productive than dwelling on problems for which he had no solution.

Better this than going mad.

Ortego Reconstruction Outpost
January 18, 2351

FRAMLING COIL twenty-three was finally up and running—the first piece of the final set of installs surrounding the Ortego site. If Mei's calculations were correct, and she wasn't sure they were, this would bring the radiation levels down enough for her team to get in there and find the source.

Whatever that entailed.

Mei and her people had driven to within a few hundred meters of the Ortego facility. They waited, geared and ready for the flippies to finish installing the final coil. John and Bart stood beside Mei, while Zoe remotely operated Dee and Dum from the back of the Dirt Cab. "How's it coming?" called Mei.

Zoe poked her head over the side of the cab. "Any second. Hold on."

"Think this'll work?" asked John, glancing at Bart.

"You questioning my craftsmanship?"

John held his hands up. "Wouldn't dream of it."

"Good," said Bart with half a grin.

"Remember, when the coil goes live, don't rush in," said Mei. "Let the flippies run their scan. We need to make sure—"

"Don't worry, Doc. We'll do this by the book," said Bart.

"There's a book for this kind of thing?" asked John.

Bart cocked his brow. "I'll send you an autographed copy when I'm done writing it."

"No accidents," reiterated Mei.

Bart nodded.

"Okay," said Zoe. "A few seconds and...we're good! Fever Killer twenty-three is up and running!"

"Do a radiation test as soon as you can," ordered Mei.

"Yes, ma'am," said Zoe. "This will only take a minute or two."

Mei took the time to recheck the seals on her suit, then John's. He didn't argue. *No more accidents*, she told herself.

After ten minutes passed, Zoe called for the others to gather at the rear of the vehicle. "So there's a few things."

"Is this a good news and bad news kind of situation?" asked John.

"Sure," she said. "First, the radiation levels are low enough for us to re-enter the area. The only problem is they're fluctuating."

"Is that the bad news?" asked John.

"Depends," said Zoe. "I don't know what it actually means."

"It means it's not stable," said Mei.

"Maybe, but it could be nothing," suggested Bart.

"We're not taking the risk unless we're certain. Zoe, continue monitoring the radiation levels. Give it a few hours. If they stay within an acceptable range, we'll move in."

Zoe didn't argue.

It killed Mei to wait. She wanted nothing more than to get back to work—her real work—but she'd do it the right way. The safe way.

She was done taking risks.

THEY WAITED three and a half hours before Mei was satisfied with the readings. They stood in the afternoon sun, baking in their suits. She gave the go-ahead to enter the Ortego site, but ordered everyone to be ready to leave at a moment's notice. Zoe would stay with the Dirt Cab, monitoring the rad levels in case there was a change. The rest of them would work, and they would do it quickly.

The primary mission for now was to determine where the source of the radiation was coming from. She and Bart had used the Framling Coils to triangulate the flow of radiation. They finally believed it to be somewhere in the basement level of the destroyed facility. They'd have to go there themselves to investigate, since the coils on the surface couldn't read anything underground.

Bart had to craft a more efficient sensor using some spare Fever Killer parts. These new scanners would allow Mei and her team to detect local radiation levels. They could also indicate which direction the flow was coming from. Handy little machines, to say the least.

Zoe also worked at outfitting the rad suits with night vision and infrared. John had suggested using parts from military-grade goggles as her foundation, which turned out to be a good idea. The suit's visor now displayed the different visual choices. Like the goggles, switching between the different sights required the use of a physical switch. This made the suits look a little awkward, but Mei would take functionality over aesthetics any day of the week.

Zoe soon activated as many flippies as possible, including Mortimer and Stanley. She stationed them throughout the grounds in an attempt to track the radiation levels. It was difficult, because the flippies weren't built to perform precision scans. They wouldn't do the whole job, but they could still detect any major spikes, should they occur. Mei hoped to use some of the flippies to continue excavating the site while her team worked on their current task, but she couldn't afford the risk. Until she had a better handle on this situation, safety would remain her top concern.

John tied the end of an extendable ladder to a spike, which he nailed into the ground. He checked its stability with his own body weight, then waved the others to him. "Ready when you are," he said.

"Let's go," said Mei, and grabbed hold of one of the ladder's metal bars. She took the lead and descended into the cavernous basement of the Ortego facility. It had been several years since she and John had been inside these walls. A lifetime ago. Yesterday. Talk about déjà vu.

The others followed shortly afterwards, climbing one at a time to ensure the ladder held. When everyone was on the floor and ready, Mei and Bart retrieved their scanners.

John insisted the trio stay together through the mission. This place was a tomb, filled with the dead and ready for more. There were so many things that could go wrong in a place like this. The radiation levels might spike at any moment. The walls could collapse and bury them alive. "Sticking together means there's less of a risk we'll run into trouble," he had said. "Progress might be slow, but it's safer this way."

The scanners detected the flow of the radiation through the corridors. They indicated the general direction of the source, but the range was severely limited. While the coils outside could handle roughly fifty to sixty meters, a handheld scanner couldn't detect more than a few dozen meters. It gave them an idea of which direction to go, but not which hallway to use. This caused a lot of backtracking as they discovered several collapsed or blocked passages.

Throughout the afternoon, Zoe radioed Mei with updates on the radiation levels. There had been a few spikes, but nothing to worry about. Not yet.

"This way," called Bart from inside one of the rooms. Mei followed, checking her own device as she moved. The flow of radiation was definitely coming from this direction, growing marginally stronger.

This room was yet another server farm. The flippies had scavenged part of it before things got out of control. Roughly a third of the basement levels were filled with places like this—ancient data hubs filled with a litany of potential secrets.

On the other side of the servers, a set of double doors stood waiting. The left side had taken some damage, cracked and unhinged. Bart opened the right door, swinging it wide and holding it for the others.

The next section appeared to be an office, roughly one thousand square meters. The ceiling was lower than the server room, but higher still than others. If not for the massive cluster of cubicles and supplies sitting in the center of the room, crushed together like a massive ball of metal and plastic, Mei might have thought nothing of the place.

"What the hell is this?" asked John. "All the furniture's been moved. Did the flippies do this?"

"I don't think so," muttered Bart. He looked at Mei, as though he doubted himself. Perhaps he hoped he was wrong.

She shook her head. "They haven't touched this one yet."

"What's the scanner say?" asked John.

Bart held the machine, taking a moment to analyze the readings. "Hold on a second..."

"What is it?" asked John.

Mei looked at her own scanner. The radiation in this room was higher than anywhere else. It was barely within safety parameters. "Crap," she said.

"Crap is right," said Bart. "If there's even a slight spike, we're toast. These suits can't take anything higher."

"What do we do?" asked John.

Mei approached the debris in the center of the room. As she did, the sensor's warning light beeped. She quickly backed away. "This is it."

"You're sure?" asked John.

She nodded. "I think this is where the radiation is coming from." She walked along the outer area of the room, keeping her distance until she was on the opposite side. Once there, she stepped a few steps toward the center. The sensor beeped. "See? This is definitely the spot."

"We should get out of here," muttered Bart. "We can come back when we have a plan. It's too dangerous to stick around talking."

"Right," said Mei. She rejoined them on the other side and

together they walked swiftly through the server room. "Bart, as soon as we're home, I want you to work on building another coil."

"Another?" asked Bart as they reached the hall. "What for?"

"We'll place it there," she said, pointing behind them. "Not too close, but enough to make a difference so it's safe."

"Not sure if you remember, Doc, but your typical coil is too tall for a room like that. They also drill themselves into the ground for stability. How do you expect to put one here?"

"All you have to do is make a few modifications, like you did with these scanners."

"Yeah, Bart, don't be so dramatic," said John, grinning.

"I guess I could put something together," he said. "But I'll need some time. A few days, maybe."

"You've got one!" snapped John, raising his finger.

"Take all the time you need, Bart," said Mei. "I've got my own work to do."

14

Ortego Outpost File Logs
Play Audio File 419
Recorded: January 18, 2351

CURIE: *Doctor Tremaine, this is Mei Curie calling with a status update.*

TREMAINE: *What do you have for me today?*

CURIE: *We managed to locate the origin point of the radiation. It's coming from underneath the Ortego ruins in one of the sub-basements. We're working on a way to contain it.*

TREMAINE: *Sounds like good news for everyone. When will you be able to shut it down?*

CURIE: *Bartholomew Higgs, one of my engineers, is working on a solution using several Framling Coils. The rest of my team and I are working on a more permanent solution.*

TREMAINE: *And what exactly is the source?*

CURIE: *My best guess is an Ortego experiment. It may have been dormant until recently.*

TREMAINE: *I see. Do you have any idea how long this will take you?*

CURIE: *A few weeks. I'll have more information soon.*

TREMAINE: *Sounds good, honey dear. So long as you keep me updated, we shouldn't have a problem.*

CURIE: *A problem?*

TREMAINE: *Don't worry about it. You're fine. Keep up the good work.*

CURIE: *Yes, Doctor.*

End Audio File

Ortego Reconstruction Outpost
January 18, 2351

Mei wasn't a fan of half-truths and keeping secrets, but she didn't see much choice in the matter. Doctor Tremaine had asked if Mei had a plan to stop the radiation and she'd told her boss part of the truth. But she wanted to do more than shut the problem down. She wanted to understand it.

Of course, if Tremaine found out, she might try to stop her and call them all home. Mei couldn't risk that. For now the plan stayed a secret, locked inside her brain where no one else could see. When the time was right, she'd tell her team the truth but not yet—not when Tremaine could still find out and stop her.

Mei ordered her team to assist Bartholomew with his work, but he declined, saying he worked better on his own.

She didn't argue.

While she waited, Mei and Zoe returned to the Ortego site. Together they had the flippies retrieve as many Ortego Disks as possible. They unloaded several floors' worth of server farms and offices, scavenging hundreds of disks in the process. Most of them were broken or trashed, but a few still functioned well enough. If nothing else came from all this, at least she'd have something to show for it.

Mei also took the time to visit and analyze the irradiated pile of trash in the basement. She couldn't get close to the source without risking injury, so most of her progress remained theoretical. She came up with a myriad of ideas for what could be causing the radiation—even a few potential solutions—but she couldn't test them. Not without Bart's machines in place to impede the radiation.

But for now, she imagined the possible scenarios and how they might unfold. What could possibly force the furniture in that room to crash together and stick? Why was it emitting such large amounts of radiation? Why this location and not somewhere else, like a lab or some other place where a dangerous experiment might take place? Why an office?

These questions lingered in her mind for hours, and she tried coming up with one solution after the next, but nothing fit. It was infuriating. She lay awake for hours, contemplating possibilities.

Her thoughts brought her back to the place where it all began. She remembered the journey here, the path through the city towards the Ortego headquarters. The image of the void, trapped behind the glass cylinder, circled in her mind, clawing at her thoughts. She pictured herself standing outside the facility with John, watching the implosion…seeing Terry die.

Then a thought occurred which gave her pause. There had been no measurable radiation the first time she'd visited this place. Not on any noticeable level. She and her team believed the radiation had simply grown over time, beginning well before the destruction of the Ortego facility, but what if they are wrong? What if the rift had something to do with it?

It seemed ridiculous at first to think a pile of trash in the basement had any relation to the original machine. How could they be the same? They were several floors removed, separated by at least a hundred meters.

But the thought lingered. It didn't take long for her to finally get out of bed. She pulled up the blueprints for the Ortego building on her pad, locating the place where the portal used to be, then compared it to where the anomaly was in the basement.

She dropped the pad on the table, staring at the blueprints. How could she not have seen this sooner? Despite being several floors apart, the machine and the anomaly were in identical locations. She couldn't believe it.

No, hold on a second, she thought. The debris in the basement didn't look anything like the portal she'd seen four years ago. The rift was three meters tall, a massive tear in space. They couldn't be the same. Unless…

Micro-wormholes, she thought. Maybe when they shut the rift down, it destabilized and fractured, sending pieces of itself into the sub-levels.

It certainly explained a few things. The unstable micro-fractures, if they existed, could be the cause of the radiation. She'd have to find a way to test for them, but how?

She needed a solution soon, before Tremaine figured out what she was doing. She was running out of time.

Ortego Reconstruction Outpost
January 22, 2351

ON THE FOURTH DAY, Bartholomew delivered on his promise. He showed Mei a set of miniature Fever Killers, mobile but extremely heavy. Zoe suggested they use the flippies to transport them into the underground basement. Mei agreed, and she got to work.

Mortimer and Stanley hauled the first coil into the basement. Dee and Dum following with another. They went slowly through the broken stairwells and cracked foundation. They would take as much time as they needed. This equipment was valuable, and they might not have time to make more. It took ten hours altogether.

Bart requested the coils be set up on opposite sides of the anomaly, roughly three meters away. "Give me some room," he told Mei and John.

They backed away, and he joined them, checking his pad for a moment. When he looked satisfied, he tapped the screen. "Here goes."

The miniature engines in the coils roared to life. They vibrated and shook the floor. For a second, Mei thought the tiles beneath her feet were going to collapse, and she'd fall into them. *That would be the end,* she told herself. What a way to go.

But after a moment, the vibrations settled, and the hum of the engines calmed into a soft purr. "So far so good," said Bart, analyzing his pad. "They're both working fine."

"I guess you're not totally worthless," said John with a chuckle.

"I've been known to do things," said Bart.

Mei retrieved her scanner and powered it on. It would take a few minutes for the radiation levels to even out. There was nothing left to do but sit and watch.

The scanner's display showed the radiation levels holding at a steady rate. A few minutes passed without so much as a flutter. Was the radiation too strong? Maybe the coils simply weren't enough. What was she going to do?

Exactly when the thought crossed her mind, the digital number on her scanner dropped a single digit. She stared at it, wondering if perhaps it had been a fluke. A moment later, another drop. Then a third.

Before long, the radiation had fallen considerably. They wouldn't be able to take their helmets off, but this was definitely an improvement. "Not bad," said Bart, who'd been monitoring his own scanner. "At this rate we might actually get somewhere."

Mei took a few steps toward the center of the room, keeping an eye on her scanner. She went to the same spot she'd gone before, but there was no warning sound this time. She pressed on, edging closer to the pile of metal until she was within an arm's length of it. She checked the scanner, confirmed it was safe, and moved her hand towards the object.

Before she could touch it, her arm twisted and stretched, becoming some kind of octopus tendril, morphing in the air. Her fingers drew long and snake-like, bending and spiraling, doubling the length of her other appendage. She jumped back and fell on the floor, letting out a sharp cry.

"What the hell was that?" snapped Bart.

John went to her side and tried to grab her arm, but she kept it close to her chest, holding her wrist with her other hand. It was normal again, with no sign anything had happened at all. "I'm okay," she said between sharp breaths. "It just took me by surprise."

"Does it hurt?" asked John.

"No," she muttered. "There wasn't even a tingle."

"What do you think it was?" he asked, helping her stand.

"I don't know. I'll need to run a few more tests. We need to find a way to get close to it without—"

John threw a rock at the pile. It stretched into a shape resembling a needle before changing back and coming out the left side, tumbling to the floor.

Bart rolled his eyes. "Or I guess we can throw a rock at it."

John shrugged. "It seemed easier."

Mei hurried to the stone to examine it. It looked like any

other rock, round and jagged, a little cracked perhaps. How was this possible? John threw it at the front of the trash pile, and the rock came out the left side. Could it have deflected off something?

She grabbed the rock and threw it again. It hit the debris, morphed, and flew toward John. He dodged out of the way. "Hey!" he snapped.

Another ninety degree change, she thought. "Sorry."

"I don't get it," said Bart. "What's causing this?"

Mei paused, licking her lips, then smiled. She stared at the pile in the center of the room. "What if the space around this thing is somehow bent?" she asked.

"Bent?" asked Bart.

She took a deep breath. Here goes nothing. "I think we're dealing with a portal," she said at last.

"A portal?" asked Bart. "You mean like the kind you found upstairs four years ago?"

"Similar, yes," she said.

"But I've seen the reports and you never mentioned anything about it bending the laws of physics or sucking objects into it."

"The one we encountered last time was at least partially stable. And really big. This is different." She held her hand up. "Hear me out. I've been trying to think of how all these phenomena could happen, like the radiation and the magnetism with the office furniture. But I wasn't sure until a few seconds ago."

"You're talking about the rock?" asked Bart.

"When John threw the rock and it broke the laws of physics, yeah."

John smiled.

"I looked at the blueprints for the entire building last night. We didn't have the whole basement, so I used the flippies' scans to fill in the gaps. Did you know we're right below where the original rift used to be? Sure, it was thirty stories above this, but this room is the exact same location, only lower."

"So you think, what? The portal fell?" asked Bart. "If so, where's the rest of it?"

"The rift doesn't exist anymore, not the same way it used to. If I'm right, what we're looking at right now are called microwormholes, fractured pieces of the original portal. There could be hundreds of these things, maybe more."

Bart furrowed his brow. "How the hell did we go from a giant portal to a bunch of microscopic ones?"

"We blew it up, remember?" asked John. "Same thing happens when you take a boulder and smash it into pebbles." He glanced at Mei, like he was searching for approval.

"Not quite the same, but good enough for this discussion," she said, meeting him halfway. "It makes more sense to say we disrupted the machine keeping it stable, and without a power source to sustain it, the portal collapsed into what we see before us."

"So what you're saying is I'm smarter than Bart," said John. "I'll take it!"

Bart ignored him. "If your theory is right, how do we fix it? Better yet, how do we even test for it?"

"All the signs are here. The radiation could be a result of the instability of the fractures. The same is true of *this*." She motioned to the debris. "But our real test will be the solution. It's the only way to make sure."

"I take it you've already got a plan in mind?" asked Bart.

She smiled. "I might have a few ideas."

Somewhere on Kant

January 22, 2351

IT WAS the dead of night. Terry leaned against the stone wall separating him from Ludo. His eyes were closed, but he was not asleep. He took slow, deep breaths, trying to relax his mind the way Ludo had taught him.

But there was a minor distraction. "What are you doing?" asked Janice.

Terry awakened to see the little girl standing before him. Her eyes were big and wide, almost cartoonish. "Quiet," he mouthed, knowing she would understand.

"You shouldn't do that," she said.

He didn't answer.

"Brother, look at me!" she snapped.

He didn't. Instead, he turned his thoughts inward, closing his eyes and focusing on his breathing exercises.

Minutes passed, perhaps longer. He could not know. In the void, he felt nothing, saw nothing, did nothing. He only drifted, lost in the dark, empty of thought, like being in the womb again, ready to wake up.

But Terry knew it could not last. The good dreams never did. He could never sustain the emptiness for very long, especially now with Janice pestering him.

Laughter echoed through the void, low and faint, but quickly rising. It tapped at the back of his brain like a piece of fractured glass.

Go away, he begged.

But she wouldn't.

He opened his eyes to find his neck and forehead covered in sweat. His heart raced with fear and dread, blood pumping, his face on fire. But the girl was gone, at least for a while.

She would return, though. She always did.

Over the last several days, the meditations had become routine—the only way to shut her out. She clearly hated them, and he was never allowed to practice for long before an interruption. But when it was over, she stayed away, and he got his peace.

He longed for silence, for one night of uninterrupted sleep. For a single day without the laughter. Without the taunts.

Oh, well. It wouldn't be long before the men in charge killed or sold him. Any day now.

He closed his eyes and recited the words his friend had taught him. "Peace of body. Peace of mind." He repeated the mantra again and again in a low whisper, minding his breaths as he did. There were many mantras, Ludo had explained, but they served the same purpose. By giving the mouth a series of words to focus on, it freed the mind of its cluttered thoughts. Terry was still having some trouble with the last part.

An hour later, he felt the urge to sleep creep over him and this time he did not fight it. The early morning would be here soon, so it would be wise to get some rest. He didn't want to be exhausted if his captors decided to stop by and cause him trouble.

He moved under the soft light of the night sky as it crept through the barred window above. Closing his eyes, he recited another mantra to calm him. "I fly to the Sea of Everlasting. I am strong. I am calm. I am at peace."

He repeated the words until he was asleep.

Terry's cell door swung open, waking him, and three large men towered before him. He recognized them immediately. Purple Eyes, Red, and Scar each entered the cell. "Get up," said Red.

"Why?" asked Terry.

Red's face twisted at the word. "You will, or we will make you." He pulled out a large knife and waved it at him.

"Fine," said Terry.

Scar turned and took a stool from the hall, placing it several steps across from the bed on the other end of the room. He stood next to it and stared at Terry. "You will not move. The Lord will ask you questions, and you will answer. Understand?"

"Okay," said Terry.

Purple Eyes went to the stool and took a seat, motioning to Red, who closed the door. "I see you understand how to listen now," said Purple Eyes. His voice was like gravel. "This is good. It will make you easier to sell. A stupid slave is a useless slave."

At this, both Red and Scar chuckled, beating their chests in approval.

"Tell me. What is your name?" asked the old man. "Where do you come from?"

"My name is Terry. I'm from—" he paused, unsure of what to tell them. "I'm from far away."

"Another country?" asked Purple Eyes. "Which one?"

"Central," said Terry.

Purple Eyes furrowed his brow and licked his lips. "I have never heard of this place. Why did you come here?"

Another tricky question. He took a few seconds to think. "I left to explore the world."

Red chuckled again, but stopped when Purple Eyes looked at him. "It is a brave thing to be on your own," said the old man. "My son knows little of such a thing."

Red lowered his face.

"Do you know who I am?" asked Purple Eyes.

"No," said Terry.

"I am Gast Maldeen, Lord of Three Waters and one of the five high priests of Xel," he said. "I have been granted dominion over this land, which means I am your master."

So his name was Gast, and he was the leader of this place. Never mind the rest. "Alright," said Terry.

"You will tell me now why you were with the traitor. Answer truthfully, or my son will cut you down where you sit."

Terry looked at Red, who smiled, rubbing the edge of his knife with his thumb. "They have a farm," said Terry. "I was attacked by an animal in the field. They helped me."

"How long were you with them?" asked Gast.

"A while," said Terry.

Gast stared at him, pursing his lips for a moment. "What do you know about them?"

"I know their names," said Terry.

Gast pointed to the wall behind Terry. "The one in the other cell used to be a temple guard. He took the high priestess Ysa Maldeen as his wife and escaped, keeping her power for his own selfish desires. The priestess's father allowed this, but now he is dead."

"Maldeen? Is she related to you?"

"Shut up!" barked Scar. "You do not ask questions."

Gast raised his hand to quiet him. "She is my niece," he said simply. "My brother allowed her to leave, but I have come to take her home where she belongs."

Terry didn't know what to say. Somehow, without realizing it, he'd found himself in the middle of an alien family feud.

"It is unfortunate for you," said Gast. "First to be caught in the woods and escape, only to find yourself living with a traitor. Perhaps your ghost would rather die than live, given how often you find yourself in trouble. But life is circular, is it not? Our mistakes repeat themselves forever, and every moment comes again."

Kill them now before it's too late, whispered Janice. He pushed the thought away. He couldn't fight them. They were too strong. He might be able to take out Red or Scar, but not Gast. He'd seen what the old man did to Ysa—the things he could do. Terry would have to wait for a real opportunity.

Gast walked to the door and stopped. "I believe your words," he said. "You will be auctioned to the highest bidder. Exotic slaves do well." He chuckled. "I'm expecting it to be quick. Perhaps a few weeks. Enjoy the wait."

Scar slammed the door behind them as they left. Terry sat on the bed, staring at the door, a panic rising in his chest. What was he going to do?

I have to get out of this room, he thought.

"You have to kill them all," said the girl, appearing to his side in the place where Gast had been sitting.

"I won't," he muttered.

She giggled and began skipping around the room, passing him repeatedly and laughing. Always laughing. He hated her. *Go away*.

"I'm with you forever and ever," she yelled. "Forever and ever and ever and ever!"

He wrapped his arms around his head and lowered it between his knees. Sweat dripped from his forehead as his heart raced. He didn't know what to do. He didn't want to be a slave. He didn't want to die. He hated this place, Gast, and the whole damned planet. If only he could—

"Terry," said a muffled voice. "Are you there?"

He shuddered at the sound of his own name.

"Did they hurt you?" It was Ludo, of course. Who else could it be? He must have heard the whole thing.

Terry wiped the sweat from his face. "Yeah, I'm here," he said, breathing quickly. "Sorry."

A short pause. "Terry, my friend, listen to me."

"Okay." His chest was pounding, like it was about to rip itself apart.

"Close your eyes and perform the mantras and the breathing. Do it quickly, please."

"Why would I—"

"Please," said Ludo.

Terry hesitated, but did as his friend requested. He crossed his legs and closed his eyes, ignoring the pain in his body. He took several deep breaths, counting them as he went. Finally, he recited the mantras. "Peace of body. Peace of mind."

"Again," said Ludo with a calm and relaxed voice.

"Peace of body. Peace of mind," said Terry. "Peace of body. Peace of mind."

"Now breathe," said Ludo. "Let your ghost fly free and out of this place."

Terry listened to Ludo's voice, letting it carry him. Like before, he was in the dark, quiet and unmoving. He was alone. He swam in a sea of thoughtlessness, in a place devoid of time. He had been here before, but now it was different. Now there was no laughter. No interruptions. He felt nothing.

He had done it.

After what felt like hours, he heard a voice saying, "Wake now, my friend."

Terry let out a sigh of relief as he opened his eyes. He was calm and relaxed. A welcome change. The pain in his body was gone, and there was no sign of the girl. How long had he been absent? "How did I do that?"

"You let go," said Ludo. "It is not easy. Continue on this path, and you will grow stronger."

"Stronger?"

"You draw strength from within. I have seen it before on our hunts together. I watched you do it when the soldiers came. You have great potential, Terry, but you must learn to control your fears."

Terry considered his friend's words. He remembered all the times he'd called upon his strength. Most of them had been under the threat of death or danger. He always assumed adrenaline was the key. Had he been mistaken? Was there a better way? He didn't quite understand how meditating could make him stronger, but he trusted his friend. If Ludo said this would help, Terry believed him. "Okay," he finally said. "Tell me what to do."

"Let us continue," said the farmer through the stone. "There is much for you to learn."

15

Doctor Mei Curie's Personal Logs
Play Audio File 190
Recorded: January 23, 2351

CURIE: *After transferring all my personal logs to a local data pad, which I've also disconnected from the network, I finally feel comfortable recording my thoughts again. Doctor Tremaine's eyes are everywhere, which she doesn't seem to try and hide during conversation. She probably thinks she knows everything we're doing here, and maybe she does, but it doesn't mean I have to make things easier for her. I had Zoe remove the network chip from this device, along with a few others throughout the camp. I don't work well with someone watching over my shoulder. No one does.*

After arriving at a hypothesis about the source of the radiation, I've been working on a way to fix it. Specifically, I'm going to reconstruct the original wormhole and then stabilize it. To do this, I'll need to create a steady magnetic field around the anomaly. Doing so should cause the micro-tears to collapse in on one another, which will reform the original rift.

Of course, there's some risk involved. If the new portal operates the same as the old one, we'll essentially be replacing radiation with Variant. And if I remember my history, the gas spreads like wildfire. The key difference this time, however, is that everyone here is safe from the gas, so the risk is minimal. We also have the added benefit of knowing what we're building, unlike the poor fools who created the original. If things go bad, I'll shut the magnetic field down, and the portal should collapse. If it doesn't, we'll bury the damned thing and that'll be the end of it.

Either way, we're almost there.

End Audio File

Ortego Reconstruction Outpost
January 23, 2351

Mei sat in the conference tent with the rest of her team, getting ready to go over the final leg of the mission. Even Tabata was there.

She cleared her throat. "Thank you all for coming. As you know, we've located the source of the radiation. The working hypothesis is that we're dealing with a series of microscopic wormholes. I've also come up with a way to test this."

"What have you found?" asked Tabata.

"I believe these micro tears are the remnants of the original wormhole John and I encountered and subsequently destroyed four years ago. In order to close the smaller tears, we'll need to reform the original portal. It's the only way to prove the hypothesis."

"You want to stabilize it?" asked Zoe.

"Correct," said Mei. She took a duffle bag from below her seat and set it on the table. "This is what we're going to use."

"What?" asked Bart.

Mei unzipped the bag and grabbed one of the metal rods inside, handing to Sophie so she could pass it around. "Ortego used a massive machine to initialize a magnetic field to create the original wormhole. We can't afford to build another one of those, but these little guys should be enough to get the job done."

An air of silence filled the tent.

Mei sighed. "If you have questions or concerns about any of this, please speak up."

Zoe fidgeted in her seat. "You're asking us to reopen the thing that killed the planet."

"It's dangerous," said Sophie.

"More than dangerous," said Tabata.

"I know," said Mei. "But if we don't do this, the radiation will continue to climb, and not even the coils will be enough to stem the tide. None of us knows how bad it will get if we let it continue. The results could be catastrophic. You all know this."

"You're right, of course," said Tabata. "But how does opening the wormhole help?"

"It confirms the hypothesis, which is the most important part. We have to know what the cause is if we're ever going to fix it."

"Why not bury it?" he asked.

"Burying it is my last option. We don't know how the anomaly will react, and I'd much rather understand what we're dealing with before I toss it in the ground," she said.

"The last time somebody did this, we got Variant," said Bart. "You're sure you wanna take the risk of a repeat apocalypse?"

"The planet's already been filled with Variant. Maybe less now than there used to be, but the gas isn't going anywhere. Opening the portal for a minute or two won't make it any worse."

"Fair enough," he finally said.

"Okay, I think we're with you so far," said Zoe. "But how does opening the portal stop the radiation?"

"These micro tears are unstable. I think the instability is what's causing the radiation. If we can unify them into a single bridge, we may actually be able to collapse it for good."

"So we'd activate it for, what, a few seconds?" asked Bart.

"Precisely long enough to see if it works, then shut it off. If we're successful, we can reactivate it later for further analysis."

"You think we'll need to?" asked Zoe.

"I don't know," admitted Mei. "But at least we'll have the option."

"There's no risk of the portal staying open after we try to shut it down?" asked Bart.

"Not this time. If you recall, the original Ortego facility used solar panels and Fever Killers for power. They couldn't shut the portal down in time, so the consistent energy supply kept the lights on. The magnetic field we're creating here is totally different. If one of these rods gets detached, the whole thing stops, and the portal destabilizes into micro-wormholes again. The risk is far lower."

"If we shut the portal down and the micro-tears reform, won't the radiation come back?" asked Bart.

"Yes, and I'm expecting it to. All we're doing right now is testing to see if I'm right. If the rift forms, we'll start looking for a better long term solution."

Zoe blinked. "When did you have time to come up with all this?"

"I don't sleep much."

"Count me in, ma'am," said Sophie.

Zoe and John both nodded.

"I have no objections," said Tabata from across the table. "I'm here if you need me."

"I appreciate the support. We'll need everyone's help."

"Okay, so what's the full plan? Break it down for us," said Zoe.

"First, Bart, I need you to work on getting a few more mobile coils up and running. The two we have are working fine, but the radiation will keep rising until we resolve this, so we'll probably need them soon. Plus, it's good to be prepared. The two we have could die at any moment."

"Not confident in my work?" he asked, raising his brow.

"You're good, but the parts we're using are ancient. It's their age I don't trust."

He gave her a thin smile. "Fair enough."

"Zoe, I need you and your flippies to keep excavating. If we have to bury this thing, I want to have as much data as possible from the basements."

"You got it," she said.

"Sophie, you'll be assisting me with installing the rods and monitoring the field."

The assistant's face lit up. "You mean I don't have to stay in the camp?"

"No, not this time. If Tremaine wants something, she can leave a message. I need my team."

Sophie grinned, but quickly composed herself. "Yes, ma'am."

Mei nodded, and turned to Tabata. "I hate to ask this of you, Doctor, but we could use your medical expertise at the site, should anything go wrong."

"Rest assured, Doctor Curie, I will be there."

"What about me?" asked John. "I'm going with you, so you'd better find something for me to do."

"Of course," she said. "Someone has to carry the supplies."

He dropped his head. "Figures."

"Everyone know their jobs?" asked Mei, lifting the duffle from the table. "I want that portal open by the end of the week, which means we have four days to excavate, build, and prepare. Let's make it happen."

Somewhere on Kant

January 25, 2351

TERRY SPENT the bulk of his days meditating in the cell. He was finally able to sustain himself in the void for as long he wanted. It was a huge relief.

"Why waste time with such a dumb game?" asked Janice. "It's so boring. You should play with me instead." She ran around the room, waving her arms. "Play play play!"

Janice hated the meditations, always taunting him before he started the process. Terry knew better than to listen. A few minutes of meditating, and he wouldn't see her again for hours.

She giggled. "Won't be long before they kill you, brother."

He ignored her, closed his eyes, and breathed. He recited the mantras, banishing his make-believe companion in the process.

Today, Ludo would teach him a new technique meant to cleanse his wings—whatever that meant. He could never understand him when he talked about flying or wings. All he knew was the lessons were working. He didn't care why.

At the appointed hour, when the suns were at their zenith, Ludo called to him from the other side of the wall, requesting he take his position. Terry did, relaxing his body and performing his routine.

"Today will be different," said Ludo.

"Different how?" asked Terry.

"Today, my friend, you will free the ghost from its cage."

Free the ghost? He wanted to ask what Ludo meant, but he didn't. For the sake of his friend, he would listen. For the sake of himself, he would try.

Ludo began the session with a new, wordless mantra. It was composed of meaningless sounds. This was something Terry had heard him do before, but never in a lesson. Ludo said each word soft, but deep, pulling the sound from his throat and stretching it out when he exhaled. He did this until Terry joined him, and together they repeated the mantra for several minutes. "Ahh-mm…" Terry let the word fill him, the deep sound of the M vibrating his mouth as he exhaled. He repeated this many times before the exercise was complete.

"We do this to strengthen our wings," said Ludo. "Now we must stretch them."

What followed was another chant, though the word changed. "Hummm…" They repeated the sound as they had the first, and Terry found himself relaxing.

By the time the hour had passed, Terry learned five sounds, each with a different function. All revolved around strengthening his supposed wings.

"Rest now," said Ludo after a long while. Terry looked at the barred window to find most of the daylight gone, replaced by the soft glow of moon. "Today, we have cleansed our wings. Tomorrow, we shall stretch them."

"I don't understand," said Terry.

"You will see, my friend. Tomorrow, you will see."

Somewhere on Kant
January 26, 2351

THE NEXT DAY CAME, and so did the meditation hour. Like before,

Ludo led with the new mantras, but this time the process was much shorter. "I will speak and you will breathe," said Ludo. "Focus on my words and let go of your thoughts."

Terry took a deep breath and released it in a long and steady sigh.

"You are jumbled inside, Terry," said Ludo. "Your ghost is tied to the ground and mangled."

Another breath. Release.

"You were not always this way," he said. "When you were born, your ghost was like an endless piece of rope, stretching far and free. The world has twisted you, however. It has made you what you are. You must untangle the knot and get back to who you used to be. You must free the ghost."

Another breath. Release.

"Inside you there are wings mightier than the strongest of birds. They have been pinned to the earth by forces in your life. Anger, greed, envy, desire, hate—these are your weights. They must be lifted."

Another breath. Release.

"Imagine yourself standing on the edge of a mountaintop," said Ludo. "The snow is cold, but you cannot feel it. The light is hot, but you cannot sense it. The wind is strong, but you cannot feel it. You are there, but not there. You are aware, but unaware. You are you, but you are not you. Now tell me, what do you see?"

In his mind, he saw the place which Ludo had described, and he saw around him all the things which Ludo told him to see. A whirling wind bellowed through the mountain, bending the necks of trees and tearing blades of blue grass from the ground to carry them into the sky. Terry walked in the snow, and he heard the crunch of his feet as he pressed the white ice with his toes. He looked behind him to find a long and endless series of footsteps following him. He had come a long way. He had traveled far.

As he moved to the edge of the mountain, he saw a great chasm stretching wide and deep, filled with forests and rivers, villages and people, and beyond them, still, a sea so vast it nearly swallowed him. Terry saw them clearly, as though he were really there. "So many things," whispered Terry. He described the sight before him, which wasn't particularly difficult. It was all so clear.

"Good," said Ludo. "You see much. Now listen, for this is important. The world before you is one we have made together, but now you must forget it."

"Forget it?" asked Terry. "It's beautiful."

"It is not yours," said Ludo. "You must craft your own world. Build it to your liking and fill it with your thoughts. You must do this, and it must be yours and yours alone. You must remember every detail. All the blades of grass, all the clouds in the sky, all the rocks at your feet. Remember these things so you may build them again and again, every time you close your eyes. Once you have mastered this new world of yours, then I will teach you to fly."

Ortego Reconstruction Outpost
January 27, 2351

Mei was optimistic. It took Bart less time to build the second set of mobile coils, which put them ahead of schedule. She thought about asking him for more, but four was enough for the moment. In the meantime, he could work on building explosives to take down the rest of the building in case they had to bury the portal.

During this, Zoe managed to collect an enormous amount of useable data from the ruins, thanks to the flippies.

John, Sophie, and Mei spent most of their time in the basement. They brought some lighting fixtures so they wouldn't have to do everything with their night vision on. The green hue gave Mei a headache.

She wanted to run experiments with the rods to make sure a magnetic field would actually do the job. Sophie observed her mentor and assisted where she could. Mei explained every detail to the girl. She wanted to make sure someone else knew how to shut the field down. If anything happened to Mei, Sophie would know what to do.

They fiddled with the rods, fine-tuning their frequency for hours. The field had to be exactly right, otherwise the rift might not form and they'd have to start all over again. Given how impatient Tremaine had gotten lately, Mei wagered she was running out of time before the old woman found out the truth. She had to act fast.

Nevertheless, Mei was staying positive. The first official test was scheduled for this afternoon, and so far she had no reason to doubt her success. Still, anything could happen. She wasn't a fool. She was prepared for failure, hence the extra coils and explosives. If the whole thing went to hell, she'd end the story here.

At half past noon, the team arrived at the Ortego site, equipment in tow, ready to make history. Bart, Mei, Sophie, John, and Mortimer the Flippy all waited in the basement of the Ortego building.

"Coils are coming online," said Bart, his eyes on his pad. "Should only be a few minutes."

"I'm good up here," said Zoe. Her face appeared in the corner of Mei's visor. She had knotted hair and looked exhausted, although the radiation suit hid most of it.

"Sophie and I will proceed with the field activation process, so I suggest everyone step back and give us some room," said Mei.

They did as she asked. She unzipped the bag and removed the first rod. She gave another to Sophie. They'd previously gone and marked each and every one of the spots where the rods would go, measuring the distance so they were equally apart from one another. "Remember," said Mei. "It's just like I showed you."

Sophie nodded. "Yes, ma'am."

Mei twisted a ring at the center of the rod, releasing the pin at its core and snapping the rod into place. The room cracked with a loud pop as the rod sent a thin needle into the floor for support. "Next."

The process repeated until both women had placed eighteen rods around the anomaly. When the last two were set, Mei and Sophie joined the others near the far end of the room.

Mei took her pad and opened a simple app Zoe created specifically to operate and monitor the wormhole. Zoe called it

"Knock Knock." With a tap of the pad, a countdown appeared on the screen to signify the startup process.

"Everyone stay back," she said as the clock counted down. When it hit zero, the rods activated, bringing no visible change. But Mei knew this wasn't so. Her pad showed a buildup of the magnetic field as it formed, spreading through the circle and slowly stabilizing itself.

A light erupted from the center of the room, flashing like a thunderstorm. "What was that?" Zoe asked, taken back.

"Some kind of electrical discharge," said Bart.

Another flash, this one brighter than the first. It snapped through the room, causing them all to shield their eyes. Behind her arms, Mei saw a series of short, bright bursts, consuming everything. The pile of metal caught on fire, sparks dancing around it. A low rumbling shook the floor, causing Sophie to fall. She screamed. Bart caught her and didn't let her go. The room was going wild with the sounds of thunder.

A massive orange spark danced atop the surface of the anomaly, weaving and expanding like a piece of yarn. After a few seconds, it lifted off the metal altogether, swirling in the air like fire in the sky, like lightning in a bottle.

In less than a moment, the string of light exploded. Mei felt the grip of John's hand around her arm. It was the Second Jolt all over again.

But suddenly the shaking ceased, and all at once the light surrendered. When she could see again, Mei lifted her eyes and saw what remained of her experiment.

It was the rift, alive and real, a massive circle of darkness, pulsing with the same steady breaths it had all those years before.

After all these years, she'd found it.

"HOLY SHIT, IT WORKED!" shouted Zoe through the com in Mei's visor.

"Look at it!" yelled Bart. "I've never seen anything like it."

"It's pitch black inside," said John.

"No, look," said Sophie, pointing to the base of the rift. "You can see something." She paused. "It looks like a flat surface."

Sophie was right. Mei could see the ground on the other side, a deep brown. What the hell was over there?

"Hey!" snapped John. "Aren't you going to shut it down?"

Mei blinked, trying to collect herself. She could make an excuse, tell them they should examine it while they had the chance, but she stopped herself. She could wait. Do things the right way. She nodded. "Okay." She took her pad and hit the deactivation icon. "Shutting it down now."

Mei expected another shakeup, perhaps even an explosion, but the portal only dissipated, fading into the air with a series of sparks. Below the rift, where the cluster of furniture had been, nothing now remained. Somehow, the debris had disappeared with the arrival of the portal. Had it been sent through? If so, then right now a ball of manmade metal and plastic was halfway across the universe. Another planet, maybe? She wasn't sure. The bridge had to go somewhere. Mei was certain of that. Whether it was a planet or the inside of a gas cloud, she couldn't say, but she knew it existed.

Variant had to come from somewhere.

Ortego Reconstruction Outpost
January 28, 2351

When the portal was activated, the scanners recorded a complete drop in radiation output. With the micro-tears reformed into a full wormhole, the problem was momentarily solved. It was by no means a permanent solution, but it gave Mei the reason she needed to try again.

The following morning, she assembled her team to discuss the next phase in the plan. "We're sending something through this time," she told them.

"Don't look at me," said John. "I hate traveling."

"What did you have in mind?" asked Bart.

"We need to scan the bridge from within the event horizon as well as the other side. It may give us the data we need to find a way to seal it for good." She looked at Zoe. "A flippy seemed like the best idea."

"Which one?" asked Zoe.

"Your call," said Mei. "I trust your judgment."

Zoe smiled a little. "You got it."

Mei dismissed everyone, asking them to meet her at the Ortego site in three hours. She planned on spending the time fine-tuning the rods. With a little work, she was fairly certain she could cut down on the activation feedback.

John drove the dirt cab with her in the passenger's seat, still tinkering with a few of the rods. "We're really doing this, huh?" he asked when they were nearly halfway there.

She didn't look up. "It's the only way to get the data."

"Okay," he said. "I just wanna make sure you're not doing this for another reason."

She paused, the rod in her hand. "What other reason?"

"Terry died from that thing," he said. "Here we are bringing it back. You sure this is what you want?"

She didn't say anything.

"It's okay. You don't have to explain. You know I've got your back."

They sat in the cab for several minutes without saying a word. Mei caught herself holding her breath, debating what to tell him, wavering somewhere between the truth and a lie. At last, she set the rod on the seat between them and looked at him. "What do you think happened to him?"

He returned her glance. "To Terry?"

She nodded.

"I don't know," he admitted, putting his eyes back on the road. "I barely understand what happened to *us*."

"If I said..." She stopped herself, not knowing if she should go on. But didn't John have a right to know what was going on? Sure he did, but what if he tried to talk her out of it? What if he thought she was crazy?

He slowed the vehicle and looked at her. "What is it?"

She stared at the dash. "What if I said the reason I'm doing this is because of him."

"Because of Terry?" he asked. He stopped the cab altogether and put it in park.

"I want to know what happened to him, John. I have to know where he went."

John stared at her with the same soft, blue eyes she'd known her entire life. She had expected doubt or even a difference of opinion, but he had none of that in him now.

He leaned across the divide of the seats and held her by the palm. He wiped her cheek with his other hand, pulling tears away. Without realizing it, she'd been crying. "It's okay," he whispered, smiling warmly. "I get it."

She gulped, pushing down the lump in her throat. "No one else can know," she said.

"They won't," he told her.

"If anyone finds out, they'll send me home and cut me out of the program. They'll say my judgment's compromised." She paused. "Maybe they're right."

"You're doing what you think is best. It's what you've always done."

"Maybe it's selfish," she muttered. "Looking for an answer just because I want to know. It doesn't help anyone but me."

"You're wrong," he said. "What about Terry? He died protecting us. We owe it to him to find out what really happened. And I want to know, too."

She nodded.

He beamed a smile her way and let go of her hand, taking

the wheel again. "We'd better hurry," said John. "Don't wanna miss the big show."

WHEN EVERYONE WAS in the basement, Mei and Sophie set the modified rods in place. The team stood a few meters from the circle, their backs against the wall and waiting.

Mortimer was sitting a few steps from the others, a long cord hooked into his side. No one knew whether a wireless signal could go through the portal or not, so Zoe had the flippy jacked into a local control box. She was sitting behind it now.

"We're doing this just like last time," said Mei, motioning to the rods. "I tweaked the equipment, but be ready for a light show in case I goofed it."

Bart gave a thumbs up. "Hit it, Doc."

Mei touched the icon for her Knock Knock app, bringing it to life on the pad. She took a deep breath, staring at the space where the bridge was about to form, and pressed the activation button.

A burst of light filled the room momentarily. It only lasted a second before dissipating into a steady, pulsing circle of darkness. The modified rods had been a success. Mei let out a sigh of relief.

"Amazing," said Zoe. "It's so different up close."

"Nice work on the mods," said Bart.

"Thanks," said Mei. She turned to Zoe. "Ready?"

"Morty's raring to go," she said, fiddling with the controls. Mortimer raised his tendrils into the air. "He's ready to party!"

"Do it," she said. "Everyone make sure you have the feed going on your visors. If you see anything, call it out and mark the timestamp for later."

Zoe positioned Mortimer in front of the rift, easing him to within a few centimeters of it. "Here goes nothing," she said.

The little window in the corner of Mei's display went black as Mortimer passed through the gateway. The flippy disappeared into the darkness, tugging his chord behind him.

"Activating night vision," said Zoe.

The screen in the corner of Mei's visor lit up the environment in a bright shade of green. What lay before the flippy left her dumbstruck—a vast room with desks and chairs, surrounded by flattened metal walls which rose higher than she thought they should. Below the flippy, a wide ramp stretched out towards the floor.

"What the hell is this?" asked Bart.

"Zoe, keep going," said Mei.

The flippy crept forward off the ramp, dragging the cord behind.

"Turn around," ordered Mei. "Let's have a look at the whole room."

Zoe rotated Mortimer's head, passing several desks and what looked like computers along the way. As it reached the rift, Mei felt her heart flutter. There, standing before the little flippy, a tall, metal ring sat elevated in the air, and at its core Mei saw herself watching from the other side.

"Holy shit," muttered Zoe, her mouth agape.

"You've got to be kidding," said Bart.

"I don't get it," said John. "Did Ortego build another one?"

Mei didn't know what to say. Could John be right? Did Ortego actually make another portal? If so, where on Earth was it?

She stopped herself, shaking her head. No, it didn't add up. Variant came through the original portal, which meant this couldn't be on Earth. Not unless Ortego created Variant themselves and accidentally released it. But why send the gas through the rift in the first place? "Zoe, keep scanning the room."

"Aren't we going to talk about the artificial ring we just saw?" asked Bart.

"Later," said Mei. "Right now we've got other priorities."

Bart grunted. "Yeah, okay."

"Doctor Curie, I've got something," said Zoe. "Look there, against the wall near the doorway. Here, let me move closer."

It took Mei a moment to realize what she was looking at. With so much going on, it was easy to overlook. But as the flippy neared the wall, she saw what it truly was: a pack, academy-issued with the name Terry stitched on its flap.

She took a step back, her legs shaking. In all her wildest dreams, in all the scenarios she played out in her mind over the last four years, she never dreamed of this. If Terry's pack could survive the trip to the other side, maybe her friend could as well. Her hands trembled at the thought of it.

"No way…" muttered Bart, shaking his head.

"It can't be," said John, dropping his pack with a loud thud. He took a few steps toward the rift. "Terry?"

"Hey, watch out," said Sophie. "Don't get too close."

John ignored the warning and edged forward. He pointed at the rift. "We have to get that!"

"We will," said Sophie. "We'll use the flippy. Now get back. It's not safe."

But he didn't listen. Before anyone could stop him, John dashed forward and leapt through the rift. He landed on the ramp with a hard *clank*, nearly falling in the process. He ran past Mortimer and quickly found the pack, grabbing it with both his hands and holding it close.

It took Mei a moment to realize what was happening. The shock of seeing Terry's pack was too much. It was like all the energy in her body had been drained. When she realized what John had done, it was too late to stop him.

"Do you know what this means?" yelled John from beyond the other side. "Terry's alive! He has to be."

Mei blinked, trying to snap herself out of it. "John, get back over here!" she shouted.

He turned, looking over his shoulder and into the gate. "But—"

"If the portal goes down, you'll be trapped. We'll figure everything out, I promise. But right now you have to come back. Please!"

He looked at the bag in his hands, pausing for a moment. "Okay."

"Pull Mortimer out of there, Zoe. As soon as John gets back, I'm closing the gate."

Zoe nodded. "Roger."

"Come on, John," said Mei. "Bring the bag and let's go."

He did as she said, clutching the pack against his chest with both his arms and running up the ramp and through the rift. A moment later he was back with them, followed by Mortimer.

Mei hit the deactivation button, watching as the void disintegrated before her. When it was over, she used the com to contact Tabata, who had been watching the experiment from the surface.

"Yes, I'm here," said Tabata. "You put on quite the show, I must say."

"If you can spare a minute, Sergeant Finn needs a checkup," she said. "I'm sure you know why."

"Of course. I'd be happy to help."

"Everyone else convene on the surface. Forget the equipment. Leave it here for now. We have a lot to do before the day is out."

After Tabata gave John a clean bill of health, Mei convened the team in the conference tent.

She unloaded the contents of Terry's pack onto the table for everyone to see. Among the belongings were a small knife, a few stained rags, and some plant residue. She placed each of the items in a sealed plastic bag for safety purposes.

John chose to stand while everyone took their seats. He stared with vacant eyes at the knife, nervously flicking his thumb against his index finger. Mei wanted to reassure him somehow, tell him everything would be okay, but it would have to wait.

"This is every item from the bag we found," said Mei, motioning to the table. "The knife appears to be made out of some kind of bone. We're running an analysis of the rotten plants, but my first guess is it's food. Sophie's running a test on the cloth and what we're assuming is blood." Mei felt a knot in her stomach. She tried not to let it show. "Suffice it to say, it's not what we expected."

"Do you think Terry might be alive?" asked Bart.

"I do, and I think it's reason enough to continue our research. We need to explore the other side of the portal."

"Don't forget the advanced technology we saw," said Zoe. "There's another reason right there."

Bart sighed. "Things are about to get complicated, aren't they?"

Zoe rolled her eyes. "As if they weren't already."

John still wasn't speaking. He only stood, staring at the table, flicking his finger. But Mei knew he wasn't really there in the tent with them. He was in the other place, standing in the dark and looking for his friend.

"Does this mean we're putting the current project on hold?" asked Sophie.

Mei looked at her. "Huh?"

"I think she means the mission to close the wormhole," said Bart.

Mei paused. She wasn't sure how to answer. If she postponed their primary objective, it might cause problems with Tremaine and the board, maybe even her team. But she couldn't walk away from this, not after today. Not with Terry's pack sitting right in front of her. "If I did sideline the mission, would anyone object?"

Bart and Zoe looked at one another, then simultaneously shook their heads.

"No objections here, ma'am," said Sophie.

Mei looked at Tabata. "Doctor?"

His eyes fell on the bloody rags resting on the table. "Technically, I'm not part of your team," he said. "Officially speaking, I'm here as a zoologist, studying the kitobora, which means I have no say in what you or your team does. However, I'm also a doctor, and I'd be remiss to ignore your medical needs, now and in the future." He scratched the tip of his chin, sweeping his short, gray whiskers. "I will be here, the same as I have these last eight months, whatever the outcome."

Mei smiled. "So we're all onboard. Good."

"Do we have a plan yet?" asked Zoe. "Seems like we should have a plan…"

"Slow down," said Bart. "We just opened a wormhole to another world and found *this* waiting for us. Give the doc at least a few hours."

Zoe wrinkled her nose. "Sorry."

"As it happens, I actually do have a plan," said Mei.

Zoe grinned at Bart. "See? Curie's always got us covered."

"The goal hasn't changed. We're still going to find a way to close the portal. It just won't be today."

John finally looked at her with a shocked expression.

She met his gaze and her voice softened. "Don't worry, though. We're adding a few steps before we get there."

John seemed to relax at this, but not completely.

"A few steps?" asked Sophie.

"Right. For starters, we'll continue to investigate the room we found. I'd like to spend some time on the other side analyzing the equipment we saw there. Maybe bring it back for proper study."

Zoe nodded. "We can use the flippies to move everything. No use risking our lives traveling through the portal."

"John already took the trip, and he's perfectly healthy. But to be safe, we'll wait until we have more time to study the portal. In the meantime, Bart, I want you analyzing the stuff the flippies bring back. Tell me what the hell it is. Sophie, learn everything you can about the three items on this table. Everyone understand?"

They did.

"Then, let's get to work."

16

Ortego Outpost File Logs
Play Audio File 652
Recorded: February 1, 2351

TREMAINE: *Morning, dear. How's the progress going? Have you found a way to stop the radiation?*

CURIE: *Still working on it, ma'am.*

TREMAINE: *I see. Perhaps you could use some assistance. I'll send another team to help you.*

CURIE: *That really isn't necessarily. I just need some time.*

TREMAINE: *More time? It has been nine days since your last report, yet you have nothing to show me. I'm sure you understand my reluctance.*

CURIE: *My team works better on our own. Sending more people would only slow everyone down.*

TREMAINE: *Perhaps if you opened up about your recent findings, I* *might be more apt to grant your request. Right now, you have me sitting in the dark.*

CURIE: *I'm sorry, but we don't have much to report at the moment. We're working hard to bring you more information.*

TREMAINE: *Doctor Curie, please. Why don't you tell me what's really going on, dear?*

CURIE: *I don't know what you mean.*

TREMAINE: *Oh, come now. We both know you do. I've been monitoring the research outpost for several months. I'm fully aware of what you've found.*

CURIE: *I don't—*

TREMAINE: *Please, let's not play pretend anymore. I know all about the wormhole.*

CURIE: *How—*

TREMAINE: *You thought by activating the Einstein-Rosen Bridge you could find a way to close the fractures. I admit it's a perfectly reasonable plan. What I don't understand is why you felt it necessary to open it a second time. You've confirmed your theory, doctor, so why continue the experiment?*

CURIE: *I don't understand. If you know all this, don't you already have the answer?*

TREMAINE: *Let's say for the sake of this discussion I don't. Please enlighten me.*

CURIE: *When the rift opened…we saw something on the other side. It was a room, maybe a cave. We couldn't tell for sure. Either way, I felt it was worth exploring.*

TREMAINE: *So what did you find?*

CURIE: *A room full of technology, another portal, and…*

TREMAINE: *What?*

CURIE: *Terry's pack.*

TREMAINE: *Terry? You mean the boy who died in the Ortego facility four years ago?*

CURIE: *Yes.*

TREMAINE: *I see.*

CURIE: *We have to keep exploring the other side. There's no telling what else we'll find. You do understand, right?*

TREMAINE: *I understand you've let your emotions impede your better judgment in this matter. Don't you see what's happened? You're too close to the mission, especially after what you found. You have to shut it down. Close off the rift for good.*

CURIE: *How? If we shut the portal down, the radiation will only grow. We need more time to find a solution.*

TREMAINE: *You will send an explosive through the wormhole and destroy the gate on the other end, which should cause the tears to close. The board and I believe they are only there because of the link they share with the alien ring. Kill the bridge and you stop the radiation.*

CURIE: *But you don't know what that might do!*

TREMAINE: *It is better than risking the lives of everyone here, or would you rather kill us all to satisfy your own curiosity?*

CURIE: *But what about all the technology? What about Terry? He could still be alive!*

TREMAINE: *One life is not worth the risk. Have you learned nothing from human history, child?*

CURIE: *I—I can't just abandon him…*

TREMAINE: *Doctor Curie, you will follow the orders I have given you. You will terminate the project immediately and have your team return to Central. Do you understand?*

CURIE: *I—*
TREMAINE: *Do you understand, doctor? Hello?*

End Audio File

Ortego Reconstruction Outpost
February 1, 2351

Mei was running out of options. Tremaine had given her orders to destroy the bridge from the other side, but she couldn't simply walk away. Especially now.

Sophie's analysis of the wraps revealed Terry's DNA. By this point, Mei was hardly surprised.

In the meantime, the flippies managed to map most of the caves on the other side of the bridge. They found dozens of rooms, including storage compartments as well as sleeping quarters. Bart and Zoe were hard at work trying to decipher the computer systems, but the technology was completely foreign and unlike anything they'd ever seen. It would be a while before any of them fully understood what they were dealing with.

By now Mei was fairly certain the portal led to another world, but she needed more evidence. If only she could find a way outside.

However, time was running out. Tremaine might send the military in to extract her team, which could complicate things.

She considered going to John about it, but the news would

only worry him. Bart, Zoe, and Sophie had little to no connections with the board, so they were out. Then she remembered Tabata. The old man was offered a seat on the board several years ago. He must know a thing or two about dealing with them.

Less than an hour after the call with Tremaine, Mei went looking for Tabata. She found him at the kitobora pen, feeding the animal a handful of blue grass. "There you are," she said at last.

"What can I do for you, Doctor Curie? Are you feeling ill?"

"Not quite. I need to talk to you, if you don't mind."

He let the kitobora lick the rest of the grass from his palm. "You sound quite serious today."

She nodded. "What do you think of the work we're doing here?"

He paused, scratching his chin with the same hand he'd fed the animal, taking a moment to think. "There are two ways to answer your question and I'm afraid I don't know which response to give."

"What do you mean?"

"On the one hand, your mission is to block the radiation coming from the anomaly, yes?" he asked.

"Right."

"On the other, you've begun a separate investigation involving a lost boy and what appears to be a cache of alien technology. Truly remarkable findings, I should think." He grabbed another handful of grass. "Of course, because the investigation is ongoing, the original mission has been postponed, delaying a solution to the radiation problem."

"But I can't ignore the findings."

"You mean you can't ignore the possibility of your friend being alive," he corrected.

She said nothing.

"Don't worry, Doctor Curie. I agree with your decision to look for the boy," he said, patting the kitobora's head.

"You do?"

"If I didn't, I would not still be here."

She relaxed. "Thank you."

He waved his hand. "No need for that. Now tell me what's really on your mind. Surely you didn't stop your work to come and ask for my approval?"

"Doctor Tremaine called me a few hours ago. It wasn't good."

He raised his brow. "Abigail? What did she want with you?"

"She ordered me to close the gate," said Mei. "She said to blow it up from the other side."

"Oh, my."

"She threatened to have me removed if I didn't comply," said Mei.

"What are you going to do?"

"I was hoping you knew someone on the board. Maybe you could put in a call."

He seemed to consider this for a moment. "I could, but I wonder if it would be enough. Abigail is the head of the Science Division. Her authority supersedes the board."

"What else can I do?" she asked.

"First, pull yourself out of the situation. You have been

looking at this from a limited perspective. Yes, Abigail is the authority in this division, but she is not the only authority in the government."

"You're talking about the military and the Motherhood," said Mei.

"Each has a leader equal in power to your opponent. Bring your case to them and rally support against her."

"How am I supposed to get their support? This is a scientific mission."

Tabata held up a finger. "Think about it. Who are the heads of those divisions?"

Mei paused as the realization hit her. "Mara Echols!"

"The very same," said Tabata, grinning.

"And Colonel Ross is a friend of hers, isn't she?" asked Mei.

"Oh, yes," he said. "Very much so."

Mei couldn't believe it. She was so stupid for not seeing it sooner. She clasped Tabata's hand in both of hers and shook it. "Thank you!"

"Think nothing of it," he told her.

It would be easy enough to contact Echols. The Matron's office was well known for its open-door policy. The problem was reaching Colonel Ross. Thankfully, she happened to know a guy with connections in the military.

He also happened to be her boyfriend.

Somewhere on Kant

February 1, 2351

TERRY SAT in the middle of a field, taking in the vibrant serenity of the forest. He listened to the flow of the river, watching the clouds move overhead along the afternoon sky. On the bark of a nearby tree, a large blue beetle scurried to the ground, shuffling through the blades of green grass.

Terry smiled, nodding at the bug as it went. He knew the insect wasn't actually there. It was only a fabrication, devised inside the fantasy of his own mind. But he didn't care. The beetle was real to him.

Since he first conceived of this place, Terry had expanded its borders and filled it with life. Insects, a few small animals, flocks of birds. Most were ancient species from Earth—creatures he'd read about in history class. He wanted people here, too, but Ludo was against the idea. "People should not be created in the mind," he told Terry. "This is your sanctuary, but it would be their prison, and before too long you would want to free them."

Terry got to his feet and walked through the valley, passing under the tree line and into the forest. He made his way to the river where dozens of salmon leapt upstream against the moving current. One of the fish jumped over a large rock only to be snatched by the mouth of a bear, which then consumed it. Terry saw this once in a nature documentary in school. He'd been appalled by it at the time, the way the animal slaughtered the fish. But now the bear, which he had since named Peter, brought him a strange sense of peace.

Peter and Terry were not the only ones to visit the river. A family of ostriches drank on the other side, while a tiger cub and a crimson fox played together several meters behind them. Terry had recreated each one from what he remembered in school. The pictures he'd seen. The movies he'd watched. They were probably inaccurate, but he didn't care. They were his and he liked them.

He sat by the riverside and listened to the rapids. He had never actually seen the Earth when it was like this, but he did his best to recreate it. But he knew it was a fraction of the truth. He could never know the world as it had been, back before the Jolt transformed everything. This version of the Earth was more alien to him than Kant, but he could not help but long for it.

Terry pushed the negative thoughts from his mind. The point of this place was not to dwell, but to remember. If only he had more time to learn this process.

He waited by the bank for a long time, lost in the flow of the water, consumed by the sounds of the rapids. The noise filled him, drowning his thoughts and allowing him to relax. He remained this way for several minutes, losing himself to the artificial environment.

After a time, he got to his feet and made his way back towards the valley. Birds chirped overhead, and Peter roared behind him. He willed the wind to blow, sending waves through the grass and bending the branches of the trees. He wished he could feel the current of air on his skin or smell the pollen. Ludo said there were a select few who could do this, but they were master flyers and had spent decades training.

Still, he was proud of his little world, and he wished he could show it to someone and share the experience. If only he could create people, perhaps John and Mei so he could talk to them. What he wouldn't do to have his friends back. His old life. His family.

He walked through the valley towards the mountain, staring at the grass beneath his feet and frowning. If only he could go home. If only—

A shadow fell over him, covering the area. He raised his head and saw a building, curiously present where nothing had been before. It was tall, two stories high, and vaguely familiar. A blue door stood at the base, lined with silver and brown. Terry stared at it, uncertain of what he should do. He knew this wasn't right, that he should wake himself now and ignore it, but he couldn't. Something was drawing him in.

The door was cracked a few centimeters. *I should leave,* he thought. *This isn't right. I should wake up.*

Instead, he touched the knob and opened it.

He knew where he was the moment he entered the old house. It was a memory. His family's house.

His mother's desk sat in the corner, her coat still on the back of the chair. The light board on the wall near the stairs beeped, and he saw a little green dot blinking steadily.

He was home.

Terry walked through the first floor of his childhood apartment, dazed and confused. How long had it been since he was last here? Yet everything was so detailed. So clear.

A loud crash filled the house, causing him to flinch. There

was nothing there, but he could hear the faint sounds of footsteps overhead. Someone was upstairs.

He stood there for a moment, fighting the urge to investigate. *I should leave,* he thought as he walked to the bottom of the stairs. *What am I doing?*

He gripped the handrail.

Against his better judgment, he climbed. The stairs creaked as he pressed his foot to them, sighing with age. Laughter rang in the distance, echoing through the walls, giving him pause. The voices were muffled, but different enough to know there was more than one. He climbed, and when he neared the top he heard them speak.

"When will I get a birthday?" asked a voice.

"You're only four, so you have to wait," said another.

Terry stood at the edge of a doorway. There were toys on the floor—blocks with letters on them in the shape of a castle and plastic soldiers. He knew these things, or he thought he knew them.

A tiny hand appeared from behind the wall, followed by a child. He had pale skin and dark hair.

Terry stared at the boy who would be him.

The little one gathered a few of the blocks and put them away.

Janice, who had been obscured by the wall, walked to the boy's side and helped put the rest of the toys away. "I wish I was seven," she said, frowning. "I want to go with you."

"I'll tell you all about it when I get home. I promise, okay?"

She smiled cheerily. "Okay!"

The boy grinned and marched out of the room, almost bumping into his older self. Terry stepped to the side to avoid him. The child didn't notice.

Janice followed after her brother, and together they went downstairs. Terry followed them, staying several steps behind. They searched the house for their mother, checking the light board, which now displayed three blinking dots instead of one. Red, blue, and green. Mother was in the kitchen.

I was just in there, thought Terry.

But there she was, sorting through her work with a hurried expression on her face—a woman he had not seen in nearly twelve years. She looked different from the way he remembered. She had the look of stress about her, with bloodshot eyes and frizzled, hastily brushed hair. Was this really how she used to be?

Terry stiffened as he recognized the moment. This was the day his mother had taken him to the academy. It was the final memory he had of his family in this apartment.

The woman placed her pad in his bag. "Come on, Terrance. We've got to get you ready and out the door. Today's your first day, after all, and we have to make a good impression."

"When will he be back?" asked Janice.

"Hurry up. Let's go, Terrance," she said, ignoring the question. She grabbed his hand and pulled him along. "We have about twenty minutes to get all the way to the education district. Hardly enough time at all."

Janice ran and hugged her brother, wrapping her little arms as far around him as she could. "Love you," she said.

"Love you, too."

She smiled. "Bye."

Their mother grasped the boy's hand and pulled him outside. They disappeared through the door, vanishing like smoke.

Terry stood there, uncertain of what had happened or why. Did Ludo ever experience this sort of thing when traversing his own mind palace? He'd never mentioned the possibility of memories manifesting themselves like this. Maybe he didn't know.

Perhaps this was happening because Terry was thinking about his friends in the field, imagining Mei and John. But if those thoughts were to blame, why wasn't he standing in the academy? Why remember something from before he even met them?

"Because this one is mine," he heard a voice say.

He turned to see Janice standing there in the same place the boy and his mother had left her. The same girl he left who, only moments ago, had hugged her older brother and said goodbye. "I'm always here," she said. "You should know, big brother."

No, this didn't make any sense.

"Aren't you happy, Terry?" she asked him. "We're home now. No more bad people ruining our fun. We can stay here forever. We can play."

A pile of blocks manifested between them. Janice fell to the floor and grabbed a few and waved them around. "Come on and play!"

This was too much. He needed to leave and quickly. He closed his eyes and concentrated, trying to pull himself out of the fantasy.

"You can't go," she said.

He ignored her, reciting the mantra to relax himself. "Peace of body. Peace of mind." He repeated the phrase several times, but nothing happened.

He could feel his heart racing. No, he shouldn't feel this way. He shouldn't feel *anything* here. What was happening to him?

"You're here to stay now," said Janice. "You and me, together forever." She tossed one of the blocks into the air.

Terry ran to the living room at the front of the apartment, to the door where he'd entered. He gripped the knob, but it didn't turn. He kicked and pushed it, but nothing happened. "Let me out!" he cried. "Let me out let me out let me out!"

Janice giggled behind him. He turned to see her standing there, arms behind her back, wide and innocent eyes looking up at him. She grinned awkwardly, the way people did when they got photographs taken, showing too many teeth.

"Leave me alone!" he shouted.

She shook her head, still grinning. "You don't mean it. I know you don't."

He tried to open the door again, but it was no good. The damned thing wouldn't budge. He screamed and punched it. Why couldn't he leave?

"Because you don't want to," said Janice.

"Liar," he said. "Get away from me!"

"No, I won't," she said. "This is my home, and you can't make me."

"This isn't a game!"

"Says you!" She walked over and pushed him, knocking him to the floor. He stared at her in disbelief. She touched him and he felt it. The pressure of her fingertips, the force of her arm. Unbelievable. "You can't boss me around!" she said, placing her foot against his neck.

He tried to move, but couldn't. The weight was too much, like a thousand bricks pressing on his body. He screamed.

"You should just go ahead and die," she told him. "No one will care."

"Shut up!" he shouted.

She ignored him. "They all hated you anyway. You couldn't even do the mission right. Alex and Cole died. Roland, too. You didn't save any of them." Her voice grew deeper and thicker as she spoke, and her eyes changed from a light gray to a deep blue.

"Stop it!" he cried.

"Mei and John are dead, you know," she said as her face began to morph. "They died trying to get away…died from the explosion you caused. It was all your fault."

"No," he said, wheezing through the pressure in his neck.

She laughed, but it was no longer Janice. The definition in her face had changed as her skin turned into putty, molding into something else. Within seconds, her hair receded and she grew much taller. Her clothes transformed into those of an academy student. "Poor little Terry," it said in a familiar voice.

Terry gripped the boot and tried to push it off.

The empty face grew eyes and a nose, forming definition like a painting come to life. It was a boy. A child from his nightmares. "You could never save anyone," said Alex. His dark blue eyes stared at Terry. "Not me or anyone else."

Terry gasped for air beneath Alex's foot. "No!"

"Don't pretend with me," said the dead boy. He chuckled, lifting his shoe from Terry's neck and backing away. He clapped his hands. "Remember what I told you before I died?"

The words entered Terry's mind without him asking, circling like water in a drain. *You're like me,* they said.

"I'm not," said Terry, slamming his fist on the floor.

Alex chuckled. "Come on, man. Don't lie to yourself."

"You tried to kill me. You tried to kill Mei and John. You wanted to. Even after we helped you. But I had to…I had to stop you. I never wanted it to end that way. I never wanted you to..."

"To die?" asked Alex.

Terry got to his feet. "I tried to save you! I tried to stop it. But all you wanted was to hurt people. Why? Why couldn't you stop? Tell me! Tell me why!"

"Because you were weak," said Alex. "Because I wanted to. I don't know."

Terry screamed, throwing himself at the dead boy, wrapping his hands around Alex's neck and flinging him to the floor. Alex didn't try to resist. He only laughed. Terry punched his face. "Stop!" he yelled, but Alex continued grinning. Blood ran from the boy's split lips, pooling on the brown carpet.

Through red and white teeth, Alex laughed. "You're a failure!" he screamed. "A failure a failure a failure a failure! Couldn't save me and you can't save yourself!"

Terry grabbed him by the neck. "No one could save you! You were insane! I tried everything, but you wouldn't stop. You wouldn't…." Tears filled his eyes. "Now you…"

Alex frowned. "Now, I'm dead," he said. "Me and Cole. Dead dead dead."

Terry paused, then shook his head. "No," he muttered. "It was your own fault. Both of you. It wasn't mine. It wasn't my fault!"

Alex's face disappeared, melting into mush before the rest of his body followed, disintegrating into the tiled floor, leaving nothing behind.

Terry stood there, gasping, huffing air and sweating.

"You're being silly," said Janice's voice inside his head.

He glanced around, but no one was there.

"Why are you fighting?" she asked. "I thought you loved me."

"Leave me alone!" he screamed.

"Never," she whispered into his ear. Her hot breath made him flinch and turned to see her standing there. "I can't leave my big brother all alone."

"Stop it," he said. "You aren't her. You aren't my sister. The real Janice is home and alive. You're just a *thing*. Not real. Just a thing inside my head, and it's time for you to go."

"Real *enough*," she said.

Maybe she had been once. Back when he was alone in the jungle and needed her, but no longer. Not anymore. He shook his head and closed his eyes, taking a breath and releasing it slowly. "Get out."

The girl tilted her head, staring at him with a blank expression. "Meanie," she said, and bits of her skin dripped like mud from her cheeks, splashing into the floor. "Meanie, meanie,

meanie." She took a step back. Clumps of hair fell from her head, vanishing in the air. "You'll be sorry. So sorry so...*sorry*..."

She collapsed, hitting the floor with a loud squish as her flesh dissolved into a puddle. The pile sank into the tiles, fizzling like acid. The smell hit him and he cringed. Rotting eggs and wilted leaves. He shuffled backwards to the door, grabbing the knob and turning. It opened.

He left the house and emerged into the valley. When he looked behind him, he found the apartment gone without a trace. Good riddance.

He sat on the ground, crossing his legs and closing his eyes. He would not come here again, not to this world. The next time he meditated, he would make another one, completely separate. Nothing like this place, but something better.

Something new.

17

Ortego Outpost File Logs
Play Audio File 652
Recorded: February 1, 2351

THISTLE: *Sergeant Finn, are you receiving? Johnny, say something if you can hear me.*

FINN: *Hey, boss, sorry for the noise. I'm reading you now.*

THISTLE: *Damn radio. Why the hell aren't you using the camp's com?*

FINN: *We think it might be bugged, sir. I couldn't risk anyone snooping.*

THISTLE: *Bugged? Why would anyone tap your com system?*

FINN: *Did you get the report I sent you? It's all in there.*

THISTLE: *Uh, yeah, I did, but I'm not sure what half of this is. By* *the look of it, it sounds like you're telling me those scientists you're with accidentally made a portal to another planet. But that's crazy.*

FINN: *I agree, but it's true. They really did.*

THISTLE: *Well, shit.*

FINN: *I know.*

THISTLE: *So this other stuff here about the alien tech…you mean to tell me this is right, too?*

FINN: *Far as we can tell, yeah.*

THISTLE: *Damn.*

FINN: *I know it's a little out there, but stick with me. When we opened the portal, we saw all those alien machines and stuff, but we also found an old military-issued pack.*

THISTLE: *A pack? You didn't say anything in the report about finding lost gear.*

FINN: *I wanted to tell you myself, sir. Too important.*

THISTLE: *Alright, go on with it, son. What happened?*

FINN: *You remember four years ago when my original squad blew up the Ortego building?*

THISTLE: *Hard to forget.*

FINN: *When that happened, we lost someone.*

THISTLE: *You're talking about Mara Echols' boy.*

FINN: *Terry. Right.*

THISTLE: *You mean to tell me you found his gear?*

FINN: *Better than that, boss. We think he's still alive.*

THISTLE: *Alive? How?*

FINN: *The pack was filled with equipment from over there. A knife made from bone. Some kind of old fruit. A few rags. None of it came from here.*

THISTLE: *Well, I'll be.*

FINN: *The only problem is Doctor Tremaine's trying to shut the portal down. She wants to blow it up. If we don't take action and get the brass involved, we'll lose the chance to bring Terry home.*

THISTLE: *I get what you're saying, Johnny, but how are you planning to convince Colonel Ross?*

FINN: *This is the son of Mara Echols, one of her best friends, right? She'll help us. If you need some extra push, explain how bringing home a hero would boost morale to an all-time high.*

THISTLE: *Ha, listen to you sounding like a politician. Alright, Johnny. You've got a deal. I'll get this info to Ross and see what we can do to help.*

FINN: *Thank you, sir. There's just one more thing.*

THISTLE: *What is it?*

FINN: *When she gives the green light on this, I want it to be my team.*

THISTLE: *You sure about that? Could be dangerous.*

FINN: *If it means bringing my friend home, boss, I'll take the risk.*

End Audio File

Ortego Reconstruction Outpost
February 1, 2351

Mei used John's remote communicator to contact the Matron's office. This allowed her to get a message to Mara Echols without having to worry about Tremaine reading over her shoulder. She explained the situation, emphasizing the evidence for Terry and how she believed he was still alive. The message went through successfully, but there was no immediate response.

The wireless com John brought from Central worked off of the military towers, rather than those used by the Science Division. She had to stay within a kilometer of them to send and receive, which meant taking a drive, parking, and waiting. She had no other choice. If she left the area, she'd never receive the response. Instead, she sat in the dirt cab, falling asleep in the process.

But after four and a half hours, a response did come.

"Doctor Curie, are you receiving us?" asked a voice on the other end.

The noise woke her, and she fumbled with the controls in an effort to reorient herself. "Here," she said, wheezing. "I'm here. I'm here!"

"Doctor Curie, this is Mara Echols. I understand you have some information regarding my son."

Mei's chest fluttered nervously. So the message really had reached the Matron after all. "Yes, ma'am," said Mei, trying to keep her composure. "We found his equipment. Did you get the documents I sent?"

"I have, yes," said the Matron. "My staff has spent the last few hours trying to verify your claims, but things have proven difficult. The Science Division is denying all knowledge of this wormhole or anything involving Terrance."

"Doctor Tremaine wants me to destroy the gate. She believes

the risk is too high," said Mei. "But I promise you, everything I've said is true! The information in those documents is accurate to the letter."

There was a short pause on the other end of the com. "I believe you, Doctor. Don't worry. When I couldn't get in touch with Tremaine, I contacted Colonel Ross. She managed to shed some light on your situation. Though, honestly, she only found out about this a few hours ago herself."

"Yes, ma'am. All of this information was considered classified under Section Nine of the Stone Charter."

"I suppose this means you're breaking the law by giving this to me," said Echols.

Mei hesitated. Despite knowing what she was doing, the treason part never quite occurred to her. "I'm not sorry, Matron," she finally said.

"I would hope not. It would be a shame for you to back out right when I'm about to give you my full support."

Mei's eyes widened. Did she hear her right? Her full support? She couldn't hardly believe it. "I don't know what to say."

"Say you'll bring my son home, Doctor." Her voice wavered as she spoke, a peek behind the curtain. She was the Matron, certainly, but she was also a mother.

Mei gulped. "Terry was my friend," she said. "He's why I'm here." She'd never told anyone that, not even John, but it was the truth. Pure and absolute.

"Then find him for us both," said the Matron. "Whatever it takes."

Ortego Reconstruction Outpost
February 2, 2351

Mei Curie sat on a slab of metal debris, staring into the solar fields. The light of the morning sun beamed a soft hue of amber across the panels as they lay there motionless, the same as they had these last four years. She stared into it, her mind free of worry and stress. She hadn't felt this way in months. She took a deep, cold breath and sighed, a puff of warm fog escaping her lips and dissolving in air.

She had done it.

In less than an hour, a squad of armed soldiers would arrive at her camp, not to arrest her but to assist. They would go through the rift and search for her friend. With any luck, they would find him.

As a scientist, Mei understood the odds were not in her favor. She would likely never see Terry again, or if she did, it might only be a corpse.

She didn't give a damn. The world had taken enough from her. She wouldn't give it the satisfaction of taking this. Not without a fight.

She would search the stars for Terry if she had to, because they were family. They had been born together, and she would not let him die alone.

Somewhere in Kant
February 2, 2351

THE GUARDS CAME in the morning to Ludo's cell. They dragged him through the hall, laughing as they went. They took him to another place to interrogate and to beat him. Terry listened from his little room, helpless.

Two hours later, they brought him back, tossing him into the cell and slamming the door behind them. "Won't be long until he's dead," said one of the guards.

The other chuckled as they left.

Every day Terry wondered if this would be the last time. The final beating before the execution. But Ludo continued to deny them.

Terry wished he could be so strong.

"Terry," muttered Ludo from his cell. His breathing was weak and garbled, like his mouth was full of blood.

"I'm here. Are you alright?"

"How is your meditation going?" he asked, ignoring the question.

"I'm making progress," he said, leaving out the part about fighting his imaginary sister.

"You have done well," said Ludo. "Your chakka is clean. I sense it. Today you are lighter, stronger. Today I—" He coughed violently and wheezed. "—Today I will teach you to fly."

"Ludo, you need to rest, please," said Terry. "You sound—"

"There is no time for that," insisted Ludo. "We don't have long before they take us, before they…" He paused.

"What?"

"It does not matter. Listen to me and understand. Please."

Terry sighed. "Okay," he said. "What do you want me to do?"

"Prepare yourself," said Ludo.

So Terry did. He sat against the wall, closed his eyes, and concentrated. Together, the two men recited the mantras.

Terry let his mind go numb and empty, easier now than ever before. What had once taken him hours now took only seconds, and in a moment, the prison cell evaporated into nothing, replaced by a void as empty as the space between the stars. He stood in the place his dream had been, in the spot where he had killed the little girl, and from this, he built again.

And in an instant, another world was born.

In a vast plain, on a planet with two suns, Terry sat outside of a farmhouse, staring at the horizon. None of it was real, but he didn't care. The old world he'd created didn't work out so well, but it was based on a long-forgotten life. This one felt more like home now. This one felt right.

"Terry," called a voice from the air—Ludo, talking to him from the real world.

"I'm here, Ludo," said Terry.

"Do you see the things you have made?"

"I do."

"What are they?"

Terry listed his creations as he had made them. He began with the sky, the suns, the grass, and the trees. He listed the insects, the animals, the birds, and even the fish in the sea.

"Now, look at these things. There are many, and they are yours. But now you must build more. Fill this place until it is overflowing. Until your mind is stretched, and you can barely contain what you see."

So Terry did. He created thousands of individual animals, insects, birds, and fish, and counted them and remembered them all. In the valley, there were deer and lions, beavermites and cheches. Every animal he could conceive of, a hundred thousand creatures from across two worlds, brought together in a young man's mind.

When he came to the point where he could barely sustain their numbers, he wavered. "Now what?" he asked.

"How many do you see?"

He did not need to count them, for he knew the answer without thinking. "Sixty thousand, eight hundred and twelve," he said.

There was a short pause. "Remarkable," muttered Ludo.

"What?"

"Nothing," he said quickly. "Do you feel the strain?"

"Yes."

"Good. Hold this for as long as you can."

So he did, and it felt like days. The pressure of the thousands built upon his mind like the weight of a mountain. He fought the urge to let go, knowing how far he had already come. To do so would mean defeat, but most of all, it would mean Janice was right. So he did not relent.

As he sat there in the valley, a fleet of creatures surrounding him, encapsulating him, a swell of pain moved through his body, beginning in his feet and rising until it found his chest. He took shorter and heavier breaths, and for a moment, he thought he might black out.

Yet, he could not stop. Not until he—

A cold breeze hit him, caressing his lips and cheeks, bringing a calmness. He paused at the sensation, here in this place where there should be none.

Suddenly, the agony left him, draining like water from a jug, and he was empty. He wondered if perhaps the animals had vanished, if he'd somehow lost them…but such was not the case. The valley and sky were as full of life as ever, not a single creature missing. Only the strain was gone. Only the weight of the world.

He stood and walked, and he felt the tips of the grass beneath his bare feet and the morning dew which covered every blade. Another gust of wind blew, tugging his face and filling his ears, bringing the smell of Variant, sweet and pure. The light of the suns beat against his face and forearms, warming him.

He sensed it all as though it were real.

Maybe it was.

"Open your eyes, Terry," said the farmer from beyond the sky. "Then, you will know what it means to fly."

Come and see.

Terry opened his eyes. He sat in the light of a rising moon as it pierced his barred window and filled the darkness of his cell. Flakes of dust fell from the ancient stone, swirling in the silver beams like leaves in a storm.

Outside his cell, a guard grunted, and Terry knew exactly where the man was. Twelve meters down the hall, tapping his holster and biting his lip. Terry saw him without seeing, heard the beating of his heart like thunder in his chest.

Two floors above, the boot of a guard pressed firmly against the floor, followed by another. This one was walking, marching to…to somewhere…a dining room with forks and plates, bustling chefs and laughing men. The smell of bread and soup, hot and spicy like the chili Terry's mother used to make. He could taste it in the air, and his stomach ached.

Far from the prison, deep inside the surrounding woods, a beavermite gnawed on the bark of a wooden stump, searching for food. Another squeaked nearby. A baby, begging for its dinner.

Terry saw every one of them. All he had to do was listen.

His time in the second world had given him focus, improved his ability to draw his strength. But he no longer felt the urge to run or fight. All of this, it came from something else.

Peace and tranquility. A quiet stillness.

He had to tell Ludo about this, to thank him for his guidance. Without him, he never would have been able to—

But Ludo wasn't there. Terry listened through the barrier of stone, but heard nothing. No movement, no breathing. He was gone.

Or worse. Those men had beaten him so much for so long. Maybe he was finally—

Terry stopped himself. Worrying would do nothing. He had to stay focused. Stay in this moment and search. Find his friend. He scanned the building, listening for the sound of Ludo's voice, for whatever sign of the farmer's life he could find.

He listened through the halls and along the staircases, passing through dozens of people in the process. Some were laughing, snarling, coughing, sleeping, eating, talking, fighting. An orchestra of noise bleeding through the walls. Terry hushed them soon, filtering the hundreds, searching for the one.

Then he found him in the corner of a room, high above the rest. A gasping farmer, whispering a prayer.

"The Eye save me," muttered Ludo, and then a stick fell against his neck.

"Coward, thief, and traitor," said Gast Madeen, the man with the purple eyes. "You are not worthy to speak such words."

Ludo's pulse was slowing, his breathing quick and fading.

It was time to go.

Terry turned his attention to the six guards in the hall—two talking and three alone, one sitting on a bench and drinking.

He walked to his door, touched the metal with the tips of his fingers. The steel was ten centimeters thick, too tough to break through on a normal day.

He took a step back. He didn't know if he could do this, but there was no other choice. Time to test these so-called wings. He formed a pair of fists and plunged himself at the door. The walls shook and the metal bent. The guards stopped what they were doing and looked in his direction.

He tried a second time, plowing into the barrier with the strength of his entire being, and this time, pieces of stone broke from the metal, falling to the floor like breadcrumbs. He did not relent. The guards arrived and shouted for him to stop, panic running through their bodies. Hearts racing. Blood pumping.

Terry pushed again. "What's he doing?" yelled a man. "The door is breaking!"

"Stop! Stop!"

"Get your weapons ready!"

With a final push, Terry broke the door free, separating it from the wall. The metal exploded into three of the guards, knocking them against the hallway. The others stood gawking for a second before reaching for their guns. They aimed and opened fire.

Terry fell to his side, trying to avoid them. The first two missed, hitting the floor and wall. The third hit him in the arm, but there was no pain.

He leapt at the men, kicking one in the stomach and knocking him several meters away. He gripped the other two by the neck and squeezed, throwing them both to the side against the nearby cell. They did not get up.

He glanced at the place in his arm where the bullet hit him and found there was no blood. Had he been mistaken? Had the bullet missed? He wasn't sure.

No time to think. He had to find Ludo.

Terry ran swiftly through the corridors, curving around the corner and into the stairwell. He climbed to the second floor, encountering a group of four guards along the way.

He didn't stop, though, not for a second. He leapt from the stairs, hurdling over them. With the heel of his foot, he kicked one in the head, and landed behind the others. Before they could turn to see him, he hurled his body at theirs, flinging them against the far wall like stones. They landed in a pile, motionless.

When he reached the third floor and entered the next room, he found another swarm of soldiers. Unlike the last group, these did not hesitate. Instead, they drew their weapons and took aim. At the head of them were two familiar faces. Red and Scar. "What are you doing here?" asked Scar, squeezing the grip of his gun. "How did you get out?"

"Let me by," said Terry.

Red scoffed. "Why would we do such a thing?"

"I'm taking my friend and leaving," said Terry. "Let me go, and there won't be a problem."

"You mean the traitor?" asked Scar. He looked at Red. "He means to go through us."

Together they laughed.

"Fine, have it your way," said Terry, and dove at the nearest soldier. He hit the guard in his chest, slamming him against another and sending them both to the floor. He took the gun in the man's hand and swung it around, slamming the butt of the weapon into another guard's nose. Blood splattered into the air, landing on Scar's chest.

"Stop him!" cried Scar, firing his weapon.

Terry was already moving. He leapt at the others, bullets hitting his legs and arms, though he felt nothing. He threw his fist into one man's cheek, breaking it. With a firm kick, he knocked the wind from another. Then, he turned his eyes to the two brothers, to his would-be captors.

"You will let me through," said Terry.

Scar unsheathed a knife. It was Ludo's blade, the one he had called *sacred.* The one he had ordered Terry to find and use against Gast at the farm. "You will die now, little boy."

Terry didn't give a damn about the knife, whatever it was, and he attacked without a second thought. Scar dodged, jumping a few steps to the side. Terry ran headfirst into the wall, missing his target.

Red plowed into him with his shoulder, but Terry barely felt it. He took the man by his wrist and twisted, and Red fell to his knees, crying out in pain. "Stop!" he begged.

"Let me through," said Terry once more.

Behind him, Scar was moving, shuffling his feet against the floor to right himself. Terry could sense him coming, so he released Red and stepped away. Scar swiped the dagger and missed, cutting the air.

"Stand still," ordered Scar.

Terry said nothing.

"Kill him already," said Red, clutching his wrist.

"I intend to," said Scar. He twirled the knife in his hand and the metal shimmered, reflecting a distant beam of moonlight. He stepped towards Terry, swiping the knife at him chaotically. Terry dodged, letting the blade slide within centimeters of his arm, feeling the wind. When the weapon was down, he kicked Scar's hand, knocking the knife free. Scar looked at him in shocked anger, then charged, wrapping his arms around Terry's chest and forcing him aside.

Red ran for the sacred vessel, taking it in his good hand.

Terry wrestled with Scar, turning him on his back and holding him. Terry pressed his knees into the man's chest. "Just leave me alone," Terry told him.

Scar spit, hitting Terry across his chin.

Behind them, Red lunged with the knife outstretched. Terry sighed and slid to the side, avoiding him, but in the process, Red fell forward, tripping onto his friend.

The tip of the blade sliced into Scar's neck.

Blood flowed quickly from the torn flesh, and Scar clasped the wound with both his hands. But it was no good. He writhed and twitched as air bubbles formed in the crimson river, stealing the life from him. He tried to scream, but all he could do was gargle as his own blood filled his lungs. He sounded like he was drowning.

Red stared in disbelief as his friend lay dying.

Terry backed away toward the wall.

Scar stopped moving rather quickly. As the last breath left his body, Red called out his name. "Garis."

Terry stared at Red. "Leave now," he said.

Red's eyes were filled with tears. "You killed him," he said in disbelief.

"You did," said Terry.

Red looked at his hands, then at the place where the knife had entered his brother. "No," he muttered.

"Leave."

Red got to his feet and backed away. He looked at Scar, then at Terry. Without another word, he turned and ran, escaping through the stairwell.

Terry waited for him to leave, then knelt beside Scar's body. He pulled the knife from the man's neck, releasing more blood. He was going to need this.

The door slammed open, hitting the wall with the sound of a lion's roar. Terry stepped forward.

He looked in the corner where Ludo lay, bound and tied by metal shackles. He was still breathing. At the other end stood Gast Madeen. Purple Eyes. One of the high priests of Xel and Lord of Three Waters. "So you're the one making all the noise," said Gast. He raised his wrinkled brow.

"Gast," muttered Terry.

The old man smiled. "How nice to be remembered."

"Let him go," demanded Terry.

"But I'm not done with this one," he said, motioning to Ludo.

"You are now," said Terry.

"You speak with such confidence. All this from the same child I fought in the grasslands."

"Things are different."

"Are they?" asked Gast, tilting his head. "I told you once that our lives *repeat*. You have lived this moment before. What makes you think it will be different?"

"Because I'm different," said Terry, and he lunged across the room at Gast. *Gotta make this quick, before he has a chance to—*

The old man dodged, touching Terry's arm with the edge of his palm, throwing him into the wall.

Terry caught himself, kicked off the stone, and turned back around. Gast grabbed him by the leg, slamming him to the floor, knocking the wind from him.

"I see you've brought the vessel," said Gast, nodding at the dagger in Terry's hand. "Took it from my son, did you?"

Terry wheezed, trying to collect himself. He shuffled back.

"You think because you've learned to fly, it means you're special. I am a high priest of Xel. My chakka is pure. My wings are wide. I fly with the strength of the Eye. You're like a newborn to me. An infant bird."

Terry got to his feet. "Shut up," he muttered and ran at him for the second time.

The old man dodged again, but this time Terry didn't try to hit him. Instead, he kept going forward.

Terry found Ludo in the corner, blood on his face and neck. He cut the rope binding his friend's hands and gave him the knife to finish the rest. "Stay back," said Terry, and swung around to place himself between the two.

Gast looked surprised. "You'd protect a dying man?" he asked.

Terry didn't answer. He dove with a low kick, hitting Gast in the leg and stealing his balance. The high priest pivoted and caught himself, countering with another kick to Terry's side, flinging him into the far side of the room.

Terry shifted his weight in the air, landing on his feet and hands. As he did, he saw his enemy fast approaching.

Gast launched high above Terry, extending his knee as he descended. Terry rolled and the knee hit the floor, shattering the stone tiles into dust.

This wasn't going to be easy.

"Stop moving so much," commanded Gast. He dashed at Terry, hitting him in the stomach.

Terry flew backwards from the blow, striking the wall. He got up immediately, no worse for it.

"You want to die then?" asked Gast, sighing. He reached under his clothing and revealed a knife similar to Ludo's. "I didn't want to kill you, but you aren't leaving me much of a choice."

Crap, thought Terry.

In a flash, Gast was on him. The weapon came at Terry's neck, but he grabbed the man's wrist with both his hands, barely deflecting it. The knife slid to the side, slicing Terry's arm and ripping his clothes. A warm stream of blood ran along his arm.

Gast did not let up. He hit Terry with the force of a wrecking ball, cutting into his shoulder like a piece of cooked meat. Terry fell to the floor.

The room distorted. His focus wavered.

Gast stepped forward, grinning at his prey. "Poor boy. Look at you." He grinned a thin smile. "I told you this would happen. I told you life repeats. You should have—"

An arm reached around Gast's neck, squeezing him. Another slammed a knife into his shoulder. The priest moaned and twisted, blood spewing from his flesh.

Ludo, half broken and bleeding, fell off the man and onto his knees. The knife dislodged and landed in the crevice of the broken tile near Terry.

"You!" cried Gast, rage in his eyes. He gripped Ludo by the throat, raising him off the floor. "Have your death if you want it so badly."

This was it. Everything was over. Ludo was going to die. Terry tried to concentrate, to call on his strength again. The pain from the knife was too much. He—

The knife. It was there, a few steps from him. If he tried, maybe he could reach it. There wasn't much time.

Terry scrambled to the blood-soaked vessel. He grasped it with both his hands, fumbling with it for a moment before managing to steady his grip. Then, with every ounce of strength he could gather, he launched himself at the enemy.

Gast reacted quickly, dropping Ludo and turning to face the attack, but he was not fast enough. The knife pierced the old man's back below the shoulder.

He backhanded Terry, knocking him down. "Enough!" cried Gast, trying to reach behind to dislodge the blade.

Before he could grasp it, Ludo gripped the handle and twisted it. Gast screamed.

Ludo withdrew the blade and stabbed him over and over. Again and again.

Gast dropped his own weapon, staggering to the floor, breathing heavily. Ludo, his eyes swollen with pain, did not hesitate with what came next.

The sacred vessel, guided by the hand of its owner, burrowed into the neck of the Lord of Three Waters, into the flesh of the man with the purple eyes.

Gast's entire body fell against the tiles, soaking the stone with his blood, spraying crimson like rain in a thunderstorm. The hot liquid pooled around Ludo's toes as he stood watching.

Gast's eyes twitched, and he smiled a crooked smile. "Everything repeats," he whispered. His lips trembled, and his eyes grew cold. A sigh left him, and a moment later he was still.

Terry ran to his friend, taking him by the shoulders. He looked like he was about to pass out. "I've got you," he said.

"I killed him," said the farmer, his voice shaking. "I never wanted to. He was Ysa's flesh. He was Talo's blood. I never meant to take his ghost."

Ludo shook his head, staring at the dead man at his feet, at the body of the one who tried to kill them.

And he wept.

Terry had no idea how they were going to get out of the prison. He couldn't fight off an army, not after his encounter with Gast. Luckily, Scar's body was sitting in the next room in full uniform.

The other guards were also there, knocked out or otherwise. Ludo found one about his size and squeezed into the outfit with some success.

Scar didn't have a helmet, but there were a few sitting against the wall. Terry didn't know what the dress code was in a place like this. He'd only seen a few guards here and there, but he was willing to take the risk.

Ludo insisted on walking on his own until they were clear of the building, despite the immense pain from his wounds. He was right. If any of the guards saw Terry carrying him, they might ask what happened or worse. Better not to risk it.

Together, they descended the stairwell and entered the foyer. There were a few guards in one of the corners, but no one stopped them.

Outside, Terry saw the prison for the first time in its full complexity. The main building was three stories tall and roughly a hundred and fifty meters wide. Surrounding it were several smaller ones shaped like the domes in the abandoned village. Around all of this was a large wall half as tall as the main facility.

The gate was directly ahead of them. Two men were standing under it.

"Let me talk to them," said Ludo.

Terry nodded. *No argument here*, he thought.

"Where are you going?" asked one of the guards.

"The lord sends us to retrieve a debt," said Ludo.

"A debt from where?" asked the guard.

"One of the slaves has been sold to the Twelfth Temple in Riverside," he lied.

"Which one? Was it the foreigner?"

"The freak," said the second guard. "I heard he was hideous."

"The very same," said Ludo. "The lord held a private auction."

"I heard about it," said the first guard.

No you didn't, thought Terry.

"Very well," said the guard, smacking his chest. "Safe travels to you."

Ludo returned the greeting, and he and Terry walked through the archway and into the field outside.

When they were far enough away, beyond the sight of the camp, Ludo collapsed. Terry caught him, carrying him a fair distance before finally stopping.

They found a small place in the woods where the trees were thick and no one would see them. They removed the armor, which smelled like a rotting animal, and cast it into the brush.

They sat for a few hours, resting.

"What should we do?" asked Terry, after a while. "What comes next?"

"I must go and find Ysa," said Ludo.

"Where is she?"

"Gast sent her home to Riverside, but she will not be there for long. In truth, I fear she has already been moved."

"Why would they take her somewhere else?" asked Terry.

"The Festival of the Eye will be here soon. It is a month of celebration held near the border of Everlasting. Ysa will be there. But…"

"What's wrong?"

"The festival is deadly. Many are killed each year."

"How can it be so dangerous?"

Ludo looked at the ground. "The borders of Everlasting are filled with guardians, great demons with unparalleled strength. Not even Ysa's wings can stand against them."

Was Ludo being serious? Demons? There was no way. "We can find her," said Terry, ignoring the superstition.

"I would not ask this of you, my friend," said Ludo.

Terry beat his chest. "You don't need to. I won't abandon this family."

Ludo smiled through his swollen cheeks. "I'm glad I met you that day in the field."

"Me, too," said Terry, and it was the truth.

Terry thought about the prison and the man called Gast Madeen. The words he told him about how life repeats, how every moment comes again, whether we realize it or not. Terry thought about his own life, the path he'd taken from his family's two-story apartment to standing in the forest of another planet, beaten and bruised.

He moved through life like a stone across a river, touching occasionally but never stopping. Always leaving someone behind. Was this his fate? Would he ever stop moving?

Of course he would. Just because events repeated, it didn't mean they couldn't change. Purple Eyes was dead, killed by the hand of a farmer. The moment had come again, but the details were different.

Anything could happen.

When the light of the two suns had faded into a red glow on the distant horizon, the two men stood and walked, heading to the north along the far-stretched road to Everlasting.

They went with uncertainty and doubt. They went with broken bodies and fractured hearts.

But they did so together.

And somehow it was enough.

18

Ortego Outpost File Logs
Play Audio File 669
Recorded: February 2, 2351

TREMAINE: *Who is this? Put Curie on the line immediately.*

MITCHELL: *This is Sophia Mitchell, apprentice grade three. I'm sorry but Doctor Curie is unable to come to the com right now. May I take a message?*

TREMAINE: *Now you listen to me, little girl—*

MITCHELL: *I am listening.*

TREMAINE: *You put Curie on here right this minute! Do you have any idea who this is?*

MITCHELL: *Yes, of course I know who you are, Doctor Tremaine.*

TREMAINE: *Then you should know full well to do as I say.*

MITCHELL: *Yes, ma'am. I completely respect and acknowledge your* *authority. Unfortunately, Doctor Curie is not here at the moment and is therefore unable to come and speak with you.*

***TREMAINE**: Don't give me that! I know exactly what she's been doing, and I won't have any of it. Do you understand? She can't break the law and go behind my back to Ross and Echols. There are consequences.*

***MITCHELL**: Yes, ma'am. Consequences. I'll be sure to let her know.*

***TREMAINE**: Wait until I clear this mess up. I'll make sure both of you wind up in the slums working in sanitation. Is that what you want, Mitchell?*

***MITCHELL**: Not particularly, ma'am, no. But as I've already explained, there simply isn't a thing I can do presently. Again, I apolog—*

End Audio File

Ortego Reconstruction Outpost
February 2, 2351

John smiled when he saw his team pull up, their gear in tow. He waved at them only to be met with a crude hand gesture from Private Hessex. John chuckled and returned the unofficial salute. Thanks to Captain Thistle's suggestion to Colonel Ross, the 1st Strategic Operations Functional Team had finally arrived.

"Looks like SOFT is here," said Bart, approaching from the side. He grinned when John glared at him. "I kid."

John nodded towards the second cab where Jackson,

Armstrong, and Hughes were unloading their packs. "See the kid in the rear there?"

Bart nodded.

"That's Mason Hughes. He's small, maybe a buck forty on a good day, but check out the stick on his back."

"The gun? What about it?"

"It's an SRS 445 rifle with an effective firing distance of over thirty-six hundred meters," said John. "They call it the Golden Ticket."

"Why?"

"One way trip to Hell," said John. "And Hughes there, he can hit the fang off a baby rab from two klicks away. He's the best. All my guys are."

Bart raised his hands. "Okay, okay, no SOFT jokes, but there goes half my material," he said, frowning. "Got another name?"

"Every squad has a nickname. There's the Guns, the Collectors, the Leatherheads, and so on," explained John. "We're the Blacks."

"Why the Blacks?" asked Bart.

"Colonel Ross thought it'd be funny," he said.

"How's that funny?"

"Jack Black was a famous rat-catcher during the bubonic plague. He became the poster child for exterminators," said John. "I guess Ross thought since we spent most of our time hunting down the local razorback population, we'd appreciate the humor."

"Seems like the name stuck," said Bart.

"The good ones usually do."

Private Jefferson waved to John and tossed him a pack. "Your stuff, LT."

John caught the bag and slung it over his shoulder, buckling the straps with a hard *click*. He watched as his troops assembled before him, their weapons at the ready, filing into formation. It had been a long time since he'd seen any of them. Almost a year, in fact. But standing here now, looking at each of their faces, it felt as though he hadn't been away at all.

"Good to see you, boys," he said with a wide grin. "Been a while."

After talking with the squad, John went to find Mei. She was sitting near the solar field on the other side of camp. As he approached, she smiled at him. He beamed and soon joined her.

They sat quietly together for a few minutes. Mei hugged his arm and placed her head on his shoulder. The wind stopped soon, and it was quiet. He heard her breathing, licking her lips as though she were about to speak.

"You did good," he said, beating her to it.

She hesitated, then smiled. "So did you."

"I do what my girlfriend tells me," he said.

She punched him in the thigh. "Don't try to play the victim with me."

"Anything you say, boss!"

Mei rolled her eyes, but John immediately wrapped his arms around her. They both grew still and quiet, breathing softly together. After a few moments, John pressed his face against her hair, taking a deep breath and closing his eyes.

She smelled like lavender shampoo, like earth and hydrazine. It was something he'd grown accustomed to in the months they'd spent together here, this blend of femininity and industry, and he wanted to remember it.

Just in case.

JOHN WAITED outside the Ortego ruins, fully geared, surrounded by his team.

Mei and her people were in the basement configuring the rods, getting them ready to open the portal. It wasn't possible for the Blacks to wear their gear as well as the radiation suits, so compromises had to be made. As such, the portal would have to be opened ahead of time to reduce the local radiation, remaining open until the area was clear, and the danger was gone. Mei said an hour ought to do the trick, and she seemed confident the rods would hold. John wasn't a scientist like the others, but he believed in Mei. He always had.

When the time came, John called his people to the basement. The Blacks descended into the ancient catacombs of the Ortego building, quiet and quick. They swept through the lower level and filed into the portal room. The Blacks would now stay in their assigned positions, utterly silent and awaiting orders. Whenever John gave the signal, they would breach the other side of the portal. Until then, they would wait. No complaints. No questions.

Mei was standing by in her radiation suit. She stared up at John, a look of concern in her eyes.

"You okay?" he asked.

"I should be asking you that," she said. "You're the one who's about to go across the universe to who-knows-where."

He nodded. "I've already made the trip once. Guess I'm not too worried now."

She frowned. "Still…"

"Don't worry," he said.

She stared at him for a moment. "I'd remove this suit if I could, but the top doesn't come off."

"Why would you do that?" he asked.

She dropped her eyes, the way she did when she was embarrassed. In a better light, she might have even blushed. "Well…" she muttered, trailing off. "I, uh…"

"What's wrong?"

She furrowed her brow. "I'd kiss you, you big idiot."

He laughed, then took her hand in his. He bent down and kissed her visor, knowing how cheesy it must have looked. "I'll see you after a while."

Mei smiled, nodding, and released his hand. She backed away and sighed. "Sophie, what's the status of the portal?"

"Holding," said Sophie.

She looked at John. "Remember, it'll be open again in three hours."

John nodded. He turned to face the rift, his team positioned. "Alright, boys," he barked. "Time to take a dive."

"Yes, sir!" they said in unison.

John took a breath. He was about to skip across the universe in an attempt to find his long lost friend and bring him back. The odds were against him. The whole thing barely made a lick of sense, but it sure was exciting.

"Breach!" he cried, his voice echoing through the basement walls. "Go!"

The Blacks filed through, their weapons aimed and hot. Two by two, they went, until John was the only one left.

He reaching the edge of the rift, but stopped and lingered. Looking over his shoulder, he saw Mei, standing there against the wall, gripping her pad between her arms, watching him. She had done all of this, made everything possible and brought him to this moment. She had done things no one else could, carried the weight of the world on her back. The portal, Terry, everything.

It was his turn now.

John faced the rift. He stared into the void, into both darkness and distance, into the other side of the universe, into the thing that killed the world.

And he walked through it.

EPILOGUE

Lena Sol watched as the data poured in from the recent excavation project in the South Sea. The digital files appeared as holograms in the air before her. With only a thought, she sorted through the documents, pulling up the summary report and magnifying the page for examination. The archeological dig had gone smoothly, resulting in several new artifacts which would soon be examined and subsequently stored in the archives. However, nothing of any true significance had been unearthed, making the bulk of the investigation somewhat fruitless.

Lena had little interest in archeology, but she was nonetheless displeased to see the lackluster results. As a citizen of Everlasting, her first priority was to the city and its people. It didn't matter what field the research was in, so long as it benefited their society. Everything else came second.

All was for the good of Everlasting.

A red emergency indicator blinked near the corner of her display. She closed the excavation file and activated the recording program—standard protocol when dealing with an emergency alert—and transferred the file to her personal visor.

A large energy discharge had occurred in the quarantine zone far to the west. Such an event was not unprecedented. Long ago, Everlasting had used this land as a testing site for early research projects but had since abandoned it. The native tribes in the area often stumbled upon caches of disregarded technology, accidentally activating them in the process. It was unfortunate but ultimately inconsequential to the welfare of the city's citizenry.

However, this blast was unusually large and had prompted the monitoring system to take further action by reporting the event to an analyst, who could then commit to more observation and request additional scans. Lena Sol was one such individual.

Her first thought was to examine the readings for evidence of an explosive, but quickly dismissed the idea. The defense system had likely already looked for such a thing. She would of course return to this idea if nothing else worked, but for now, protocol suggested she move on.

She initialized a detailed scan of the surrounding area, something which required the use of the Rosenthal satellite, which could only be accessed by a grade five analyst or higher. The satellite would observe and detail the movements of all detectable energy patterns in the affected area, dividing the findings into categories based on the level of relevance and triangulating the source of the event.

This would then permit the user to track and monitor the

incident in question and to assess the potential threat. The whole process took about three minutes.

While the system worked, she decided to see what other anomalies were recorded in the quarantine zone over the last three months. Again, standard protocol.

To her surprise, there had been almost a dozen similar events, but they had only lasted for a few minutes each. The system catalogued these and moved on, but with each additional event, the threat assessment rating grew.

Lena closed the file and called for the results of the scan from the Rosenthal satellite. The report showed a large emission of energy coming from underneath one of the unfinished, half-constructed settlements. These buildings were meant for housing and storage but were abandoned along with everything else in the quarantine zone roughly two centuries ago.

But Lena had never heard of an underground facility in this particular location. Odd, considering she'd memorized all four hundred and nineteen points of interest. Had she forgotten this one? Given her recall scores, it seemed unlikely, but she supposed anything was possible.

As a precaution, she called for a full list of her POIs and looked for any falling under the grid in question. 1103-29, 1103-30, 1103-31, and so on.

No matches for the location in question. How very odd. Had the site been blacklisted? Maybe. She'd never seen the practice herself, but there were stories from other analysts. Perhaps this location was one of them.

In any case, the next step was to determine whether further investigation was warranted, which she—

A light flashed on her display, followed quickly by an alert message.

Report to Master Analyst Foster Gel immediately.

Lena paused at the message. She'd never been called into Master Gel's office before. What could he possibly want from her?

Within seconds, another alert appeared. This time the words were larger.

She blinked. *Alert acknowledged*, she thought, and the message disappeared. She got to her feet and calmly left the room and proceeded to the elevator. "Floor sixty-eight," she said, once the doors were closed. The machine gave a light chime, accepting the command.

A few moments later, the doors opened, and she entered the entrance lounge—a large room which acted as a hub for all the department heads and their staff members. Despite only coming here a few times, she had no trouble navigating the halls to Gel's office. After all, she memorized the architecture of the building during her first year as a junior analyst.

On the way to his office, she passed the Office of Special Education and Rehabilitative Services, the Office of Compliance, the Department of Civil Protection, and the Department of Corrections. Each of them looked identical to the last, except for the plaque outside the door.

Once she was at her destination, she touched the scanner on

the wall and waited for it to verify her identity. A second later, the doors slid open.

"Analyst Sol?" asked a young man in a receptionist uniform. "Master Gel is waiting for you. Please proceed." He motioned to the back of the room to a paned glass window and another door.

She could see the master analyst on the other side of the glass, sitting behind his desk and talking to the air around him. He was probably in a meeting with someone on his visor.

Lena went to the door and waited to be recognized by her superior. He made eye contact with her within seconds but didn't acknowledge her arrival. She waited several minutes, presumably because he was still in the middle of his conversation and didn't want to be interrupted. She understood. He was an important man.

Finally, after about fifteen minutes, he removed his visor and motioned for her to enter and take a seat. She did, saying nothing. It was impolite for a subordinate to speak first.

"Thank you for responding so quickly to my invitation," said the master analyst.

"Yes, sir," she said.

"Do you know why you have been called to this office?" he asked.

"No, sir," she said.

"Would you care to speculate on the cause?"

She paused, trying to look as though she were giving it more thought. "I honestly cannot think of anything, sir," she said. Of course, this was a lie. She knew exactly why she was here. Discovering an energy anomaly at a potentially blacklisted site in the quarantine zone was not a common occurrence. Not as far as she was aware.

"You are here because you received a priority message from the defense system in regards to grid 1103. Is this accurate?"

"It is," she said.

"Did you find this report to be unconventional?" he asked.

"Yes, sir," she responded.

"Why?"

"Because the source of the discharge did not originate from a listed asset. The energy appears to have come from an underground facility, though there are no records of such a place in the database."

He nodded. "You are sure?"

"If the Rosenthal scans are to be believed, sir."

"Why do you think the site was unlisted?" he asked.

"A variety of reasons, sir, but I couldn't say with any certainty."

The master analyst took his visor and placed it over his eye. Immediately, his pupil dilated, indicating the neural connection.

His eyes left hers and seemed to focus on the air above the desk. "Lena Sol, level-5 analyst, eight years' experience beginning at age thirteen. Several commendations for excellence and dedication to service." He looked at her. "A superb portfolio. No infractions noted. You should be very proud."

"Thank you, sir."

"You seem to be quite adept at your station, Lena Sol," he said. "I have a hard time believing you don't have a single theory regarding this unusual event."

She stiffened.

"It's okay. Go ahead and tell me what you think. I assure you, I will not file a report."

She let out a small sigh. "Yes, sir."

"So what do you think?" he asked.

"There are a few possibilities. To begin with, the database may have simply been corrupted and never fixed. The scans are not as accurate when dealing with underground sites."

"And the other possibility?" asked Gel.

"Someone may have blacklisted the facility," she said.

"Have you ever heard of such a thing?" he asked.

She shook her head. "No, of course not."

"Really?" he asked. "I find that surprising. I hear rumors all the time."

She shifted in her seat. "I've heard a rumor or two, sir, but never anything believable."

"Would it bother you to learn those rumors were true?"

"If they were, I'm sure the government had its reasons." A non-answer, but a safe one. She was in dangerous territory.

"I agree. But such things, if they exist, would likely be considered classified and confidential. As a grade-5 analyst, you are several levels shy of receiving the necessary clearance to even speak about these matters."

Oh, no, she thought, feeling panicked. She shouldn't have said anything about a blacklisted site. What was she thinking?

Master Gel gave a thin smile. "Don't worry, Ms. Sol. You can relax. You are not being reprimanded. On the contrary, you're about to be promoted."

Her jaw fell. "Sir?"

"The fact of the matter is that you are correct. This is a classified location. You received this alert by accident through a fault in the system. It should not have gone to you. Policy states I have two options now. Either I can send you to a memory facility and have the information extracted, potentially damaging your brain in the process, or I can promote you and give you the necessary security clearance. Given your exemplary history with the department, I'd rather side with the latter. What do you think?"

"Y-Yes, thank you, sir," she said, struggling to get the words out.

"Very good," he responded. "Now, if you'll join me, please link your visor with mine, so I can finalize the promotion."

She did as he told her. A moment later, he called for a document to appear between them, detailing Lena's work history and current position as a level-5 systems analyst. In an instant, the title changed to level-9, causing Lena to gasp quite suddenly. She had never heard of anyone jumping four levels in a single promotion.

Master Gel removed his visor. "There," he said. "Now you are authorized to hear what I am about to tell you."

She didn't know what to say.

"As you have already surmised, Ms. Sol, the location you received is indeed blacklisted from lower level personnel. The question you're surely asking yourself is why? Are you aware of the history surrounding that area? I'm sure you know the general story about the tribal conflicts and toxicity of the land, yes?"

She nodded.

"All true," he assured her. "However, there's a little more to it. The reason behind the pollution and radiation has to do with the facility in question. You see, under the mountain is an abandoned city, largely undetectable. The only reason you were able to find it was because of the Rosenthal satellite, which was only recently launched." He shook his head. "It seems no one thought to delete the details of this location from the satellite's scans, but I suppose mistakes happen. Regardless, this facility exists and has been there for roughly two hundred and sixty years."

Two hundred and sixty years? Lena considered this. If Gel's math was accurate, then this place was the oldest structure in the quarantine zone by at least a decade.

Master Gel went on. "The purpose of this location was to carry out a wide variety of classified scientific research. Due to the dangers this work entailed, the order was given to establish an outpost far from Everlasting, should anything go wrong."

"What sort of work could be so dangerous?" asked Lena.

"There was a project," explained the master analyst. "An experiment dealing with cutting edge quantum theory, specifically aimed at discovering and potentially developing a means for matter transference through a singularity."

"Matter transference?" asked Lena.

"A wormhole," he replied. "A means of moving from one point to another, no matter the distance, in a matter of seconds."

"I see," she said, surprised.

"Indeed, but after a few decades of research, a discovery was made. Quite accidentally, I might add."

"What kind?" she asked.

"The dangerous sort," he said. "The scientists did indeed find a way to open a bridge, but what they found on the other side was not what they expected. In attempting to create a means of traveling great distances through space, they inadvertently opened a door to another universe. A separate reality, if you will."

"Another reality?" she asked, a little taken back. "Incredible."

"What followed was a disaster," said Gel. "The machine activated successfully, but the gate caused a power surge throughout the facility, damaging several systems in the process. This in turn caused an immediate containment breach in one of the fission reactors, which was our main source of energy at the time. The resulting radiation swept through the compound, killing everyone in a matter of minutes. Those who managed to escape died a few days later."

Lena was stunned. "Sir, this is…I don't know what to say."

"It's hard to believe, I know," he said. "The machine and the underground city associated with it were considered lost. The intense levels of radiation were beyond deadly, and the government at the time refused to risk more lives. Thirteen thousand people were lost that day."

"What happened to the portal, sir?"

"It was believed to have shut down after the power failure," said Gel. "With no energy to draw from, how could it continue working? But four years ago there was a disturbance, an energy spike which bore a striking resemblance to the signature of the portal. An investigation was performed, but there were no conclusive results. However, several theories have been surmised."

"What kind of theories?"

"That the portal was never closed," said the master analyst. "That it remained open for two hundred years, only shutting down on the day in question, when the energy surge occurred suddenly and without warning, right in the heart of the quarantine zone."

"Sir, would this be the same energy—"

"Yes," he answered. "The event from four years ago is identical to the one you stumbled upon only a short while ago. What's more, they have been occurring with some frequency these last few weeks, and as you might expect, we are concerned."

"Yes, sir," she said.

"Unfortunately, the Rosenthal satellite is not capable of giving us the status of the machine, nor can it detail the state of the facility. As such, we find ourselves in a situation requiring a more hands-on approach."

"You mean the government is looking to send a research team?" she asked.

"Exactly true, yes," said Master Analyst Gel. "Several departments have been tasked with providing an experienced and qualified member for this joint operation." He grinned and arched his brow. "As it happens, Lena Sol, I think you'd make an excellent candidate."

TERRY, MEI, and JOHN will return in HOPE EVERLASTING, available right now, exclusively on Amazon.

For more updates, join the Facebook group and become a Renegade Reader today.

CONNECT WITH J.N. CHANEY

Join the conversation and get updates in the Facebook group called "JN Chaney's Renegade Readers." This is a hotspot where readers come together and share their lives and interests, discuss the series, and speak directly to J.N. Chaney and his co-authors.

https://www.facebook.com/groups/jnchaneyreaders/

He also post updates, official art, and other awesome stuff on his website and you can also follow him on Instagram, Facebook, and Twitter.

For email updates about new releases, as well as exclusive promotions, visit his website and enter your email address.

https://www.jnchaney.com/variant-saga-subscribe

Enjoying the series? Help others discover the *Variant Saga* by leaving a review on Amazon.

ABOUT THE AUTHOR

J. N. Chaney is a USA Today Bestselling author and has a Master's of Fine Arts in Creative Writing. He fancies himself quite the Super Mario Bros. fan. When he isn't writing or gaming, you can find him online at **www.jnchaney.com**.

He migrates often, but was last seen in Las Vegas, NV. Any sightings should be reported, as they are rare.

You can also actively engage with him on his Facebook group, **JN Chaney's Renegade Readers**.